LOVE AND SHENANIGANS

BALLYBEG, BOOK 1

ZARA KEANE

BEAVERSTONE PRESS LLC

LOVE AND SHENANIGANS
(Ballybeg, Book 1)

Falling for the groom...

Gavin Maguire's life is low on drama, high on stability, and free of pets. But he hadn't reckoned on Fiona Byrne blasting back into his life and crashing his wedding. In the space of twenty-four hours, he loses a fiancée and a job, and gains a wife and a labradoodle. Can Gavin salvage his bland-but-stable life? Or will he lose his heart to Fiona all over again?

THE BALLYBEG SERIES

Love and Shenanigans
Love and Blarney
Love and Leprechauns
Love and Mistletoe
Love and Shamrocks

Be the first to know when there's a new Ballybeg story. Join my mailing list and get a FREE copy of *Love and Blarney*!

http://zarakeane.com/newsletter

For C.A.L.L.

1

Ballybeg, County Cork, Ireland

If an evil fairy conjured Fiona's personal hell, it would be this wedding.

"Isn't your dress gorgeous?" The evil fairy of the moment, Fiona's cousin, Muireann, displayed dazzling white teeth set in a saccharine smile. "Since you're my maid of honor, I wanted you to wear something special."

Fiona tongued her lip ring and squinted at the satin monstrosity hanging in her cousin's walk-in wardrobe. No, she wasn't hallucinating. Muireann wanted her to wear snot green.

"You're in the chartreuse." Muireann's smirk widened. She took down the hanger and held the dress against Fiona. "Maroon is so draining on brunettes, don't you think?"

Fiona grimaced. Who the feck chose chartreuse and maroon for their wedding colors? And what in the bejaysus was that thing at the end of the dress? “Is that a fin?” She poked at the stiff fabric. With a bit of luck, it was detachable. She’d “lose” it somewhere between here and the church.

“It’s a mermaid bottom. I thought the design particularly well suited to someone with your physique.”

My physique. Riiight.

In other words, she knew the dress would draw attention to Fiona’s childbearing hips and thunder thighs. What better way for Muireann to emphasize her own petite figure than to contrast it with her heifer of a cousin?

A lot had changed in the eight years since Fiona left Ballybeg, but her cousin had not. And neither, it seemed, had Fiona’s reactions to Muireann’s jibes. Over the years in Dublin, she’d shed her body-image issues and learned to embrace her curves. Half an hour back in Ballybeg and Muireann’s company, and all her old insecurities had come flooding back.

“Plus,” continued Muireann, “the long sleeves will cover your tattoos.”

Fiona shifted her weight from one lace-up boot to the other. “If you find my appearance offensive, why did you ask me to be your maid of honor?”

“Mummy insisted. But she doesn’t feel it’s proper to show tattoos in church.”

“In that case, I guess your groom will be wearing a high-necked collar.”

Her cousin’s eyes narrowed to slits. “What do you know about Gavin’s tattoos?”

Feck! Curse her for a fool for speaking without thinking. She cleared her throat. "The one on his neck's pretty obvious."

"Gavin's a man," Muireann said with a sniff. "Tattoos aren't ladylike."

But being a total bitch was? Fiona gave a mental headshake. Why had she let Bridie talk her into participating in this farce? She'd bloody well known Muireann would do something to humiliate her.

Muireann draped the dress across the queen-sized bed and pivoted on her heels. "I'll leave you to get ready. Claudette, my designer, needs to check the fit. Such a shame you couldn't make it to Cork to attend the earlier fittings. Claudette was most distressed."

"I had to work. I was teaching summer school up until yesterday. It's hardly my fault you scheduled the fittings for weekdays." Fiona fingered the hooks at the back of the dress. "Am I going to manage to do it up myself?"

Her cousin waved one French-manicured hand in a dismissive gesture, the other already turning the crystal doorknob. "I'll send Olivia in to help. Be quick about it, will you? Claudette doesn't have all day."

The door half closed, leaving Fiona to contemplate fish tails and dresses the color of infected sinuses.

Muireann's head popped round the door again. "By the way, Fiona?"

"Yeah?"

"Lose the boots."

The door clicked closed.

Fiona slumped onto the four-poster bed. Three days. Three days until freedom and white sandy beaches. Three days until she embarked on the trip of a lifetime. The catch was surviving the next seventy-two hours.

Someone tapped on the door, making her sit bolt upright.

"Are you decent?" Olivia, her best friend and only ally at this infernal shindig, slipped into the room. She wore a simple maroon bridesmaid's gown that complemented her auburn hair and slim figure. She held a bottle in one hand and two champagne flutes in the other.

Fiona leaped to her feet and enveloped her in a bear hug. "Liv!"

"If you're initiating physical contact, it's got to be bad." Olivia spied the dress draped across the bed and recoiled. "Oh, my gawd! The color's hideous."

"It's a shade I associate more with sinus infections than weddings." Fiona scrunched her nose. "What the hell was Muireann smoking?"

"It's odd. She's got a good reputation as an interior designer."

"Obviously her good taste in color schemes doesn't extend to clothing."

Olivia cast another look at the offending garment and gave an exaggerated shudder. "I'm so glad I nicked the champagne. You're going to need it if you're to model that dress before your aunt Deirdre and the evil twins."

"The twins are here, too?" Fiona groaned. "In that case, bring it on."

Olivia popped the cork and poured. She handed a glass to Fiona. "Get that down you. If there's a silver lining to this wedding, it's the Cristal."

"*Sláinte*."

The bubbly liquid coated Fiona's tongue like a caress. "Delicious. Uncle Bernard's wine cellar can't compensate for the fugly dress, but it certainly helps."

Olivia peered at Fiona over the brim of her champagne flute. "Jokes aside, how are you coping? This can't be easy, especially after the breakup with Philip."

Fiona swallowed hard. The concern in her friend's gaze almost persuaded her to succumb to her inner blub fest. "I'm grand," she said, ignoring the quaver in her voice.

Olivia reached out to squeeze her hand. "You're a crap liar. You always were."

She gave a wry laugh. "That's why we sent *you* to buy alcohol when we were teenagers."

"Ah, Fee. Queen of the witty diversion." Olivia wagged a finger. "You won't distract me that easily."

"Consider it a deferred conversation." Fiona took another sip of champagne before placing her glass on the bedside table. "Are you going to help me into this crime against fashion or what?"

Olivia cast her a knowing glance. "I'm only letting you change the subject because Muireann will do her nut if we don't hurry up."

"Not to mention Claudette." Fiona grinned, slipping off her jeans and T-shirt. "Is she as terrifying as Muireann makes out?"

"Worse. Even Deirdre quakes in her Jimmy Choo's when Claudette's around."

Fiona removed the dress from its hanger. "It looks kind of tight."

"There's not much give in the material, but never fear. I'll wrestle you into it."

Fiona groaned. "That's what I'm afraid of."

"Ah, it's your own fault. You should have told Muireann to feck off."

"*She* didn't ask me to be her maid of honor. It was Aunt Deirdre's idea, and I let Aunt Bridie guilt me into agreeing. She said it would be healthy to bury the hatchet."

"Where? In Muireann's back? How's making you her maid of honor supposed to compensate for years of bullying?"

"Given the state of the maid of honor's dress," Fiona said morosely, "I suspect my role is to lumber down the aisle behind her looking like a luminous green sausage. How did you get roped into being a bridesmaid, anyway? You and Muireann aren't exactly besties."

"Aidan's in cahoots with your uncle Bernard." Olivia rolled her eyes. "Long story short, he's got a stake in the new shopping center Bernard's building, and Bernard's got a stake in his political career."

"Aidan's serious about running for the town council?" Fiona was tempted to add something disparaging about sleazy lawyers and politicians and had to bite her tongue in time. Aidan was odious, but he was Olivia's husband, even if Fiona couldn't fathom what she saw in the man.

"Town council? Sweetheart, you're behind the times. Aidan's already on the council, and he won't stop there. He wants to be mayor of Ballybeg when O'Shaughnessy retires next year."

Fiona gave an internal shudder. The thought of Aidan

Gant wielding so much power was terrifying. "I'm sorry you have to suffer through this with me, Liv, but I won't lie—I'm damn glad you're here."

"At least it'll be over in a couple of days." Olivia tossed her rich red hair over her shoulder. "Then I'll return to my exciting existence as a lady who lunches, and you'll be off gallivanting around the world. You lucky sod. I wish I were a teacher and could take a year off work."

Fiona laughed. "No, you don't. Teaching's a bloody hard job these days. The kids are obnoxious, and the parents are worse. Yeah, the opportunity to take a sabbatical is fantastic, but I don't get paid for the year I don't work. However, I figure if I don't go traveling now while I'm still relatively young and definitely single, I'll never do it."

"Where's your first stop?"

"Singapore, home of the Singapore Sling, then on to Melbourne." Fiona tugged the dress over her hips. "Gosh, this *is* tight."

"The color is revolting." Olivia shuddered, and topped up their champagne glasses. "It's typical of Muireann to pick horrible bridesmaid dresses so none of us upstage her. She told you about the shoes, right?"

"That I'm to lose the Docs? Yeah, that was mentioned."

"Ah. It gets worse." She strode to the wardrobe and extracted a shoebox. "These are your wedding shoes." Reaching into the box, she withdrew a pair of five-inch stilettos the same shade as Fiona's dress.

Fiona's stomach lurched, and the prickling sensation of panic climbed her spine. "Muireann remembers I have a limp, right? How does she expect me to walk in those?"

"You'll practice," Olivia said with determined cheer. "You've got until tomorrow. Besides, you hardly ever limp anymore."

"If I have to stagger around in those heels all day, trust me, I'll be limping." Fiona groaned and reached for her glass. "I need more champagne."

Olivia examined every inch of Fiona, pausing when she came to her backside.

Fiona drained her glass. "How bad does it look?"

"You can see your knickers through the fabric."

"So?"

"So you'll have to go commando."

"No effing way."

"It's only for this evening. You can get a thong to wear on the day."

"I don't do thongs."

"Fee." Olivia thrust her chest out. "Shut up and lose the knickers."

"Some pal you are." She struggled out of the offending garment.

"No more VPL," Olivia said with triumph. "Much better."

"I doubt anything could improve this dress." Fiona had managed to squeeze herself into it, but breathing was a challenge. "Can you help me with the hooks at the back?"

Olivia yanked the back panels together. "Are you sure it wasn't mislabeled? It's meant to be formfitting, but this is awfully tight."

"I don't think so. I'm the only one wearing chartreuse."

When her friend started lacing up the hooks, Fiona gasped.

Olivia tugged. "Breathe out."

"I can't. Breathe. At. All."

"Okay, Fee. Let's try this lying down."

"Damn," Fiona said, wheezing. "I sent Muireann my measurements. The dress should fit."

She lay on her stomach. Olivia straddled her and pulled at the material with force.

"Ouch. You're after digging a hook into my back."

The bedroom door swung open. Aunt Deirdre stood in the frame, her lips forming an O. "Girls! What are you doing?"

"I'm trying to get Fiona into her dress," snapped Olivia. "What does it look like?"

"I thought perhaps…" Deirdre trailed off, her bony hands aflutter. "Well, chop, chop. Claudette is waiting."

"There's a problem with the fit," Fiona gasped from the bed.

"What?" Deirdre sounded like she'd been sucking on helium. "Then hurry up and come out." She slammed the door behind her.

They lay frozen on the bed for a moment, then burst into simultaneous laughter.

"Did Deirdre think we were in a lesbian clinch?" Fiona asked. "Oh, damn. I shouldn't have laughed. The hooks have burst."

Olivia made a few more attempts to force the back of the dress to close. "Sorry, Fee. It's hopeless."

She climbed off Fiona and picked up the matching chartreuse shawl from the dressing table. "Chuck this around your shoulders, and let's see what Claudette can do."

Fiona struggled to her feet. "I'm not sure I can walk in this thing." She eyed the mermaid bottom with suspicion. "Or in these shoes."

"Can you shuffle?"

"I can try."

"Give me your arm."

Fiona took a deep breath and laced her arm through Olivia's. "Let's go face my demons."

2

Gavin steered his BMW down the winding road leading to Clonmore Lodge, windows down, and punk rock blaring. Through the gaps in the trees, he glimpsed the sea. He inhaled deeply, tasted the salty air on his tongue, and felt it sting his nose.

Ballybeg was the best place on earth. He'd loved this area from the first moment he'd seen it. Adored the wildness of the sea, the rolling green fields, and the seaweed-scented wind. He couldn't imagine living anywhere else. While he liked to travel, the best part of every holiday was coming back home.

He rounded a last bend in the road and turned into the drive that led to a spacious three-level house. It was gorgeous; of that there was no doubt. Built in the mid-nineteenth century, it combined the quaint elegance of Old Ireland with modern comforts. It boasted five bedrooms, a sauna in the basement, and a small tennis court out the back. As his fiancée assured him daily, it would be the perfect home to raise kids.

And yet he'd trade it in for his cozy cottage any day. Yes, the cottage was too small for a family. Yes, it wasn't as fancy as this house. And yes, it wasn't in the most desirable area of Ballybeg. But the cottage was the first place he'd called home, and leaving it was heartbreaking.

He pulled his car to a halt outside the ivy-framed door of his new home. He was on the verge of opening his car door when his mobile phone flashed a message. A glance at the glowing display made his stomach cramp. He read the message several times. By the time he shoved the phone back into his pocket, the words were imprinted on his brain.

> *Hi, Gavin. Best wishes on your wedding day. Sorry we can't make it. Too much to do on the farm. I know you'll understand. All the best, Mum xx*

He exhaled sharply. He was used to his mother's offhandedness. Resigned to her disinterest in his life. So why did this latest rejection hurt so damn much? He was thirty-two years old. Too old to get maudlin over her lack of interest, and old enough to have developed a thicker skin.

He grabbed his briefcase and architect's tool bag, climbed out of the car, and slammed the door. What he needed was a break. A couple of weeks of rest and relaxation, far away from his domineering future in-laws and disinterested family. He and Muireann had been under so much stress over the last few months that they'd fought more often than they'd ever had in the several years they'd been a couple. Hopefully, their honeymoon would provide them with the respite they needed.

Inside the house, seventies pop music drifted down the hallway. Gavin laughed softly. One thing he and his fiancée definitely did not have in common was their taste in music. Either she'd forgotten to switch off the music system before she'd left for her wedding dress fitting, or she was running late. Knowing Muireann, both possibilities were likely.

"Muireann," he called. "I'm home."

Over Abba's crooning, he heard what sounded like a dog barking. He frowned. That couldn't be right. He and Muireann had a strict "no pets" rule.

Gavin dumped his bag and briefcase and headed toward the living room to investigate. And reared back at the sight before him. "What the hell?"

He stared at the scene before him, slack-jawed. There was an overturned vase, claw marks on the leather sofa, and a suspicious yellow stain on the hearthrug. A curly-haired puppy sat in the middle of the chaos, chewing on one of Gavin's running shoes.

On the coffee table lay a note written on Muireann's signature pink scented notepaper. Gavin grabbed it and scanned his fiancé's elegant looping letters.

> *Hey, Gavin. When Daddy heard about your allergies, he bought us an Australian Labradoodle as an early wedding present. His name is Wiggly Poo. Could you make sure he's fed before you leave for my parents' house? Thanks! xxx*

"Oh, hell, no." He slipped his phone out of his pocket and rang his fiancée's number.

She answered on the fourth ring, breathless and irritated. "What's up, Gavin?"

"What's up is me coming home to the apocalypse playing out in our living room."

Muireann sucked in a breath. "Oh, dear. Did Wiggly Poo cause a mess?"

"A mess is an understatement," Gavin said, eyeing the chaos. "What does your father mean by foisting a puppy on us? He knows I'm allergic to dogs."

"Yes, but Daddy knows how much I've always wanted a puppy, so he did some research and discovered Labradoodles. They're a cross between a Labrador and a poodle, and they're supposed to be hypoallergenic."

"*Supposed* to be," he drawled. "That's reassuring."

"You're not suggesting we give him back?"

An icy edge had entered his fiancée's tone, but Gavin wasn't biting.

"We discussed marriage. We discussed babies. We never discussed labrawhatsits."

"If you want rid of him, *you* talk to Daddy."

"You can be damn sure I'll talk to Bernard. I bowed to pressure over the house. No way am I allowing him to force a pet on us."

This wedding business was getting out of control. The sooner the ceremony was over and they were sunning themselves in Mauritius, the better.

"I realize you wanted us to live in your cottage," Muireann said coldly, "but you must see it's not practical."

Gavin sighed. "Yeah, I do. That's the reason I agreed to move in with you rather than vice versa."

Her tone softened. "We've been spoiled by our years of living in separate homes. It'll take time to adjust. For both of us."

The dog barked, drawing his attention back to his unwanted guest. "Who came up with the daft name?"

Muireann giggled. "Mummy. Wiggly Poo wouldn't be my first choice, but I didn't want to offend her. Besides, it rather suits him."

Gavin eyed the animal with suspicion. It resembled a walking bath mat. The dog panted and batted canine eyelashes at him.

"Who's minding the mutt while we're in Mauritius?"

"Aunt Bridie."

"What about her bad hip?" That was the sort of detail Muireann and her parents were likely to overlook.

Muireann sniffed. "After all Daddy's done for her over the years, it's the least she can do."

"Why can't your parents dog-sit?"

"It would be too much for Mummy's Chihuahuas. Wiggly Poo's a little wild."

Gavin's gaze dropped to the stained rug. "You don't say."

"Mummy called boarding kennels," she said, a hint of defensiveness in her voice. "None had a free place at such short notice."

"I'm not happy about having a dog thrust upon me," Gavin said. "By the time we get back from our honeymoon, I want him gone."

Muireann gave an exaggerated sigh. "It's the day

before our wedding. I don't want any unpleasantness between us."

"I'm not backing down. You got your way over the house, the wedding, and the honeymoon. I am not agreeing to keep a pet."

"Fine," she snapped. "Can we discuss this later? I'm in the middle of a dress fitting with my bridesmaids."

The puppy edged closer to Gavin, sniffing cautiously around his legs. "What am I supposed to do with the dog while we're out for dinner?"

"Oh, leave him at home," she said airily. "It's only for a couple of hours. He'll be fine."

"He might be fine, but will the house?"

Muireann sighed. "It's natural for Wiggly Poo to want to explore his new terrain."

"His new terrain is our house. Our heavily mortgaged house, complete with expensive furnishings."

"Gavin, don't make a fuss. My interior-design business is picking up. And once Daddy promotes you, we'll easily afford the mortgage. Besides—" she lowered her voice, "—we're getting the house for a steal. Daddy gave us a great price."

"He gave us a good deal on a very expensive house. And you're trying to distract me from talking about the dog. If I don't bring him with me to your parents' house, where will he sleep tonight? You're staying overnight with your parents and say you can't bring him with you, and I'm staying at my old house with Jonas. We can't leave him here alone."

"Can't you take him to your cottage? Jonas's kid can play with him. Kids love dogs."

"Luca's staying with his grandparents. It's only me and Jonas at the cottage."

"Look, I have to go, Gavin. Claudette is calling me. She wants to finish the fitting. You'll figure something out."

With these not very reassuring words, Gavin's future bride hung up on him.

He stared at the phone in his hand for a long moment. Then he returned his attention to the puppy clawing at his shoe. "No offense, mate, but you have got to go."

Gavin reached down, scooped the puppy into his arms, and marched into the hallway. On his way out of the house, he grabbed an empty moving box from beside the front door.

The little dog buried his snout into Gavin's chest. The small body felt warm and vulnerable. "I will not be manipulated by small, cute creatures," he said out loud. "We're not keeping this puppy." Gavin opened the passenger door and deposited the box on the seat and placed the dog inside it. He wagged a finger at the puppy. "No funny business, you hear?"

The dog's only response was a not very reassuring bark. With a sigh, Gavin slid behind the wheel and started the engine.

Muireann's parents lived a five-minute drive from Clonmore Lodge. Too far for Muireann's taste, and too near for Gavin's. He followed the curve of the road until Clonmore House was thrown into view. He whistled softly, as he did every time he saw the house. It was an impressive Georgian construction, nestled on a cliff overlooking the beach. The building was large, imposing, and pompous—rather like Gavin's future father-in-law, he thought with a grin.

Like the Lodge, Clonmore House had been part of the estate of the Earl of Clonmore, back in the bad old days of British rule in Ireland and near-slave conditions for the native Irish. Whereas his and Muireann's new home used to be the gatekeeper's residence, Clonmore House was the former dower house. Obviously, the Earls of Clonmore had liked their mammies.

"Woof!"

Gavin peeked at the moving-box-cum-puppy transporter on the passenger seat. The dog was urinating. "Aw, hell. Not again!"

Yellow liquid seeped out of the box onto the leather seat and all over the bunch of flowers destined for his future mother-in-law.

He glared at the dog. "First you wreck my rug and my running shoe, and now you piss in my car."

The small dog whimpered and retreated into the recesses of his box.

Gavin ran one hand through his short blond hair and gripped the steering wheel with the other. "Sorry, Wiggly Poo. I'm not mad at you. I'm mad at your dog mammy."

Actually, he was more annoyed with Wiggly Poo's dog granddad for foisting a dog into his life.

"And you interrupted my nostalgic moment." He banged the steering wheel, warming to his theme. "After months of wedding crap, I was savoring it. I've had Muireann morphing into Bridezilla, Bernard behaving like a boor, and Claudette trying to strangle me with cravats." He turned to the dog, which was staring at him with huge brown eyes. "Seriously, when did people in Ballybeg start referring to ties as cravats?"

Wiggly Poo's tongue lolled.

"I'm a simple man with simple tastes. I was happy in my cottage. And now I've got a McMansion with a mortgage and a koi pond." Gavin eyed the dog. "I don't suppose you eat fish?"

Wiggly Poo continued to stare at him.

"No, I guess that's more cat territory." He rolled up the automatic windows. "Ah, well. I'm hoping the koi pond is the extent of Muireann's garden monstrosities. She's always been a perfectionist, but she's lost the plot over the last few months. She needs a holiday. *We* need a holiday."

He nodded to himself and drummed the steering wheel. "It'll all be grand when we get back from Mauritius. We'll get back into our comfortable routine. She'll concentrate on her career, and I'll concentrate on mine. We'll put the stresses and strains of the last few months behind us."

The car crunched over the gravel courtyard, and he pulled up beside Muireann's Mini.

He hopped out of the car, retrieved the peed-on flowers from the front seat, and grabbed the dog out of its makeshift home. Wiggly Poo was thrilled to escape the confines of the box. The puppy licked Gavin's face and whined in excitement.

He was struggling to keep a grip on the wriggling dog when the front door was thrown open.

"Gavin," boomed Bernard from the top step. "Delighted to see you."

Bernard Byrne was a large man—in width as well as in

height. He had a bushy walrus mustache to complement his bushy eyebrows, a florid complexion, and a bulbous nose. The crowning glory—literally and figuratively—was a jet-black toupee perched precariously on his scalp.

Gavin glowered at Bernard's twitching mustache. "You have an extra dinner guest."

"Giving you gray hairs already, is he?"

"I'm allergic to dogs," Gavin said tersely.

"Muireann isn't." Bernard grinned, and stepped aside to allow him entry. "And she loves dogs. I don't see why she should be deprived of a pet because you're allergic. Sure, isn't she delighted with the little fellow?"

"It's not about me depriving Muireann of a pet. Dogs and cats trigger my asthma."

Bernard shrugged. "I made sure to buy one that's hypoallergenic."

A muscle twitched in Gavin's cheek. "So why am I sneezing?"

"Hay fever. Those flowers will be to blame." Bernard clapped him on the back. "Gavin, be a man. Once you get used to him, you'll be grand."

Gavin clenched his jaw. "You bought the dog, Bernard. You can deal with him. Find him a new home before we get back from our honeymoon."

"What'll Muireann say? She'll be devastated if she finds him gone."

"I'll talk to her. Make her see reason."

"Ah, you're a hard man." Bernard allowed his mustache to droop for dramatic effect. "We won't argue about it now. Can I offer you a drink? Some fortification before the big day?" The man's grin was back in place.

Gavin glanced around the small entrance hall. "Where's Muireann?"

"The ladies are still trying on their wedding finery."

Wiggly Poo's claws slid over Gavin's shirt, leaving tracks in the material. "In that case, perhaps we can discuss the shopping center plans while we have that drink. I have a few suggestions to make about parking—"

Bernard cut him off with an imperious gesture. "Yeah, yeah. Leave that for when you get back from your honeymoon."

A mobile phone began to buzz.

Bernard's sausage fingers fumbled over his smart phone's display. "Gant? Hang on a minute." Bernard cocked an eyebrow at Gavin. "Go on into the library and pour yourself a drink. I won't be long. And keep the dog under control. Deirdre will go mad if he breaks her ornaments." With these encouraging words, Bernard turned his large back on Gavin and lumbered down the hall.

"Typical," muttered Gavin. "Bloody typical. He lands me with an untrained puppy that wreaks havoc in my house, and then he expects me to keep it under control in his."

Wiggly Poo treated his nose to a generous lick.

He scowled at him. "Keep that up and I'll walk down the aisle with a rash on my face."

A shriek of laughter from one of the rooms proved too much excitement for the puppy. He leaped out of Gavin's arms, slid across the marble floor, and shot off in the direction of the noise.

"Come back, you blaggard!" Gavin chucked Deirdre's roses on the floor and took off after the dog.

He pounded down the narrow hallway that led to the downstairs guest bedrooms. One door was slightly ajar. He caught sight of a curly canine arse disappearing behind it.

He barged into the room without knocking.

A chorus of feminine gasps greeted his appearance. Apart from the French designer, all the women were wearing satin dresses of various hues. Deirdre was in a lavender creation, complete with puffy sleeves. The bridesmaids—Olivia, Mona, and Brona—wore maroon dresses that reminded him of the costumes in the deadly dull Jane Austen adaptations his fiancée adored. Muireann's wedding dress was a meringue concoction with skirts that took up half the room. It didn't suit her, but he'd lie tomorrow and tell her it looked great.

The *pièce de résistance* was the woman poured into a greenish-yellow frock with a weird fishtail bottom. The bodice of the dress was so tight that half her breasts were squeezed into view. He drank in the woman's face. Her mouth formed an O of horror at the sight of him.

His stomach performed a stunt worthy of an acrobat. He knew those breasts. He knew that face. He knew that mouth.

Fiona.

Bloody hell! What was she doing at the wedding? What was she doing *in* the wedding?

Her intelligent green eyes pinned him in place. A slide show of memories flashed through his mind—some good, some bad, some X-rated.

"Gavin!" Muireann screeched, jolting him back to the present. "You're not supposed to see my dress!"

He flushed to the roots. Had he been remembering sleeping with another woman while his bride-to-be stood in front of him? Jaysus. He needed to pull himself together.

Deirdre grabbed a swath of fabric from the speechless Claudette and threw it around her daughter. "Get out, Gavin. You'll jinx the wedding!"

"Sorry for barging in. Wiggly Poo is in here somewhere."

Muireann's jaw dropped. "You brought him here? I told you to leave him at home."

"Baby, I couldn't leave him alone," he said in mounting exasperation. "He was wrecking the place. He pulled down the curtains and attacked my stereo speakers."

"Ah, Gavin. Why didn't you stop him? He's only a puppy."

"Are you sure? I'd label him a hellhound."

Fiona snorted with laughter. Muireann shot her cousin a look of pure venom.

No love lost between them.

In a split second, Wiggly Poo emerged from underneath an antique chair and charged at a basket near Deirdre's feet.

"Watch out!" Gavin cried. "There he goes."

"Stop him!" Deirdre screamed, veiled hat askew. "He's attacking Mitzi and Bitzi."

Fiona lurched forward on her high heels and half fell, half dive-bombed the dog basket.

The sound of ripping fabric tore a horrified gasp from the crowd. The material at the back of the dress split open, revealing two luscious, creamy buttocks.

3

Ohmygawd! Her arse was on display.

Her fat, white arse.

Why did these things happen to her? One weekend without incident. That was all she'd asked for. Yet within an hour of arriving in Ballybeg, she was lying prostrate on top of a dog basket with the man she'd hoped to avoid staring at her cellulite.

Feck.

"*Mon dieu*!" Claudette clutched her necklace. "What have you done to my dress?"

"Fiona!" Muireann shrieked. "How could you?"

"Never mind the dress. She's squashing Mitzi and Bitzi." Deirdre darted forward and yanked the dog basket to safety. Fiona's face landed on the Persian carpet with a thud.

"What's wrong with you people?" a male voice demanded. *His* voice. "Help her up, for heaven's sake."

Muscular arms reached around her rib cage and hauled her to her feet.

"Here." Olivia retrieved the shawl from the floor. "Get this around her."

Gavin wrapped the shawl around Fiona's waist, careful not to touch her bare flesh. When his fingers skimmed her satin-encased hips, she felt a jolt of something she didn't care to define. Their eyes clashed for a millisecond. Too short to mean anything to him, too long not to mean something to her.

She exhaled sharply, her cheeks aflame. Why hadn't he had the decency to develop a beer gut over the past decade? Or a receding hairline? Life was so unfair.

"Grr!" Wiggly Poo was growling at the Chihuahuas, now held aloft in Deirdre's scrawny arms.

"My poor babies." Deirdre fussed over the tiny dogs and fixed Gavin with a quelling gaze. "I blame you for this debacle. If you hadn't let that mongrel loose, none of this would have happened."

"Me?" Gavin's tone exuded outraged incredulity. "I didn't ask to be saddled with a dog."

"Mitzi and Bitzi are sensitive around strange dogs, and that one is positively rabid."

Gavin's sky-blue eyes darkened. "Wiggly Poo probably mistook them for vermin. An easy mistake to make."

"Well," Deirdre said, aghast. "I never."

Laughter bubbled up Fiona's throat. "Wiggly Poo?" She gasped, struggling to keep her composure. "What sort of name is that?"

Deirdre glowered at her. "This is no laughing matter,

Fiona. My pets were brutally attacked by that savage beast."

"Bollocks." Gavin scooped up the puppy. "He didn't touch them."

"He didn't, Deirdre," Fiona said. "I got to him before he had a chance to do anything more than bark."

Deirdre's thin lips parted, baring teeth whitened to a radioactive glow.

"Mummy." Muireann laid a hand on Deirdre's arm. "Wiggly Poo's young. He needs time to adjust."

"Until he's tamed, that creature is not welcome in this house."

Fiona convulsed, losing the battle against laughter.

Deirdre rounded on her. "You're in no position to laugh, young lady. You've destroyed a very expensive dress."

"Yes." Muireann smirked. "I invited you to be my maid of honor in good faith, and now…this." She gestured in the direction of Fiona's arse.

Fiona's cheeks grew even hotter, anger mingling with embarrassment. "The dress is too small. I'm sorry it tore, but I wasn't going to get down the aisle in this frock. Nor in these shoes." She kicked off the offending footwear and sighed with relief as her stockinged feet sank into the plush carpet.

Deirdre pursed her mouth. "Did you lie about your measurements?"

Fiona gave her aunt the stink eye. "Of course not. Do you think I wanted to humiliate myself by busting out of the dress?"

"In that case, you must have put on weight."

Muireann tittered. "With the amount you eat, it's hardly surprising."

"Steady on," Gavin said. "Fiona's not fat."

Muireann and Deirdre cast him withering looks.

"Get out, Gavin," Deirdre said. "And take that dog with you. You've caused enough trouble for one day."

Gavin met her glare for glare. "If you want to cast blame, Deirdre, look no further than your husband. He bought the dog."

Deirdre opened her mouth as if to protest. Gavin cut her off. "What am I supposed to do with Wiggly Poo while we have dinner? I can hardly lock him in the car."

Muireann regarded the wriggling puppy doubtfully. "Can't you ask Jonas to look after him? Just for this evening? We can sort out what to do with him later."

"I can ask. If he has any sense, he'll say no." Gavin sighed. "Right. I'll leave you ladies to change."

Fiona caught his eye, and her heart skipped a beat. She mouthed thanks, and he gave a curt nod. He hoisted the puppy onto his shoulder and left the room.

All eyes focused on Fiona.

"I knew you were too fat for that dress." Muireann's spray-tanned face creased into a smirk.

The suspicion that had been forming in Fiona's mind crystallized. "You did this deliberately. You gave Claudette the wrong measurements, and you made damn sure to schedule the fittings for when you knew I wouldn't be able to attend."

"I most certainly did not." Muireann's smirk faded, but there was a wicked gleam in her eyes. "I'd hardly want to wreck my own wedding."

"Don't be absurd, Fiona." Deirdre waved a hand in impatience. "Muireann would never play such a nasty trick."

"No?" She placed her hands on her hips. "I sent her my exact measurements, and I haven't put on weight in the meantime. The moment I saw the dress, I doubted it would fit. If Muireann received my e-mail, I assume she passed on the information to Claudette."

"*Naturellement*," Claudette said in her musical Parisian accent. "And I followed them exactly. If you are the size you say, the dress will fit."

"If the dress reflected the measurements I sent Muireann, it should fit, yes."

"Are you calling me a liar?" Muireann's blue eyes widened in faux horror.

Fiona tilted her chin. "Yes, I am."

"Girls," Deirdre snapped. "Enough. Whatever happened cannot be undone. I don't suppose there's time to make a replacement dress?"

"Not in the chartreuse." Claudette gave a Gallic shrug "The material was a special order for Madame."

Quelle surprise. Most people had better taste.

"Mummy, we can't let Fiona wear one of her Goth getups to the wedding. She's supposed to be my maid of honor."

"Here's an idea." Fiona's voice rose a notch. "Why don't I resign as maid of honor? I'll spare you the indignity of having me and my unsuitable wardrobe following you down the aisle."

"You can't quit," Deirdre said. "There'll be an uneven number of bridesmaids."

"Far be it from us to screw with symmetry." Olivia stepped forward to stand beside Fiona. "If Fee's no longer in the wedding party, then neither am I."

"Are you quitting on me?" Muireann's nose quivered. "Your husband won't like that."

"Feck Aidan." Olivia's jaw jutted belligerently. "And feck you. You set Fiona up."

"Girls, please," Deirdre said weakly. "I can feel a migraine coming on." She pronounced it 'mee-graine'.

Fiona caught Olivia's eye and smiled. She'd rather be just about anyplace on earth than here, but having a friend by her side made everything better. Well, that and having a getaway car at the ready. "If we're done here, I'm going to change back into my highly unsuitable clothes." She fingered the torn garment. "I don't suppose you want the remnants of my dress?"

The twins tittered. Claudette stood mute. Muireann smirked. Aunt Deirdre quivered with outraged disapproval.

"Excellent. In that case, I'll keep it as a memento." Fiona removed the shawl from around her waist and tossed it at Muireann. "You can have this back, cuz. After all, you wanted to see me humiliated. I'd hate to deprive you of the pleasure."

Feeling cheerful for the first time since she'd arrived in Ballybeg, Fiona turned on her heel and marched across the room, swinging her naked arse for all to see.

~

*T*HIS TIME TOMORROW, *I'll be a married man.*

The sick sensation that had been building in the pit of Gavin's stomach rose up his throat. He swallowed hard, tried to stem the surge of panic.

Breathe in. Breathe out.

Everything was going to be fine, he thought, flexing his fingers over the steering wheel. He was experiencing a bout of the pre-wedding jitters. Everyone got them, and everyone got past them.

He'd been on edge for the past few days, anxious to get the wedding over and done with.

Not that he didn't want to marry Muireann. Of course he did. Marrying her made perfect sense. They both wanted kids, eventually, and they'd been a couple since university. They were good together. Content. Not the most passionate of relationships, but he'd gladly sacrifice wild passion for stability and security. In short, he and Muireann were the polar opposite of his mother and the numerous men who'd paraded through his train wreck of a childhood.

With a grim sense of déjà vu, Gavin pulled his car to a stop beside Muireann's Mini. He'd left Wiggly Poo with Jonas's parents for the night. At least that was one problem sorted.

The other problem was a little trickier.

Fiona.

His stomach lurched. If only she hadn't blasted back into his life. Fiona was the last person he needed right now. He'd been stunned to see her standing in Deirdre's parlor wearing that awful dress. No one had mentioned she was invited to the wedding, let alone the maid of honor.

What the hell had Muireann been thinking? She loathed Fiona. Always had.

And the feeling was mutual.

A vision of Fiona's exposed backside danced before his eyes, and he quashed the memory with a mental sledgehammer.

Fiona was in his past. His distant past. A short interlude that had ended badly. In all likelihood, she barely remembered their drunken night together in Las Vegas. Unfortunately, he remembered it only too well…in all its pixilated glory.

He sighed and pushed open his door. He'd barely had time to lock his car before Muireann appeared in the doorframe. She looked radiant. And happy. And if her happiness were accompanied by a hint of smugness…well, she'd make a beautiful bride.

"You look lovely." He kissed her on the cheek, careful not to ruin her makeup.

She put a hand on his arm. "I'm sorry about Mummy earlier. You know what she's like about her Chihuahuas."

"Don't worry about it. We're all on edge at the moment."

She nodded and looked past him at the car. "What did you do with Wiggly Poo?"

"He's with Jonas's parents, wreaking havoc."

She slipped her hand into his. "Come through to the living room. We're having a drink before dinner."

In the Byrne's antique-ridden living room, Bernard stood before the fireplace. One bulky arm rested on the mantelpiece, while the other hand clutched a tumbler of whiskey. His florid cheeks were redder than usual. This was not his first drink of the day.

Gavin swallowed a sigh. Bernard was hard to deal with sober. Drunk, he was a nightmare.

"The man of the moment." Bernard's smile was a rictus of protruding teeth. "How are you enjoying your last hours of freedom?"

The acid in his stomach gnawed his insides. "Apart from dealing with an untrained puppy, I'm grand."

"What are you drinking, Gavin?" Deirdre sniffed, not looking in his direction. Mitzi and Bitzi were by her side, ears cocked. They glowered at him with their rat-like eyes.

"Fizzy water's fine. I'm driving."

"Nonsense. The boy will have a whiskey. The MacAllan nineteen seventy-four." Bernard leaned closer. His breath alone was fit to put a man over the limit. "I'm cheating by going for Scotch over Irish, but this is worth it. Retails for over eight thousand euros a bottle."

"That's obscene."

"That's success, my boy." Bernard's mustache bobbed. "Success in a glass. Go on. Taste it."

Gavin took a dubious sip.

Bernard's self-satisfied smirk widened.

"Isn't it perfect?"

"Hmm…not bad." To Gavin's undiscerning palate, it tasted like any other whiskey. He put the glass on the mantelpiece and turned to his fiancée. "All set for tomorrow?"

She beamed. "I can't wait. It's going to be the best day of our lives."

"You'll make a beautiful bride." Deirdre patted her daughter on the arm in a rare display of physical affection. "The neighbors will be pea green with envy."

"Screw the neighbors," Gavin said. "Once Muireann's happy and having a good time, that's all that counts."

Bernard snorted. "Impressions matter, especially in business. You'll learn, lad."

Gavin refrained from comment. The Byrnes never missed an opportunity to network. He shouldn't be surprised that Muireann's parents saw her wedding as yet another opportunity to grandstand and lick the right arses.

"Take this house, for instance." Bernard was warming to his theme, his voice increasing in volume with every sentence. "Do you think it's an accident that I bought it? No. Generations of my family worked the land on the Clonmore estate. They were treated little better than slaves and left to starve during the Great Famine. Now here I am, master of the house, while the present Earl of Clonmore lives in a shack on the other side of Ballybeg. That's success in modern Ireland."

Gavin had heard the tale a thousand times. "The Major's not exactly living in poverty. His house is a nice bungalow. Hardly what I'd call a shack. And if I recall correctly, this was the dower house, not the Earl's residence."

Bernard shrugged. He wasn't a man to let a few inaccuracies interfere with a good story. "But now that the old house has been converted into a hotel, Clonmore House is the largest *private* residence on the old estate."

The gong sounded, producing a melodious echo. The

gong was a relatively new affectation in the Byrne household, and Gavin cringed every time he heard it.

"Time for dinner." Deirdre led the way into the ornate dining room, complete with an ugly table centerpiece Deirdre called an epergne.

Gavin sat across from Muireann. Judging by the place settings, it was going to be a five-course meal. The acid burned deeper into his stomach lining. He took a deep gulp from his water glass.

The food was perfectly prepared, but it tasted like sandpaper. He had to get a grip. Being nervous about tomorrow was one thing. Being a nervous wreck was quite another.

He stared across the table at his bride-to-be. Muireann was fine-boned and classically beautiful with straight blond hair and large blue eyes. She was tiny next to his six-two frame, even in heels. Her soft-spoken manner charmed most men, but she didn't find it easy to make female friends.

Although Fiona and Muireann were first cousins, their surname was the only thing they had in common. Where Muireann was petite, Fiona was tall and curvaceous. Where Muireann was fair-haired, Fiona had a tumble of dark curls. And where Muireann was cool and collected, Fiona was fiery and chaotic.

Unless, of course, she'd changed over the years. Remembering the spark of rage in Fiona's eyes when Muireann and Deirdre called her fat, he doubted the past eight years had tamed her temper.

He continued to pick at his food. Bernard had seconds

at every course, wolfing his food and washing it down with several glasses of red wine.

Deirdre and Muireann maintained a seemingly endless prattle about the wedding and who was planning to wear what and who had gained or lost weight or had "a little work" done on various parts of their anatomy.

"I can't believe Fiona split her dress." Muireann tittered with ill-disguised glee. "What a fright she looked!"

"She has no manners and no breeding." Deirdre sniffed. "Hardly surprising, given her upbringing. I'd hoped a few years in Dublin would improve her sense of fashion."

"She'd need to be a lot skinnier to fit into fashionable clothes, Mummy."

"Fiona's not fat," Gavin said firmly. "She split the dress because it was the wrong size."

"Nonsense," Deirdre said. "Claudette is a professional. She followed the measurements exactly. Fiona either lied about her size or ate too much in the meantime."

"The sight of her pasty bottom!" Muireann laughed. "I haven't seen anything so funny in all my life."

"If that's true, you need to get out more," he said tersely. "Fiona's not skinny, but neither is she fat. And the more you go on about her weight, the more I suspect you deliberately sabotaged the dress fitting."

"What?" Muireann's face turned chalky white, and her bottom lip began to quiver. "You're blaming me for that fat cow destroying her dress?"

"Gavin!" Deirdre radiated disapproval. "What a dreadful thing to say."

"Well, Muireann? Did you give Claudette the wrong measurements?"

Her eyes darted to the side, then refocused. "Of course not. Why would I want to waste Daddy's money like that?"

"For a good laugh at Fiona's expense? It wouldn't be the first time." He tossed his fork on the table and leaned forward in his seat. "For whatever reason, Fiona brings your inner bitch out to play. Always has, probably always will."

"Don't be silly. I played a few pranks on her when we were younger. Isn't that what schoolgirls do? It doesn't mean I'd do anything so childish now."

"So you're saying Claudette screwed up?"

"She must have." Muireann fiddled with her napkin, her engagement ring glinting in the light. "Either that or Fiona sent the wrong measurements." Her blue eyes grew large, and she leaned across the table to take his hand in hers. "We never argue, yet today we've had two disagreements. First about the dog, and now over Fiona."

He focused on Deirdre's silver epergne. The center bowl overflowed with exotic fruit. Each of the small dishes extending in branches from the centerpiece contained different-colored flowers. His nose itched from all the pollen.

Raising his eyes, he looked at his fiancée. "All right." He reached for his water glass. "We'll leave it for now. I don't want to fight with you, Muireann."

Especially not the night before their wedding.

4

The church bells chimed the hour. Eleven o'clock. Fiona increased her pace, dodged a bike, and crossed the square over to Patrick Street. Despite the late hour, Ballybeg town center was busy. People spilled out of pubs onto the pavement, their laughter floating on the light autumn breeze.

So much had changed since she'd lived in Ballybeg, yet so much remained the same. The terraced houses along Patrick Street retained their brightly colored facades, but several of the businesses on the ground floors had changed. The fish-and-chipper was gone, replaced by a Chinese take-away. The old pound shop was now the tourist information office. The butcher's had been converted into a private residence.

She was a stranger in her hometown, every difference a sharp shock of reality. Time passed, people evolved, places altered. Memories froze a place in time, and change seemed a violation.

Not everything in Ballybeg was different, though, nor everyone. Her aunt's bookshop was still on Patrick Street, the familiar turquoise paint a welcome sight. Olivia was as warm and welcoming as the first day they'd met in primary school. And Muireann was still a first-class cow.

After the arse-baring disaster, she and Olivia had gone out for a drink. Now it was time to return to Bridie's house and face the music.

Feckity feck.

She hated disappointing her aunt. Requesting she consider being Muireann's maid of honor was the first time Bridie had asked her to do anything family-related for years. She went through phases of promoting family togetherness before giving it up as a lost cause.

Fiona turned into Beach Road, each step slower than its predecessor. The tide was out, and the smell of damp seaweed was overpowering.

Most of the homes along Beach Road were old cottages that had endured the strong Atlantic wind for over a century. Each cottage was painted a different shade, but none was as remarkable as Bridie's. Under the faint light of the street lamps, it was a lurid pink—an eyesore, even in the context of colorful Ballybeg. It suited its owner perfectly.

Said owner was standing on her doorstep, plump hands on broad hips. Her peach-rinsed hair was in tight curlers, and she wore a voluminous fluffy bathrobe the same shade as her hair.

Next door, the lights were out in Gavin's cottage. Did he still own it now that he'd moved in with Muireann? Fiona's cheeks burned at the memory of him rescuing her this evening. Trust her to get into such an embarrassing situation, and trust Muireann to orchestrate it.

"What's all this about you being fired from the wedding?"

"It's past eleven." Fiona shut the gate behind her. "Shouldn't a person of your advanced years be asleep?"

"Cheeky minx. I'm sixty-four, not dead. Now get inside and tell me what happened."

Bridie stood to the side, and Fiona squeezed past into the small cottage. She shrugged off her coat and walked by the multitude of knickknacks and ornaments that adorned every nook and cranny of Bridie's home.

"We'll have cocoa," her aunt announced when they reached the cluttered but cozy kitchen. "And you're making it. After listening to Deirdre screech down the phone at me for an hour, you owe me one."

Fiona laughed and rummaged in the cupboard where the tea and other hot beverages were stored. "Any chance I'm disinvited from the wedding in addition to being fired from my post as maid of honor?"

"Not a hope. Deirdre particularly said she'd like you to attend."

"Bollocks. She doesn't want the neighbors gossiping about a family feud."

Her aunt's bushy eyebrows formed a unibrow of disapproval. "How did you manage to have a major falling out with Muireann within an hour of arriving in Ballybeg?"

"It's a talent." She poured milk into a small saucepan and added cocoa powder. "I'm aware you were angling for a reconciliation between us. I told you it wouldn't happen."

"I know you did, missy." Bridie lowered herself into a kitchen chair, wincing from the effort. "I should have listened. But your dad would have wanted you to go to Muireann's wedding, and I sometimes get to wondering if the rift between you two isn't partly my fault."

"What makes you say that?" She turned mid-stir and regarded her aunt. "Muireann and I have been sparking off one another since preschool."

"Yes, but I've made no secret of my feelings toward Bernard. Maybe that wasn't fair."

"Under the circumstances, you're entitled to feel bitter."

"Perhaps, but Mammy's will shouldn't affect your relationship with your cousin. It's not her fault Bernard inherited so much and the rest of us so little."

"Nana's will has nothing to do with my issues with Muireann. She managed to piss me off all on her own."

Fiona stirred the cocoa a final time and divided the frothy liquid between two mugs. She placed one in front of her aunt and took the seat across the table.

Lines of pain etched Bridie's forehead, the grooves deeper than Fiona remembered.

"Are you okay? You look like you're in discomfort."

"Ah, I'm grand," Bridie said. "My hip's paining me this evening."

"Arthritis?"

"So Dr. Mulligan says. It's worse in the winter. Now stop stalling and tell me what led to you being fired as maid of honor. I only have Deirdre's rant to go by, and I don't place much store by her account."

"Long story short, my maid of honor dress was too small. It ripped." Fiona's cheeks grew warm at the memory of Gavin's big hands on her waist.

"Didn't you send your measurements to Muireann?"

"Yeah, I did." She took a sip of cocoa. "She swears she passed on the correct measurements to the dressmaker. I don't believe her."

"Hmm. And you had a fight?"

"Yeah. It ended with Olivia and me no longer welcome in the wedding party. Whether we quit or were fired is open to debate. At any rate, we won't be trailing down the aisle after Muireann."

"Olivia too?" Bridie licked cocoa off her upper lip. "Aidan won't be pleased."

"Not much pleases Aidan Gant." Fiona scrunched up her nose. "I don't get what she sees in him."

"Financial security is not to be scoffed at. Take it from one who knows. Gant stands to make a lot of money from Bernard's new shopping center."

"Olivia mentioned that. Where are they building it?"

"Out by Fir Road."

Fiona frowned. "Isn't that part of the land Bernard inherited from Nana?"

"Yes. He's been angling to build on it for years, but the old guard on the town council wouldn't approve the plans. Now that his cronies Aidan Gant and George Jobson are on the council, the plans got pushed through."

"Nice for Bernard."

A bitter half smile twisted Bridie's lips. "Nice for Bernard's bank account."

"Speaking of money…there's something I've been meaning to ask you."

"Ask away."

"I can't help noticing the house is looking a bit—"

"Shabby?" Bridie looked her straight in the eye.

"Well, yeah," she said awkwardly. "But it's more than that. It's fairly obvious you need to get a new washing machine, and the sink in the bathroom leaks. Are you doing all right? Moneywise, I mean."

"I get by." A muscle in her aunt's cheek twitched. "I can afford to put food on the table and pay my bills. That's more than most can say in this economy."

"Right. And the Book Mark?"

"It's a bookshop." Her aunt's eyes dropped to the worn kitchen linoleum. "People don't have money to spare for new books, and the used book exchange is more a service to my customers than a big earner. Those who can afford to buy books are going the digital route with the capsule thingies."

Fiona suppressed a smile. "Tablets?"

"Yeah. That's what they're called." Bridie drained the last dregs of cocoa from her mug and stood. Her stance was awkward, and she was favoring one side. "I'd better get to sleep. Listen, if you decide you're not going to the wedding tomorrow, would you sort your old stuff? There are at least three boxes of junk in your old room. If you haven't touched them in eight years, I doubt they contain anything important."

"Yes, boss." She gave a mock salute. "What time's the

ceremony?"

"Eleven." Bridie put a hand on her shoulder. "I'm sorry you came down to Ballybeg for nothing, love."

A pang of guilt nagged Fiona's conscience. She should visit more often. Or at least call more than once every few months. She squeezed her aunt's hand. "Not for nothing. I'm glad to see you."

"It's great to catch up with you before you head off to the other side of the world."

She beamed. "I can't believe it's actually happening. I've been planning this trip for so long it seems surreal."

"I remember you talking about going to Australia when you were barely old enough to find it on a globe."

"Bridie," Fiona asked tentatively, "how important is it to you that I go to the wedding?"

"For better or worse, I'd like to put the past behind us and behave like a proper family for one day. Your dad was always the peacemaker. Now that he's gone..."

"In that case, I'll go to the ceremony, at the very least." She planted a kiss on her aunt's plump cheek. "And when I get back from Oz, I'll come down to Ballybeg more often. I promise. You'll be sick of the sight of me."

THE REST of Gavin's pre-wedding meal with the Byrnes passed without incident.

After dessert, Muireann and Deirdre returned to the living room to discuss the last wedding details. Although what there was to be decided, he had no idea. How much more micromanaging could they achieve between now and tomorrow morning?

"Let's go into the library." Bernard rose unsteadily to his feet. "We'll have another glass of the MacAllan."

Bernard's library was yet another affectation in a house full of affectations. The oak bookshelves were stuffed with valuable first editions of the classics, yet no one in the Byrne household would ever consider reading one.

Gavin sat in a stiff leather armchair and gazed at the spine of Thomas Hardy's *The Mayor of Casterbridge*. How much had it set Bernard back? A few hundred? A few thousand? All for a book the man would never read.

A cigar clenched between his front teeth, Bernard sloshed whiskey into a tumbler and shoved it toward Gavin. He poured himself an even larger glass. "Pre-wedding nerves, lad?" He took a gulp of whiskey, then a puff of his cigar. "We've all been there."

Gavin coughed discreetly through the plumes of pungent smoke. "I'm grand. The joking about Fiona went too far for my taste."

"Fond of Fiona, are you?" Bernard's shrewd gaze speared him to the spot.

"Before today, I hadn't seen her for years." *And had tried not to think of her*. "But yeah, we always got on well." *Better than you'll ever know.*

Memories of that crazy night in Vegas surfaced again. Hazy, colorful, loud. And the look of hurt and betrayal on Fiona's face the next morning when he announced he was leaving.

"Fiona has an inferiority complex. And no sense of

style. My sister is hardly a good influence on her. She'd have been better off coming to live with us after her parents died."

"From my understanding, no such offer was extended."

Bernard's mustache bristled. "Nonsense. We'd have been happy to have her. But enough about my niece. Let's talk business."

Gavin's ears pricked up. The contract. It had to be about the contract.

"Aidan Gant's drawn up the papers to make you our new design director. They'll be ready to sign when you get back from your honeymoon."

And not a moment before. Bernard was loving having him on a chain.

He swallowed a mouthful of MacAllan. "I'd hoped to get it all sorted out before we left. That was the original plan."

Bernard swirled his glass. "Yes. I've been distracted by the wedding prep." He regarded him with a steely expression. "I'm confident you'll make my daughter very happy."

He stared at the paisley-patterned carpet. "I'll certainly do my best."

"Excellent." The older man stood and flashed him a snake-like smile. "I'll have the contract ready for you to sign as soon as you're back from Mauritius."

He was tempted to tell Bernard where to stick his contract, but common sense prevailed. Too much was at stake here, not least Muireann's feelings. If working for her father for a couple more years was the price he had to pay for financial stability, well, we all made sacrifices.

He got to his feet. "Right. I'll see you tomorrow."

Deirdre was rearranging flowers in the hallway when he emerged from Bernard's lair. "Muireann's already gone to bed," she said, poking and prodding at a yellow floral arrangement that was making his nose itch. "A bride needs her beauty sleep."

"I'll nip up and say good-bye."

Upstairs, he knocked on Muireann's bedroom door and went in. She was already in her nightie, brushing her long blond hair. She paused midstroke when she saw his reflection in her dressing table mirror.

"I'm sorry about earlier. Let's assume Claudette messed up." He put his hands on her bare shoulders and kissed her neck.

She pulled away and resumed her hair brushing. "Forget it. You're probably just nervous about the wedding."

He let his arms drop to his side. "I'm not fond of public speaking, but it's more than that. These past few months haven't been easy—for either of us."

She tugged at a tangle. "Planning a wedding is stressful. As is moving house. We've done both this year."

"At least it'll be all over by tomorrow night."

She turned to look at him, an odd expression on her face. "That's a funny thing to say about your wedding day."

"Big events with tons of guests aren't my thing."

"Why did you agree to it?"

He shrugged. "I know how much a traditional wedding means to you."

She bit her lip. "You're looking forward to the honeymoon at least?"

"Yes. Yeah. Of course I am. A holiday is exactly what we need." He bent down and pecked her on the cheek. "I'd better let you get some sleep. Besides, Jonas will be waiting for me at the cottage."

Her baby blue eyes met his. "I love you, Gavin. I'll be a good wife to you."

"I know you will. I love you, too."

And he did. Of course he did. So why did the words weigh down his tongue like lead?

5

On his wedding day, Gavin rose early for his morning run. Dawn was breaking when he closed the door of his cottage. His hand stilled on the door handle, and his eyes strayed to the nameplate on the wall.

Abhaile, the Irish word for home.

He'd loved this house the moment he'd seen it, ramshackle though it was. Where his mother saw a dump, he saw potential. Where she saw a financial drain, he saw an opportunity. And where she saw an unwanted abode, he saw a home.

Now it was no longer his home.

If his mother had despaired of the cottage, Muireann despised it. She'd set her heart on a big house, and her parents were willing to sell them Clonmore Lodge. Gavin had caved, acknowledging the cottage was too small to raise a family. The cottage was up for sale, but no interesting offers had come through yet. He was relieved, even though they needed the money. If a buyer didn't materialize soon, he'd have to find a tenant. But that was a concern for another day.

He headed down the short path and out the gate. He crossed the road and stood at the railings overlooking the beach.

What a view. The tide was out, exposing a vast expanse of wet sand. It was rocky in places, sandy in others.

He took the steps down to the beach two at a time. At the bottom, his trainers sank into damp sand. After a few preliminary stretches, he began to run.

He pounded down the strand, his lungs burning, his mind free. The only activity more calming than this was swimming, but even he wasn't crazy enough to wade in today.

After a couple of kilometers, he stopped to catch his breath. He wiped sweat from his brow and took a swig from his water bottle. The sea was wild and the tide had turned. The waves crashed and foamed, and the blue-green water crept up the sand.

He should get back to the cottage. There was a lot to do before he left for the church. Plus he had a guest. Yeah, breakfast with Jonas was something to look forward to. He hooked his water bottle.

"Gav!"

He whipped round.

Jonas was pounding down the sand toward him, clad in an old T-shirt and what appeared to be swimming trunks. A lit cigarette dangled from one hand. His dark hair stood on end, and thick stubble shadowed his jawline. Despite his disheveled appearance, he looked better than Gavin felt.

"Morning." He grinned at his friend. "Didn't expect to see you up this early, never mind jogging."

"Trying to get fit. The sedentary lifestyle and all that."

"Bollocks," Gavin said with a laugh. "You're sickeningly fit for a man who sits on his arse all day and writes."

"Mental exertion, mate. Crafting stories uses a lot of energy."

"Yeah, right. More like a high metabolism and good genes. Enjoy it while it lasts."

"I'm jogging, aren't I?" Jonas took a drag from his cigarette. "I'm trying to set an example for Luca."

"With fags and beer?"

"Shut up." Jonas grinned. "At least I'm not about to get hitched."

"You could give it consideration. Luca's nearly six."

A shadow flitted across Jonas's tanned face. "You're distracted, mate. I told you Susanne and I are on a break."

"Another one?" How many times had they broken up since Luca's birth? Four? Five?

Jonas shrugged. "Nah. Same break as last time we spoke of it. This one's just lasting a while. Luca's diagnosis hit Susanne hard."

"For feck's sake. He's on the autism spectrum, not terminally ill."

His friend gave him a sharp look. "It'll be fine, okay? I don't need relationship advice from a reluctant groom."

If Jonas had punched him in the gut, Gavin couldn't have felt more stunned. "Reluctant? Where did you get that impression?"

"Come on, Gav. We've been friends since secondary school. You're not exactly what I'd term a blushing groom."

"A bout of pre-wedding jitters. It'll pass."

"Make sure it passes before eleven this morning."

Gavin stared out to sea. "Why don't you worry about your own relationship and let me worry about mine?"

"Sorry, mate. I'll back off."

"Forget about it. How about a full Irish breakfast back at the cottage?"

Jonas grinned. "Last one there cooks?"

"You're on."

They raced down the beach, neck and neck for the first while until Gavin gained the advantage. He bounded up the slippery stone steps, across Beach Road, and waited for Jonas at the door of the cottage.

"Ha," he said when Jonas hauled himself up the garden path, gasping for breath. "You'd make the perfect ad for an anti-smoking campaign."

"Feck off," said Jonas, panting. "I lost on purpose."

"Sure you did." Gavin inserted his key into the lock.

"Self-preservation, mate. You can't cook for shite."

Gavin opened the door of the cottage. They were greeted by the sound of retching.

Gavin froze, then legged it into his bedroom, Jonas close behind. "Aw, no."

"Jaysus," Jonas said. "Is it my imagination, or is Wiggly Poo regurgitating your wedding suit?"

~

"Morning, Sleeping Beauty. Time to play happy families."

Bridie wrenched open the curtains. Sunlight flooded Fiona's old bedroom, revealing faded posters of rock bands she'd loved as a teenager and Bridie's bright orange dress.

"Ugh." Blinking, she buried her head beneath her pillow. "Not time yet."

"Olivia's drinking tea in the kitchen. Says she's here to lend you a hand getting ready for the wedding."

Fiona emerged from underneath the pillow. "Does no one trust me to wear appropriate footwear to the church?"

"Frankly, no."

"Your faith in me is touching." She threw off her duvet and found her feet. In the wardrobe's full-length mirror, her reflection stared back. A wild bush of dark curls on her head, bags under her eyes, and five kilos above her ideal weight.

"Now that you're no longer maid of honor, do you have an outfit to wear to the wedding?"

"Nothing fancy," replied Fiona. "I have a black dress I can jazz up with jewelry."

"Sounds grand. Don't forget to remove your lip ring. Deirdre made particular mention of it."

Fiona stuck her tongue out. "Oh, all right."

"In that case, I'll leave you girls to get ready." She fastened a matching orange hat to her head. "I'm due to give the Major a lift to the church. And check his attire. That man cannot be trusted to wear a matching tie."

Fiona bit back a laugh. The Earl of Clonmore—more commonly known as the Major—was Olivia's grandfather and Bridie's favorite frenemy. They argued about life, the universe, and everything during bridge, bingo, and flower shows.

Fiona threw on her dressing gown and went out into the kitchen.

Olivia was seated at the kitchen table, drinking tea and perusing the morning paper. She wore a beautiful emerald dress, and her auburn hair was pulled into a chic chignon. She looked up when Fiona came in. "Wow, Fee. Conditioner is your friend."

"Morning to you, too, Liv."

"Right, girls. I'm off." Bridie grabbed her handbag off the kitchen counter. "Be at the church before eleven."

"Yes, Bridie," they chorused.

When she left, Fiona turned to Olivia. "I love her to bits, but she's driving me mad. As far as she's concerned, I'm still a kid. And when I'm around her, I revert."

"Tea?" Olivia indicated the half-full pot on the table.

"No, thanks. I'll hit the shower and get dressed; then we can spend a productive hour cyberstalking people we used to know way back when."

Olivia laughed. "Sounds like a plan."

Fiona showered, dressed, and applied more makeup than she usually wore. She was fiddling with her hair when Olivia knocked on her bedroom door.

"Shall I?" She pointed to Fiona's hair straighteners.

"It's hopeless. I can't seem to tame it."

"Never fear. Olivia is here."

Within fifteen minutes, Olivia had Fiona's hair straightened and tamed.

A glamorous stranger stared back at her from the

vanity mirror, straight-haired and red-lipped. "You're a genius. Thank you."

"No problem." Olivia glanced at her phone. "We have over an hour before we're due at the church."

"My aunt asked me to clear out my storage boxes. Want to laugh at our school yearbook photos?"

"Sounds like the sort of thing mature adults would do," Olivia said. "Go get them."

"Bridie's got my old photo albums and mementos stored under the bed." Fiona bent down and pulled out a couple of boxes. "I keep meaning to sort through them and take the ones I want to save home to my apartment in Dublin. I guess this weekend is as good a time as any."

Olivia lifted the lid off the first box and leafed through a small photo album. "These are from our school trip to Berlin in third year. Oh, my God. That was the time I shaved my head, and the nuns had a conniption."

"There are even worse ones of you in here," Fiona said. "Irish college the summer before the Leaving Cert. You dyed your hair pink, and I dyed mine blue."

"Gosh, we look a state."

Olivia lifted the lid off the second container and rifled through its contents. "Looks like this one is from your year in the States. I have fond memories of the time we met up in San Francisco. Hey, here's a picture of you with your host family. Do you keep in touch?"

"Christmas cards."

"Oh, wow!" Olivia held up an elegant wooden box emblazoned with Chinese characters. "You still have your little memory box."

"What?" Fiona dropped the envelope she was holding.

A prickle of foreboding snaked down her spine. What had she kept in that box?

"I have no idea what happened to mine," Olivia said. "Do you remember the day we bought them in that little shop in Chinatown?"

Gavin...Las Vegas...*oh, feck*! She tried to yank it out of Olivia's grasp.

"No way." Olivia was grinning. "I want to know what you hid in the false bottom."

"Give it here."

Olivia had already opened the box and located its false bottom.

Fiona's heart rate accelerated into the fast lane. *Feck, feck, feck!*

Olivia was holding papers in her hand. "Ah, you're a sly one. Photos, eh?"

"I'm serious. Give me the box."

"Hold on a sec...here's one of you and Gavin. Huh?" Olivia raised an eyebrow questioningly. "You look pretty cozy. Where was this taken?"

Fiona's stomach performed a stunt worthy of an acrobat. "Las Vegas."

"Vegas, eh? Where's Muireann in these pictures?" Olivia put her hand back into the box and extracted more photos and papers. She flipped through them and then paused. "What the hell?"

Shite! Olivia must have found the photo of her and Gavin kissing. Why hadn't she destroyed it years ago? Why had she been soppy and sentimental and kept it?

"Fiona." Olivia's rosy cheeks were pale, her voice uncharacteristically tremulous. "Is this a marriage certificate?"

6

"Aw, fuck!" Gavin tossed his water bottle to the ground and inspected the damage.

Wiggly Poo gave a final retch, then bounded up to Gavin and licked his hand.

"Get off me, you bad dog. Look what you've done."

Wiggly Poo retrieved the remnants of Gavin's wedding suit trousers from his dog basket and deposited them at his master's feet.

"Are you expecting praise for massacring my trousers?"

The dog wagged his tail.

"Do you think we should call the vet?" Jonas leaned against the doorframe of Gavin's bedroom, a smile curving his lips.

"That fecker ate my wedding suit." Gavin held up the shredded trousers. "He deserves to be sick."

"You're a heartless dog daddy." Jonas was laughing. The traitor!

"For the last time, it's not my dog."

"Whatever you say, mate." His friend straightened and reached for Gavin's suit jacket. "He's after puking all over this, too."

"What the hell am I going to do?" He threw open his wardrobe and rifled through his clothes. "Muireann's going to kill me."

"An unfortunate start to married life," Jonas said dryly. "Have you no other suit you could wear?"

"None Muireann would deem acceptable. It has to be a morning suit."

"Okay. You hop in the shower, and I'll ring the suit rental place on Patrick Street."

"Shouldn't we take the dog to the vet first? If I need to take him, it'd better be now. We're not due at the church until eleven."

"Nah. He looks remarkably cheerful for a dog that just threw up. We'll give him breakfast and see how he fares."

"Right." Gavin leaned his head against the wardrobe door, thoughts racing, chest heaving. "Dammit. Muireann will be pissed. She was dead set on me wearing that suit."

"Shower. Shave. I'll take care of the dog and the phone call."

"Jonas, you're a star. Thank you."

"No worries. Now get moving." Jonas picked up Wiggly Poo. "And don't have a panic attack in the shower."

"Not panic. Asthma." Gavin gestured toward Wiggly Poo.

Jonas arched an eyebrow. "Yeah, right."

Gavin stripped in his en suite bathroom and stepped into the shower. He blasted it at top power, relishing the feeling of the needles of water stabbing his back. Everything would be fine. He'd find a solution. Even if he couldn't wear the suit Muireann had chosen, he wouldn't show up at the church in his birthday suit.

He washed, shaved, and dressed with as much speed as he could muster in his groggy state. Jeans and a T-shirt would do until he got a suit at The Black Tie. By the time he entered the kitchen, Jonas had breakfast on the table.

Gavin sniffed the air in appreciation. "A full Irish. Jonas, I might marry you instead."

"I figured a culinary coronary would be a fitting end to the morning."

"Woof!" Wiggly Poo dashed under the kitchen table and buried his snout in Gavin's crotch.

"Wiggly Poo. We need to have a word about your manners. Crotch sniffing is not socially acceptable."

"You're not seriously going to leave the poor creature saddled with that name?"

"I dunno." Gavin examined the dog. "It sort of suits him."

Jonas speared a fried mushroom. "I spoke to Nora at The Black Tie. She's rooting in the back for a couple of suits for you. Said it's a pity you're so tall."

"I won't be shrinking between now and the ceremony. Whatever she has will have to do."

"Right-o. Eat up, and we'll go by after we drop the dog off."

"Sure your aunt realizes what she's letting herself in for?"

"Ignorance is bliss, my friend. Besides, Mary's good with dogs. She'll be grand."

"It's her house I'm worried about."

He piled his plate high with rashers, sausages, black and white puddings, fried mushrooms, and tomatoes. On one point Jonas was correct: he was the superior cook. "Delicious."

"The dog seems to like it, too."

"What the..." Wiggly Poo had hopped up on the chair next to Gavin's and was helping himself from Gavin's plate. "Ugh. That's disgusting." He scooped up the puppy and placed him beside his food bowl. "Bad doggy. You've worse table manners than Bernard."

"If he tucked into your grub with such gusto, looks like he won't be needing a vet," Jonas said, grinning.

Gavin's mobile rang. He glanced at caller display.

His fiancée. What was he going say about the suit?

"Muireann." His voice rang with false cheer.

Jonas mimed a hangman's noose, complete with comical facial expressions.

Gavin flipped him the finger. He strode into his bedroom and closed the door behind him. "How are you this morning? All ready for the wedding?"

"What's wrong, Gavin?" She sounded peevish. "Did something happen?"

"What makes you ask that?"

"Your tone of voice. Is Wiggly Poo okay? You took him for a morning walk, right?"

Damn. He knew he'd forgotten something. "Yeah, sure."

"Good." Her tone was clipped. "I'm calling to remind you to bring the rings."

"That's Jonas's job."

"Exactly. That's why I'm calling *you*. Jonas is about as reliable as a leaking boat."

"That's a bit harsh."

"But accurate."

"Jonas is my friend, Muireann. I don't bitch about the twins."

Silence.

"Sorry. I want today to be perfect," she said.

"Fine," Gavin said. "I'll make sure he has them."

"By the way, there's something I've been meaning to tell you." She lowered her voice to a whisper. "I wanted to mention it to you last night, but we had that disagreement."

"What's up?"

"I'm late."

"Late?"

"My period, silly."

Gavin's blood turned to ice. "Come again?"

"It might be due to wedding stress, but I'm usually so regular."

His mouth formed silent words. Seconds of tense silence stretched into a minute.

"Aren't you going to say anything, Gavin?"

"I...that's...great." He tasted bile and swallowed hard.

"I know we hadn't planned to start trying for another few months. Sometimes, these things just happen."

They did? Surely not when people were vigilant about birth control.

"I knew you'd be pleased," she continued. "I haven't bought a pregnancy test yet, but I thought the news would cheer you up before you have to face the crowd in the church."

"That's great," he repeated, feeling sick.

"I'll see you at the church in a couple of hours. This wedding is going to be perfect."

"WHAT'S THIS?" Olivia clutched a piece of paper in her hand.

Fiona stared at her, and her heart began to race. "It's nothing," she said and tried to snatch it from Olivia.

Olivia took a step back and held the certificate out of reach. "Like hell it's nothing. This says you married Gavin Maguire in Las Vegas eight years ago."

"We didn't, though. Not really." Fiona's voice cracked with desperation, and her palms began to sweat.

"You didn't really marry?" Olivia's eyebrows reached the ceiling. "You'll need to rephrase that for me, Fee. Perhaps I'm slow on the uptake after last night's debauchery. I thought one was either married or not, no in between."

"We exchanged vows. However, the officiant didn't register the marriage."

"Whoa! Back up a sec. Officiant?" Olivia blinked. "If you had an officiant, how is the marriage not legal?"

"It's…complicated."

"So explain it to me in easy-peasy words."

Fiona regarded Olivia's stubborn expression and sighed. "You're not going to let me off the hook, are you?"

"No way. I see a marriage certificate between you and

Gavin—the groom in the wedding we're about to attend—and I want answers."

"Okay, fine. It's not what you think. This is only a provisional cert and the officiant was a drunk Elvis impersonator."

"Fee! Tell me what happened."

"Remember when Muireann and her pals came to stay during my year in Flagstaff, Arizona?"

"Uninvited, if I recall correctly."

"Yeah. You know Muireann. She showed up with Gavin, the twins, and a couple of other lads in tow. She wasn't going out with Gavin yet, but it was only a matter of time. They stayed in the Flagstaff area for a few days and planned a trip to the Grand Canyon."

"And didn't invite you." Olivia finished her thought.

"Of course not. It was kind of embarrassing. My host family let me have the weekend free to spend with them, and they took off without me."

"Sounds like the Muireann we know and love," Olivia said dryly. "How did this all lead to you, Gavin, and a dude in an Elvis suit?"

"I'm getting there, Liv. Bear with me. Anyway, they'd been gone a couple of hours when I got a call from Gavin. He'd realized I'd been left behind against my will and told Muireann and the others to go on without him. They'd left him somewhere along Route 64. He called me to come collect him because he was stranded."

"And muggins complied." Olivia shook her head. "Thank goodness you've developed backbone in the intervening years."

"Oy! Do you want me to finish telling the story, or not?"

Olivia picked up her mug of tea. "Sorry. Go on."

"I collected Gavin. He was in a pisser of a mood. I asked if he wanted us to drive to the Grand Canyon. He said no. Didn't want to run the risk of running into Muireann and the others until he'd had time to calm down. He wanted to know what I planned to do with my weekend off. I said I was toying with the idea of heading to Vegas but wasn't sure I had the nerve to go on my own."

"Ha! So says the woman about to embark on a world trip alone."

Fiona gave a wry smile. "We're talking about twenty-one-year-old me. The idea of walking into a restaurant on my own terrified me. A bar or casino? Forget it."

"And Gavin oh-so-conveniently suggested he accompany you?"

"Yeah. I was shocked, to be honest. Also a little excited. I'd always had a crush on Gavin, but it was clear Muireann was making a play for him, and Muireann always gets what she wants. I didn't seriously think anything would happen between us that weekend, but I was willing to go and have a laugh."

"By the look of that photo, you had more than a laugh."

"Put it this way—turns out Long Island iced tea contains five shots of alcohol. Who knew?"

"Oh, dear," Olivia said with a laugh. "How many did you down?"

"I lost count after the third."

Olivia winced. "Ouch."

"Indeed. I vaguely recall chatting to a drunk Elvis

impersonator in a bar. Either we bought him a drink, or he bought us a round. He'd lost his job and his wife had kicked him out. Anyway, he told us he'd worked as a wedding officiant at a local chapel until they fired him a couple of weeks before. We thought this was funny. With the alcohol flowing, we thought everything was funny.

"Drunk Elvis started going on about the number of couples he'd married and how he always knew whether they'd last. He said he could see we were the real deal, and we should definitely tie the knot. At first, it was all a drunken joke. But the more we drank, the more convinced Gavin became that we should do it."

"Wow. How drunk was he?"

"Very. If even I noticed he was hammered, he had to be in a state." Fiona began to pace. "Drunk Elvis offered to do us a special offer on the ceremony. He'd say a few words, sing a song, and we'd sign the papers. I don't know why I went along with it. It was insane. For a moment, I actually hoped Gavin would fall in love with me."

"And that didn't happen," Olivia said.

"No. We had sex. That much I remember. I also remember it was fantastic, but I digress."

"Digress all you want," Olivia said. "I'm intrigued."

"You can stay intrigued. You're getting no details out of me."

"Ah, Fee. You're no fun."

"The morning after was no fun, put it that way. When I was done retching, Gavin made it clear he wanted out of the marriage and was going to talk to Drunk Elvis. He'd read the fine print in our marriage guide and realized our marriage wouldn't be legally binding until Drunk Elvis lodged the papers with the marriage bureau. Gavin wanted to offer to pay for him to stay in the motel for a couple of weeks, give him time to get on his feet after his personal drama. In return, he would agree to forget the ceremony ever happened."

"And did he?"

"I guess. I never heard anything to the contrary. For all I know, Drunk Elvis wasn't a real officiant. And even if he was, maybe the marriage isn't valid because we were all under the influence at the time."

"Aidan's had clients who married in Vegas. It's easy enough to check if the papers were registered. It's all online."

Fiona's stomach flipped. "If he said he wouldn't register the papers, why would he have done so?"

"Don't you want to be certain?"

"I'm not the one about to walk down the aisle."

"In that case, you've got nothing to lose by checking. Why don't we look up your Drunk Elvis and see if he's genuine?"

"Okay," Fiona said, thinking of all the reasons it was not okay. "I'll fire up my laptop."

"Right." Olivia glanced at the provisional certificate. "Drew Draper. What a name. Come on, Google, do your magic."

"Wow," Fiona said. "Who knew there were so many Drew Drapers in the world?"

"Here we go," Olivia said. "Drew Draper, preacher. Wow. He doesn't look like an Elvis preacher, but he seems legit. I say we check the online registry."

"Do we have to?" The room was starting to spin around Fiona.

"If you're convinced Drew Draper destroyed those papers, why are you afraid to look up the wedding registry?"

"I don't know." Fiona took a deep breath. "Sometimes it's best to leave well alone. Gavin's about to marry Muireann."

"Exactly. That's my point." Olivia tapped the keyboard keys. "Here goes. What year was it, again?"

"Two thousand six. June two thousand six."

"Right. Oh…there's a match."

"What? No. No way." Fiona stared at the screen.

Olivia read the entry aloud. "Fiona Mary Byrne and Gavin Aloysius Maguire. Gavin's middle name is Aloysius?"

The room tilted under Fiona's feet. "This can't be happening."

Olivia drew back from the computer screen, her face a mirror of Fiona's emotions. "Fee, what are you going to do?"

7

"What do you think?" Nora Fitzgerald, proprietor of The Black Tie, Ballybeg's only suit rental establishment, stood back and admired her handiwork.

Gavin stared at his reflection in the shop mirror, poleaxed. "It...it's..." he stuttered.

Jonas regarded it dubiously. "It fits. Which is probably its only redeeming feature."

"I look like a character in an old John Travolta film."

"You're certainly rocking a seventies vibe." Jonas's voice cracked under the strain of repressing his laughter. "The matching boots are a great touch."

Gavin looked down at the white, fur-trimmed boots and cringed. "Have you no other suit, Nora?" he asked, wide-eyed. "Anything except this one."

Nora compressed her lips into a scarlet slash. "Sure, it's hardly my fault you left it till the last minute, Gavin. It's still wedding season, and the debs season is starting. I don't have many suits in stock for men your height."

"If I take it, we'll need to double back to the cottage and get different shoes."

Jonas pointed to his watch. "I hate to break it to you, mate. Your bride is due at the church in fifteen minutes, and you're supposed to be there before her."

"Fuck." Gavin ran his hands through his hair. "Fuck, fuck, fuck."

"That's terrible language to be coming out of a man on his wedding day," said Nora, pretending to be shocked.

"Sorry, Nora." Why hadn't he remembered to wear a pair of formal shoes when he'd left the house? Now he was stuck with the prospect of wearing his runners, going barefoot, or keeping on the furry boots. He rubbed his chin. With everything that had gone wrong this morning, at least he'd remembered to shave.

Nora crossed her skinny arms over her bony chest. "Are you taking the outfit or not?"

"Fine," he said with a sigh. "I'll take it."

If Muireann reacted the way he suspected she would, theirs would be a very short marriage.

FIONA STARED at the computer screen. "Please tell me I'm hallucinating."

"'Fraid not, Fee."

"Surely to goodness they checked Gavin's marital status before issuing his marriage license?"

"If the local Registrar couldn't find a record of him

being married in Ireland or the UK, they'd issue the license," Olivia said. "Aidan's dealt with cases of bigamy before, so I'm familiar with these issues. Unlike some countries, Ireland doesn't keep tabs on weddings performed abroad. We don't have the resources."

"Seriously?" Were they living in a banana republic? Ireland was a first-world country, for feck's sake. "Not even an Internet search like we did?"

"But we knew where to look. There's no single worldwide registry of marriages, and the Irish are scattered across the globe."

"So any fool can lie and say they're single? That's disgraceful."

Olivia shrugged. "This is Ireland, Fee. We don't do paperwork. And when we do, we fuck it up."

Fiona massaged her temples. "This can't be happening."

"What are you going to do? You'll have to tell him."

"What? Wait a minute, Liv. Let me think this through. What do you expect me to do? Crash into the church and announce it to the whole congregation?"

Olivia pointed to the bedside clock. "Whatever you're doing, you'd better do it fast. The wedding starts in ten minutes."

"Please tell me you're joking."

"Nope. Grab your bag and let's go."

"Wait." Fiona's voice broke on a note of desperation. "What am I going to say? I can't barge in and wreck his wedding."

"You'd seriously let him marry another woman when he's already married to you?"

"I don't know." Fiona slumped into a chair and buried her head in her hands. "Why does life have to be so damn complicated?"

"Take a deep breath and come on. We can figure out a plan in the car."

Olivia drove even faster than she talked, which meant Fiona prayed for her life.

"I can simply ask to have a word with Gavin, right? Discreetly. No need to barge in and announce we're married."

"Right," Olivia said, swerving to avoid a tractor. "Great idea. What then?"

"I dunno. Drag him into the vestry?"

"Sounds indecent."

"I can hardly have a private talk with him in front of three-hundred-plus people."

"Point taken. But what happens after? Let's say you tell him. What are you going to do if he tells you to forget it and marries her anyway?"

"Then that's what he does," Fiona said. "And let's face it, that's probably what he will do. Muireann will kill him if he jilts her."

Olivia took a sharp turn, almost collided with a taxi, and applied the brakes. "Will you keep mum if he does marry her?"

"Yeah. Yeah, I will." Fiona rubbed her neck. She'd have whiplash by the time they reached the church. "I'll have done my duty and told him about the Vegas wedding."

"What if you want to get married in a few years' time?"

"I guess I'll deal with it if and when the situation arises."

"It'll be a hell of a lot messier if you need to divorce Gavin after he's already married."

The spire of St. Mary's was visible now. Fiona's stomach lurched. "Can't we divorce quietly in Vegas?"

"Nope. Not unless one of you is a legal resident. Sure, if divorce were that simple, people would be hopping over to Vegas all the time instead of dealing with our poxy legal system."

"There goes that plan. How long does divorce take in Ireland?"

"Ages." Olivia rolled to a stop at a red light. "You need to have been living apart for a few years before you can apply. Then add however long it takes for the case to go through the system."

"What the feck?"

"Didn't you know that?"

"I'd heard it took longer to get a divorce in Ireland than in many places, but I didn't realize it was that long. That's insane."

"Oh, yeah." Olivia hit the accelerator. "I don't know how long it will be for you and Gavin, though. You'll need to talk to Aidan or another lawyer." She screeched to a halt in front of St. Mary's Church. "Here we are."

"Damn. The doors are closed."

"So?" Olivia turned to face her. "You're going in there and saying what you have to say. Whatever that is."

Fiona took a deep breath. "I can do this."

"Fee, you're still wearing your slippers."

"What?" Fiona glanced at her feet. Two bunny slippers stared back at her. "There's no time to go back."

"You can't go into a church wearing bunny slippers."

Fiona pushed open the car door. "At least I'm not in my Docs. Aunt Deirdre will be pleased."

"I'll follow you in once I've found a parking space."

"Thanks, Liv. Wish me luck." Fiona ran up the path to the church's imposing wooden doors and stopped.

Could she do this? Should she do this? How could she not?

She pushed open the door and stepped inside.

Dragging oxygen into her lungs, she uttered the words that would damn her in the eyes of her family, friends, and half the town of Ballybeg. "Stop the wedding."

8

Three hundred hats swiveled in Fiona's direction.

She stood in the doorway of St. Mary's Church, heart pounding, legs quaking.

A sea of spray-tanned faces stared back at her. The guests blurred together in a jumble of wedding finery, ostentatious hats, bling jewelry, fake nails, and even faker expressions of horror. Fiona would bet her comic collection that most were thrilled by this turn of events. Who hadn't wondered what it would be like if a wedding ceremony were to be disrupted?

They were about to find out. *What a bloody nightmare.*

She glanced down at her fluffy bedroom slippers. Had she known "Disrupt a Wedding" was on today's to-do list, she'd have dressed for the occasion.

Fiona wet her lips and shifted her weight from one leg to the other. "I said, stop the wedding." Her voice was stronger now, less croaky.

For an instant, silence thick with tension strained the walls. Then came a feminine shriek, followed by an almighty crash.

Fiona's gaze was drawn to the front of the church and the bridal couple. With their blond hair and blue eyes, they looked more like brother and sister than future man and wife, albeit with a significant difference in height. In a gesture of togetherness, they both wore white. Muire-ann's dress was a meringue creation with skirts wide enough to make Scarlett O'Hara jealous. Gavin wore a hideous satin and velvet suit, teamed with a pair of furry white boots. Had it been the seventies, he might have been fashionable.

Muireann sagged against a pillar, clutching a statue of the Virgin Mary for support. The remnants of a floral arrangement lay at her feet in a tableau of petals and smashed porcelain.

Gavin stood by the altar, stock-still and slack-jawed. Despite his ridiculous outfit, he was bone-meltingly gorgeous. His broad shoulders strained his suit jacket, reminding her of what lay beneath. She'd loved running her fingers over those shoulders, feeling the taut muscles of his upper arms.

Her stomach did a rollercoaster flip. *Oh, hell.* If only they'd never found that piece of paper.

"What is the meaning of this, young lady?" The stern tones of the parish priest boomed through the church. For such a small man, Father Fagin had a powerful voice. He placed the bible on the pulpit with trembling aged hands, and creaked down the aisle. When he was a few steps away, he paused and squinted at her through rheumy eyes. “Is that you, Fiona?” The furrows on his brow deepened. “What’s this about?”

Her legs wobbled but she stood her ground. “I need to speak to Gavin.”

Father Fagin’s furry gray eyebrows shot north. “Can’t it wait until the reception?”

“No. I need to speak to him now.” There was a hint of exasperation in her voice. “In private.”

“What nonsense.” Uncle Bernard stomped out of his pew to loom over her. His walrus moustache bobbed in indignation. “You’ve always been eccentric, Fiona, but this…this is outrageous.”

“I’m sorry, but I don’t have a choice.”

“Why?”

Fiona’s neck jerked. The old zing of awareness made the hairs on the nape of her neck spring to attention. In his ludicrous white velvet wedding suit, Gavin resembled a cross between the blond fella from Abba and the yeti. How he still managed to exude sex appeal was a conundrum she’d rather not contemplate.

“Why do you need to speak to me?” His deep voice broke in panic. Somewhere in the recesses of his mind he must remember Drew Draper.

Guilt gnawed her insides. “It’s best discussed in private.”

His mouth opened and closed, fish-like. Eventually, he nodded. “Is there somewhere we can go, Father?”

“Well, I…Yes. There’s the vestry.” Father Fagin appeared flummoxed. She could hardly blame him. It wasn’t every day a crazy lady burst into his church and crashed a wedding.

The vestry of St. Mary's was a small wood-paneled room located at the back of the church. Fiona followed Gavin inside and shut the door behind them.

He was pale and flustered. "What's going on, Fiona?"

"Do you remember Las Vegas?"

"You want to discuss that now? Seconds before I marry your cousin?"

"I don't have a choice, not morally." *Not to mention legally.*

"What do you mean?" He was pacing the small room, his face the same shade as his suit.

"We got married, Gavin."

"No, we didn't. The papers were never registered."

She exhaled in a rush. "Unfortunately, they were."

"What?" His stopped short, his handsome face frozen in an expression of horror. "That's impossible. Your man —what was his name?"

"Drew Draper."

"He said he wouldn't register the papers with the wedding bureau."

"Well, he did register them, or someone else did it on his behalf. Olivia and I checked the Las Vegas online register, and our wedding details are in there."

"No way."

"Yes way." She pulled up the search results on her smart phone and shoved the display in front of Gavin's face. "See? Fiona Mary Byrne and Gavin Aloysius Maguire, 16 June, 2006."

His eyes met hers briefly, then moved toward the glow of the screen. He hesitated before taking the phone, a flash of uncertainty quickly replaced by determination. When he reached out, it was with steady hands.

As he scanned the contents of the display, his jaw tightened.

Sick fear sent Fiona's world into a spin. This was pure sensory overload. A smorgasbord of emotions, and none of them were positive.

An eternity passed before his eyes rose to meet hers. Those sea-blue eyes framed with dark blond lashes. She'd loved him once. Fiona's heart did a slow thump and roll.

"Please tell me this is a joke." His voice was low and gravelly. The deep bass had always reminded her of James Earl Jones.

"No joke, Gav. We're married." She attempted a nonchalant shrug, but her shoulders were pliable as cement. "By the way, I didn't know your middle name was Aloysius."

"Not something I care to share." Gavin put the phone on a large mahogany desk and ran a hand over his rugged features. "I don't fucking believe this. I'm supposed to be getting married today. What am I going to tell Muireann?"

"It's up to you what you tell her." She paused and took a deep breath. "It's up to you *if* you tell her."

His eyes shot up, clashing with hers. "What do you mean?"

"I mean we can invent a reason for my crashing the wedding. I'm willing to play the part of the loony cousin, keep my trap shut, and pretend the document doesn't exist."

"You mean lie?" he asked in a monotone, his brow creased in thought.

"Why not? No one will ever know." *Apart from Olivia, Drew Draper, and who-the-hell-else in Las Vegas.*

"We'll know. For feck's sake, Fiona. I can't commit bigamy."

"That's your decision. I've done my duty by telling you. What you do with the information is your call."

She was dangling a carrot of hope before him, a way to get out of this bloody mess. A myriad of emotions flickered across his face—jerky, blurry, hypnotic, like an old film reel.

The door to the vestry burst open.

"What's going on in here?" roared Bernard. "What's the meaning of this, Fiona? Have you lost your mind?"

"I'm sorry, Uncle Bernard. I had to speak to Gavin."

"What? He's in the middle of marrying my daughter. How dare you interrupt their wedding?"

"I realize this is a question of some delicacy," said Father Fagin, his creaky tread following in Bernard's blustery wake, "but is there any reason the ceremony should not proceed?"

"Of course there isn't." Bernard glowered at Gavin. "Get out there right now and marry my daughter."

Gavin straightened, swaying slightly. He brushed off the desk and sent Fiona's phone flying.

Bernard caught it and scrutinized the display screen.

Then he let out an unholy roar.

9

Gavin had a split second to react before Bernard lunged. The punch caught him on the chin. He reeled back, and sidestepped a second blow. "Steady on. It's not what you think."

Bernard's face was mottled, and his eyes were wild. "Not what I think? What the hell should I think? You're already married to Fiona, yet you were about to marry my daughter."

His bellows reverberated off the wooden walls of the vestry. There was little chance the people in the church hadn't heard. Poor Muireann. Poor Fiona. What a flaming mess.

"Bernard," said Father Fagin in the same authoritative voice he'd used when he'd had the misfortune to be Gavin's secondary school religion teacher. "I will not tolerate violence in my church."

Bernard glared at the elderly priest, but Father Fagin stood resolute. Bernard's jowls spasmed with rage before settling into a stiff mask.

"May I see the phone?" Father Fagin extended a gnarled hand.

Bernard's grip on Fiona's phone was tight enough to render his knuckles white. He handed it to the priest. "Is this genuine?" he asked.

"Is what genuine?" Muireann appeared in the doorway of the vestry. Her breathing was shallow. Each breath made her narrow chest heave. Despite the silly dress, she was beautiful—like a porcelain doll in an antique shop.

Gavin squeezed his eyes shut. This could not be happening. His orderly life was unraveling faster than the curtains Wiggly Poo had desecrated the previous day.

He opened his eyes and addressed his bride. "I can explain."

"Explain what?" She sounded shrill. She looked beseechingly at Bernard. "Daddy, what's going on?"

Her father opened and closed his gob, but no words came out.

"Muireann, my dear, let me examine this for a moment." Father Fagin peered at the phone through lenses thicker than triple glazing. He lowered the device and shook his head. "Until I know whether or not this is legitimate, I have to assume there's an impediment to proceeding with today's ceremony."

Muireann's eyes narrowed to mascaraed slits. "What impediment?"

Gavin's stiff bow tie was tighter than a noose. "I married Fiona in Las Vegas eight years ago."

She turned chalky white under her tan. "What? You married *her*?" She half walked, half stumbled into the room, hampered by the meringue dress. Her blond hair was teased into a bouffant style that, like the dress, engulfed her tiny frame. She looked from Gavin to Fiona, then back to Gavin. "Tell me this is a joke."

Sweat gathered beneath the collar of his ridiculous suit. "I wish I could."

She slapped him. Despite her petite stature, she delivered a decent hit. "Tell. Me. Everything."

He tried to clear the frog in his throat, but his voice still sounded croaky. "Until a few minutes ago, I had no idea the marriage was legally valid."

"If you got married, why wouldn't it be valid?" Her voice was reaching a crescendo.

His jaw twitched, and his gaze slid toward Fiona. "Because the wedding officiant was drunk, and I paid him off the next morning. A Vegas wedding must be registered within ten days of the ceremony. I gave the guy who married us money not to file the papers."

"When did this happen? When we visited Fiona on her *au pair* year?"

"Yes," Fiona said. With her pale face whiter than usual, she looked as wretched as he felt. "The rest of you had a falling out with Gavin and left him stranded on Route 64. I collected him, and we headed for Vegas while you went on to the Grand Canyon."

The nostrils of Muireann's button nose flared. "You wasted no time getting your clutches into him. Well, you can't have him." She pivoted on a stiletto heel. "Father, surely you're not taking this seriously?"

"I can't perform the ceremony until I've confirmed their marriage isn't valid."

She placed a delicate hand on the elderly priest's sleeve. "Everyone's here," she said in an imploring tone. "You have to marry us."

"Not if I have reason to believe one of the partners might already be married," Father Fagin said sternly. "It would be bigamy."

Her lower lip trembled, and tears filled her large blue eyes. "But it's my wedding day. Everything's ready. Everyone's here. Everything's supposed to be perfect."

"I'll fix this," Gavin said. "I don't know how, but I'll fix it."

Her tears were falling now, forming jagged lines of color down her face. "I should have listened to my parents. They always said you were beneath me. You've wrecked everything."

"Muireann—"

"Don't 'Muireann' me," she screamed. "Look at the state of you. You stink of mothballs. Where's the beautiful suit Claudette made for you?"

He swallowed a treacherous laugh. "Wiggly Poo ate it."

"You're blaming the dog?" She was shaking now, rage emanating from her every pore. "You're unbelievable."

"It's true," he said. "Ask Jonas."

"Jonas is a writer. He lies for a living."

"I had to swing by Nora Fitzgerald's suit rental place. I'm sorry about the suit, but it was the only one she had in my size and I was desperate."

"Desperate is right," she said, indicating his feet. "So desperate you let her kit you out in one of her husband's old Elvis impersonator costumes."

"What?" Gavin looked down at the suit and the furry

boots. Now she mentioned it, they did have an Elvis vibe. *Jaysus.* He was being haunted by Elvis impersonators today, all intent on ruining his life.

"Tell me, Gavin. Did you sleep with Fiona? Was it a once-off, or did you regularly cheat on me with my first cousin?"

"He didn't cheat on you," Fiona said with quiet determination. "You and Gavin weren't an item yet."

"Why should I believe a word you say?" Muireann snarled.

"It's true," Gavin said. "It was just a one-night stand."

Fiona teetered as though he'd punched her.

Aw, crap.

"A one-night stand that ended in marriage," Muireann snapped. "Let's not gloss over the salient part." She stepped forward and jabbed a talon into his chest. "You're going to tell our guests the wedding's off, and you're going to tell them why. You screwed up, Gavin. You face them."

"We'll both go." Fiona placed a firm hand on his arm. "This mess is of both our making." She stood regal in her plain black dress and bunny slippers. He'd always admired her fiery determination, appreciated her dry sense of humor. Fiona was as much a victim of this cock-up as Muireann.

He squared his shoulders and inclined his head a fraction—it was the best he could do with the tight bow tie around his neck. "Fair enough. Let's get this over with."

WITH THE NOTABLE exception of the rip-his-clothes-off-and-shag-him-senseless variety, walking up the aisle with Gavin Maguire had been Fiona's favorite teenage fantasy. Strangely, her daydreams skipped a few details: the yeti suit, the bunny slippers, the bigamy.

United in matrimony and bad footwear—what a flaming nightmare.

During the short journey from the vestry to the altar, the collective gaze of the wedding guests bore into their backs.

She kept her head down and struggled to keep up with Gavin's long strides. His broad shoulders strained his suit jacket, and the trousers were several centimeters too short. A treacherous fit of the giggles threatened, like they always did whenever she found herself in a situation where laughter would be deemed inappropriate.

The entire scenario was absurd. How could vows they had been too drunk to enunciate be legally binding? How could Drew Draper be a legit wedding officiant? And how the feck had her weekend turned into such a train wreck that running back to Dublin and the faithless, feckless Philip seemed preferable?

They reached the altar and turned to face the guests.

The murmurs faded into expectant silence.

Fiona surveyed the crowd. Deirdre wore an expression of petulant impatience. Bridie's brow was crinkled in confusion. Olivia sat next to the odious Aidan, tense as a wound spring.

The other guests' faces displayed a myriad of emotions. Some were thrilled by the unfolding drama, others horrified.

Well, their emotions are about to be amplified.

When Gavin spoke, his voice was thick. "I'm sure you're wondering what's going on. Long story short, the wedding's off. I accept full responsibility for the situation." He paused to clear his throat. "Eight years ago, I had a drunken night out with Fiona in Las Vegas. It seems we got married."

There was a gasp from the crowd, followed by a scream.

Deirdre rose from her pew like an avenging Valkyrie. Her thin lips quivered, and her body vibrated with tension. "You're calling off the wedding? Now? In front of everyone? Because you married *her*?" On each sentence, her voice rose higher.

"I have no choice." He squirmed in his yeti suit. "I can't marry Muireann until I annul my marriage to Fiona."

Bridie sat stunned in the pew next to Deirdre. Fiona read shock and anger in her expression. Bridie's gaze met hers, and she flinched at her aunt's look of hurt disbelief.

Deirdre advanced, wielding her wedding handbag like a weapon. She grabbed Fiona's arm and dug sharp nails into her skin. "You were determined to ruin Muireann's big day. I knew it the moment you ripped your dress."

Fiona backed into the stone altar and jerked her arm free. "Get off me. You know perfectly well the dress was the wrong fit."

"You've always been jealous of her." She was up in Fiona's face now, wafting breath mints and Chanel No. 5. Her veiled hat was askew, making her resemble a Cyclops.

The hard stone of the altar dug into Fiona's back.

"Don't be daft. Muireann and I aren't close, but I wouldn't wish this experience on anyone."

"As for you, Gavin Maguire." Deirdre eyes burned with hatred. "How dare you humiliate my daughter?"

"I'm sorry, Deirdre. I truly am."

"Sorry isn't good enough. Do you know how much we've spent on this wedding?"

Fiona rubbed her sore arm and sidled out of Deirdre's reach.

"I've a fair notion," he said. "After all, I've paid half."

"I expect you to reimburse our share of the wedding expenses."

"Of course, but this is hardly the time—"

Deirdre hurled her handbag at Gavin's head. "Get out of my sight, both of you. Get out!"

Gavin ducked, but he needn't have bothered. Deirdre's aim was lousy. The bag hurtled through the air, hit a vase on the altar, and sent shattered porcelain, water, and flowers flying.

As if jolted out of a stupor, Bridie blinked, stood, and marched up behind Deirdre. "Stop the carry-on," she said, grabbing her sister-in-law's arm. "Hurling handbags won't fix this problem. Why don't we sit down with a cup of tea in the vestry? Aidan Gant is a solicitor. He'll know what to do."

Aidan, stiff in his wedding suit, sat beside an ashen-faced Olivia a couple of rows behind the bridal family. "I'd be happy to give my legal opinion on the matter."

"I don't want tea," sobbed Deirdre. "I don't want a solicitor. I want a wedding!"

"Unfortunately, there won't be a wedding today."

Bridie looped her arm through Deirdre's and guided her toward the vestry.

Muireann emerged from the small room, supported by Bernard's hammy arms on one side and Father Fagin's frail ones on the other. "Oh, Mummy," she said, tears fluttering on the ends of her eyelashes. "What am I going to do?"

Deirdre stepped forward to embrace her daughter and lost her footing on a wet patch of smashed vase and broken flowers.

The next few seconds passed in slow motion. Deirdre's bony hands groped the air as she fell, finally grabbing on to Bridie's leg for support.

Bridie was wrenched sideways, lost her balance, and crashed onto the hard marble floor.

10

There was a second of stunned silence followed by a guttural moan from Bridie.

Gavin was the first to react.

He closed the space between him and Bridie and squatted beside her. His stomach lurched. Her face was leached of color, and she was lying at an odd angle. Moving on instinct, his hand slipped into one of his suit's many pockets and felt for his phone. "Can you move your legs?"

She tensed and scrunched her face with effort before collapsing onto the hard tiles. "My hip," she gasped. "I think it's broken."

Fiona knelt by her aunt's other side and took her plump hand. "It's okay. I'll call an ambulance."

"I'm on it." He punched numbers into his mobile phone. A woman from the emergency services answered his call on the first ring. "We need an ambulance," he said without preamble. "St. Mary's Church in Ballybeg. Possible broken leg or hip." He listened for a few seconds while she repeated the information back to him. "Yeah, that's correct."

"The ambulance should be with you in fifteen minutes," she said in the calm, authoritative tone teachers and medical professionals seemed to be born with.

He thanked her and disconnected.

"An ambulance is on its way. Should be here in within a quarter of an hour."

The crowd parted, and Jonas emerged carrying an armful of cushions. "I raided the vestry."

"Good man." Gavin eased Bridie's head and shoulders off the ground, and Jonas slipped a couple of cushions beneath her. "I'm reluctant to move her any more than this," Gavin said, wiping his brow. "Not before the paramedics arrive."

"Can I get you a glass of water, Bridie?" Fiona's foot tapped an anxious rhythm on the stone tiles. He was close enough that the fruity smell of her shampoo teased his senses.

"Feck water. I want alcohol. Can't you give me some of that there wine?" She gestured at the chalice on the altar.

"What?" exclaimed Father Fagin. "That's holy wine."

"I don't give a feck what it is. I need something to take the edge off the pain, and I'll be damned if I stoop to taking a nip out of Deirdre's hip flask."

Deirdre's sinewy hands fluttered to her throat. "What do you mean?"

"The hip flask filled with gin you always keep in your handbag. Why do you think your little bag had the power to topple a huge vase?"

"Ladies, please," said Father Fagin, radiating desperation from every creaky joint. "Stop bickering. If Bridie wants wine, I'll bring her the chalice. I suppose a small sip won't do too much harm."

"Small sip me arse. I'm in agony."

Father Fagin handed the large vessel to Gavin with trembling hands, and Gavin held it to Bridie's lips.

She downed a considerable quantity of the watery red liquid before shoving it toward the flabbergasted priest. She shuddered. "Rotgut. How do you priests stand this stuff?" Weary with pain and shock, she slumped onto her pillows, and her eyelids drooped.

"Rotgut or not, it appears to have done the trick," Gavin said.

Bridie was sliding into unconsciousness. "So sore," she whispered.

Panic flitted across Fiona's pale features. "Did she hit her head when she fell? Could she have a concussion?"

"From what I could tell, her right side took the brunt of the fall." He gave her a tired half smile. "I'm sure they'll check her thoroughly at the hospital."

In the distance, the sound of sirens echoed. Within minutes, the paramedics had placed Bridie on a stretcher and bundled her into the ambulance. The vehicle pulled away from the curb, blue lights flashing.

Muireann pushed herself through the crowd and glowered at Fiona, who was being comforted by Olivia. "This is all your fault." She hissed. "And as for you…" She tugged her diamond engagement ring off her finger and hurled it at Gavin. It bounced off his velvet-ruffled chest and tumbled to the ground with a clang. "You can sell the ring to pay back my parents."

He took a step toward her and reached for her arm. "Muireann, please. Can't we discuss this?"

She shrugged herself free. "Leave me alone. I never want to see either of you again." Sobbing, she collapsed into Deirdre's arms. "Oh, Mummy."

Deirdre gave her daughter an ineffectual hug, artfully shielding her clothes from Muireann's streaky mascara.

"Come back into the vestry, my dear." Father Fagin hooked his arm through Muireann's. "Let's get you away from the crowd."

Muireann allowed herself to be led away, supported on one side by the reluctant Deirdre and on the other by the elderly priest.

Gavin bent to retrieve the ring. In the palm of his hand, it felt light and inconsequential. He closed his fist, wincing when the sharply cut diamond dug into his flesh.

His gaze met the crowd's, stare for stare.

Mercifully, no one spoke. They didn't need to. Their expressions said it all.

THE HOSPITAL WAITING room was packed. To Fiona's right, a woman with a screaming toddler tried to placate the child with a packet of crisps. In one corner, an elderly man was muttering to himself and sneaking sips from a hip flask. Everyone was giving the guy with an open leg wound a wide berth.

She checked her watch for the thousandth time. Two

hours since Bridie had been admitted to hospital. Two hours without news.

Just when she'd allowed herself to hope this weekend couldn't possibly get any worse, it had.

And how.

Bridie's fall was partly her fault. Yeah, she hadn't been the one hurling vases around the church, but if she hadn't gone there in the first place, the fall never would have happened.

Olivia returned from the vending machine bearing two steaming plastic cups. "Get that down you," she said and handed one to Fiona before taking the seat beside her.

Fiona took a cautious sip. "Ugh. Vile. What is it supposed to be?"

"A mochaccino. I thought you could do with the sugar."

"At least it's hot and sweet." Fiona's gaze darted from her watch to the clock on the waiting room wall. "Why is it taking so long for news?"

"A two-hour wait is nothing in A&E." Olivia grimaced at her coffee cup. "Bridie will be fine. She's a tough old bird."

Fiona stilled her tapping foot. "I feel terrible about this. If only I'd kept silent..."

"If you'd not come down to Ballybeg for the wedding...yadda, yadda. It was an accident, Fee. If anyone's to blame for this fiasco, it's Deirdre for chucking flowers and water all over the church."

"Fiona Byrne?" A white-clad nurse stood in the doorway, a medical chart in her hand.

Fiona shot out of her seat, spilling hot coffee on her hand. "Yes?"

"Your auntie's finished her tests. She's resting in her room."

"Is she okay?" *Please, please, please.*

"I'll let her explain it to you. She's on St. Ignatius ward, up on the second floor. Room six."

"Thanks for letting me know."

The nurse nodded and disappeared into the throng of patients, visitors, and medical staff.

Fiona shook the dark liquid off her hand and tossed her half-full cup in the bin. "Thanks for waiting with me."

"No bother." Olivia scrunched her nose. "To be honest, I'm not looking forward to going home and facing Aidan's wrath. He's pissed I got mixed up in this."

"I'm sorry."

"Stop apologizing. Listen, why don't I wait for you in the car? We can grab a bite to eat at MacCarthy's before I go home."

"I'm not sure I can face people. Everyone'll want to ask about the non-wedding."

"Sod them. You're leaving Ballybeg on Monday, anyway. Let them talk."

"True," Fiona said with a sigh. "Ballybeg, *baile beag*. It's not called 'small town' for nothing. Yeah, all right. We'll need to stop off at Bridie's for me to pick up shoes first. I'm sick of the sight of these bunny slippers."

They parted in the hallway, Olivia for the car park and Fiona for St. Ignatius ward.

Fiona took the stairs to the second floor. On the walls, menacing posters warned about hospital hygiene for staff and guests due to the prevalence of MRSA and other resilient bugs. The accompanying photographs were enough to give one nightmares. She disinfected her hands for the third time before entering Bridie's room.

Her aunt was lying in a bed by the window in a room shared with five other patients. Fiona exhaled at the sight of her. She was shockingly pale, her skin taut and gray. When had she started to get old? She'd always seemed ageless, frozen in middle age.

Bridie looked up when she approached. "Still in the bunny slippers, Fiona?" Her smile was wan. "Or should I call you Mrs. Maguire?"

She bit her lip. "Bridie…"

Her aunt held up a palm. "I knew you were soft on Gavin, but to marry him in Las Vegas?" Her expression of hurt and confusion sliced Fiona to the core. "Why didn't you tell me?"

"Because I didn't know we were married." She pulled up a spare chair and sat by her aunt's side. "The morning after we said vows and signed papers, Gavin asked the officiant not to register them. He agreed, and we assumed it was sorted."

"But the papers somehow ended up being registered?"

"So it would appear. But enough about me. How are you feeling? Or should I rephrase to how *bad* are you feeling?"

Bridie laughed hoarsely. "I've felt better, but I'll live."

Fiona leaned forward. "What did the doctors say? Is your hip broken?"

"Yes, unfortunately."

Feck. Poor old Bridie. She didn't deserve this.

"Do you need surgery? Or can they put you in a cast until it heals?"

"It's a little more complicated than that." The lines around her eyes were deeper, pinched. "I need a hip replacement."

"What?" Fiona gasped. "Isn't that extreme for a broken hip?"

"Having a hip replacement's been on the cards for a while. My arthritis is getting worse. The accident's made it a matter for sooner rather than later."

"I had no idea your arthritis was that bad."

"Why would you? You hardly ever call."

Fiona sucked in air.

Her aunt reached for her hand. "I'm not chastising you, pet. You've your own life in Dublin. There's nothing for you in Ballybeg except bad memories."

"They're not all bad. You were always kind to me."

"Sure, you were an easy child to be kind to." She shifted position and winced.

Fiona leaped to her feet. "Should I call a nurse?"

"Ah, no. I'll be grand. Will you call in to see me before you leave tomorrow?"

"Of course. When's the operation happening?"

"Monday morning."

"How complicated is the procedure?"

"Hip replacements are routine these days. I'll be fine."

"What will happen when you get out? Will you need help around the house? What about the Book Mark?"

"Don't worry. I'll get it sorted."

But would she? Or was she merely fobbing Fiona off? She thought of the plane tickets in her bedside drawer in

Dublin, of Singapore Slings and outback adventures. She'd saved for this trip for years, had dreamed about it for longer.

She regarded Bridie's pinched face and took a deep breath. "I'll postpone my trip for a week. I want to be here when you get out of hospital."

"There's no need, pet. You're looking forward to going to Australia."

"I know, but it'll still be there in a week's time." She bent to kiss her aunt's pale cheek. "Get some sleep. I'll pop by to see you tomorrow."

11

"You did what?" Olivia stared at Fiona, aghast. "Have you lost your mind?"

They were standing in a queue of people waiting to get into MacCarthy's pub.

The wind off the sea was strong tonight. Fiona pulled her jacket tighter. "I've not lost my mind. I'm just postponing the start of the trip by a week."

"But you've been talking about Australia since we were at school. I know how much this trip means to you."

"Like I said to Bridie, Australia will still be there next week. Barring an alien invasion or some other catastrophe."

"Knowing your track record," Olivia said with a wry smile, "nothing is beyond the realms of possibility."

"Thanks for the vote of confidence."

"No problem. That's what friends are for."

They shuffled to the top of the queue.

"That'll be ten euros each, ladies," said the beefy bouncer guarding the door.

"Ten euros? To get into a pub?" Fiona waited for the punch line. The man stared at her, his expression blank. "Gareth, that's moonlight robbery!"

Gareth shrugged. "We're a club now, Fiona. We've got a dance floor and all."

"You mean the shed out the back? Sure, that's always been there."

He rolled his eyes. "Either pay up or leave, Wedding Crasher. You're not on our VIP list, and there's a queue of thirsty customers behind you."

"My newfound notoriety doesn't land me on the VIP list?" Fiona asked in mock horror. "I'm crushed." She rummaged through her purse and extracted a crumpled twenty-euro note. So much for a cheap night out. It was a lot easier to argue with an anonymous stranger than a guy she'd known since primary school.

Inside, the pub was packed. As the only venue in several towns to cater to punk rock and metal fans—albeit only on Fridays and Saturdays—MacCarthy's attracted a plentiful clientele. With the exception of the punk rock blasting through the speakers, MacCarthy's made no effort to appear either alternative or trendy.

While they squeezed through the throng, Fiona scanned the room. A lot had changed in the years she'd been away, but MacCarthy's was as shabby as ever. It was a far cry from the trendy clubs in Dublin. The same pictures of long-dead martyred heroes adorned the walls —men who had fallen during Ireland's troubled history. The leather seats were even more ripped and patched than they'd been eight years ago. The wooden bar was the old-fashioned kind, once richly polished, now dulled and scratched in places. Guinness was on tap as were several other beers. The drink selection was impressive for a country pub, but that was Ireland for you.

The boisterous crowd fell silent watching Fiona battle her way through to the bar. Everyone stared, some piteous, others gleeful.

Shame burned a fiery path from her cheeks to her temples. Perhaps coming out this evening hadn't been the smartest move, but what was the alternative? Hole up at the cottage and hide? That wasn't her style.

She took a shuddery breath and jutted her chin. Feck them. Feck them all. Let them talk. Let them laugh. Let them jeer. By the end of next week, she'd be gone, and they'd have found another hot topic of gossip.

Olivia gave her a nudge. "There's a free table in the snug. It'll be quieter in there if we want to have a chat."

In times gone by, the snug was a place of privacy in an Irish pub. People whose presence was frowned upon in a public house could enjoy a drink away from the crowd—women, priests, and policemen. Nowadays, many snugs had been converted into coveted seating areas for patrons seeking peace and quiet.

Fiona tapped her purse. "I'll order the drinks and food if you grab a table. Tonight's on me."

"We can argue about money later."

"Nothing to argue about." Fiona waved her friend in the direction of the snug and headed for the bar.

Behind the counter, a bear of a man was pulling a pint. He had the crooked nose and stocky build of a man more suited to playing on a Rugby pitch than serving in a country pub. When she reached the bar, he looked up and his bulldog face broke into a broad smile. "Hey, Fiona. Long time, no see."

His smile was infectious—all the more so because he was the first person pleased to see her since the debacle in the church. "Ruairí. I heard you were working in New York. Stockbroking, right?"

"Yeah." He inclined his thick neck in a nod. "I worked on Wall Street for a few years."

She looked him up and down and laughed. "I can't imagine you in a business suit."

The smile widened, making his huge hazel eyes—his only claim to beauty—sparkle. "Me neither."

"Are you over for a holiday?"

An emotion flitted across his hard features, too quick to pinpoint. "No. I run the pub now. Da's getting on in years, and Ma...she hasn't been well."

"I'm sorry to hear that." She trailed off, stopping herself from uttering the question on her lips. Had the MacCarthys patched things up? Bridie had mentioned Ruairí leaving Ireland following a massive row with his father, but now was hardly the moment to pry into someone else's family business. Lord knew she had enough of her own.

He set his elbows on the counter. "What are you drinking?"

"Two gin and tonics, plus two plates of fish and chips."

"Right-o. Pay here, and I'll give you your drinks. We'll bring the food over when it's ready. Where are you sitting?"

"We're in the snug."

"Ah. We've fixed the bell in there, you know. Only took us thirty years." He gave her a wink. "Give us a buzz if you want a second drink."

"Will do. Thanks, Ruairí."

While she waited for him to get her drinks, her gaze drifted over the crowd.

And froze.

Gavin Maguire sat slumped at a corner table, looking the worse for wear.

Oh, feck. Of all the beer joints in Ballybeg, he had to pick this one.

Jonas O'Mahony sat beside him, sporting a pained expression.

At that moment, Gavin looked up, his sky blue eyes riveting her in place. Her stomach lurched and she averted her gaze.

"Well, if it isn't my missus." His speech was slurred. If the collection of empty glasses in front of him was any indication, he'd been here for a while.

Jonas nodded to her, making an unsuccessful attempt to smother a smile.

"Ah, go ahead and laugh," she said, leaning against the bar. "You know you want to."

"I can't believe you two eejits eloped in Vegas. What the fuck were you thinking?"

"Of our next Long Island iced tea?"

He shuddered. "Jaysus. Those things are lethal."

"Alas, no. We were still alive the next day and so was Drunk Elvis."

Ruairí shoved Fiona's drinks across the bar counter.

"Drunk Elvis? Sure, we have one of those in Ballybeg. Do you remember John-Joe Fitzgerald? Looks like your husband is wearing one of his costumes."

Fiona surveyed Gavin's ensemble. "Gawd, you're right. Speaking of Elvis, that suit's seen better days."

"I know." Jonas groaned. "Nora Fitzgerald will kill us when she sees the state of it. I tried to get him to stay home, but after he'd lashed into a bottle of vodka, there was no stopping him. I had no choice but to go with him and try to keep him in check."

Fiona regarded the collection of empty glasses on their table and Gavin's disheveled appearance. "Looks like you're doing a fantastic job of it. I gotta ask…is the wedding-suit-eating dog the same puppy who caused my public humiliation?"

Jonas choked with laughter.

"You heard about me splitting my dress?" Fiona crossed her arms over her chest and looked at him defiantly.

"Muireann might have mentioned it."

"To the entire population of Ballybeg, no doubt."

"Didja plan today as revenge?" Gavin sloshed whiskey down his formerly white suit.

Fiona sucked in a breath. What an arsehole. Did he seriously think she'd go to such extremes to get one up on Muireann? "No," she snapped. "I did not. Oddly enough, I have no desire to be married to you, not even to humiliate my cousin. Not to worry, Gavin. As usual, it's all about you."

He squinted at her through unfocused eyes. "Whaja mean?"

"We've known each other off and on for, what, twenty years?"

He considered a moment, arithmetic clearly beyond him in his inebriated state. "Something along those lines."

"In all that time, you've treated me with nothing but condescension, even when you were pretending to be nice. Poor orphaned Fiona. Poor plain Fiona. Do you know how I felt when you abandoned me in Vegas?"

"I didn't abanjun...abandon you. Jush left."

"Exactly. You up and fucking left." She placed her hands on her hips and stared him down. "You left me alone in a strange city. So screw you, Gavin Maguire."

"Steady on. I didn't mean—"

"You never do, do you? You're not capable of looking beyond yourself. I'm not even sure you love Muireann."

"Hey, now." He made a futile effort to straighten his slumped form. "That's below the belt, especially given the day I've had."

"What about *my* day? What about Muireann's? Surely, of all of us, Bridie's had the shittiest day?" What the hell had she ever seen in this man? He was totally and utterly self-centered. It was a damn shame he couldn't marry her witch of a cousin. They deserved each other.

Gavin scrunched his forehead. "How's Bridie doing?"

"She was carted off in an ambulance, and it's taken you this long to ask after her state of health?"

"Stop, Fiona. Please. I'm sick of people nagging at me today. My life was fine this morning, and now it's a fricking mess. I've hurt Muireann. I owe her parents their share of the wedding costs. I have a ginormous house with a ginormous mortgage. Considering I've just jilted and humiliated my boss's daughter, I think it's a safe bet to say I'm unemployed."

Ruairí's stocky figure loomed. "Tone it down, Gavin. I've been tolerant up to now because I know you've had a tough day. You've had more than enough to drink. It's time for you to leave."

"Ah, no. Come on—"

"No arguments." Ruairí turned to Jonas. "Are you good to get him home?"

Jonas regarded his drunk friend dubiously. "I'll haul him there somehow."

The bartender sighed. "Give me a minute. I'll ask Marcella to cover me while I drive you to his place."

"Thanks, mate. Appreciate it."

"By the way, your food's ready," Ruairí said to Fiona. "Janine's brought it to the snug."

Food. Her tummy was in knots. The absolute last thing she wanted right now was to eat. "Thanks," she said in a shaky voice. "Sorry for making a scene."

He nodded curtly and went to help Jonas drag Gavin out of the pub.

Back in the snug, two plates laden with fish and chips were on their table. They smelled heavenly. Shame she'd lost her appetite.

"Are you okay?" Olivia asked when she took the seat across from her. "Did someone say something?"

"I bumped into Gavin. Literally."

"Oh, feck. How is he?"

"Inebriated and loose-tongued. Apparently, I've wrecked his life, and it's my fault we're legally married."

"Screw him."

"I would, but he's an arsehole."

Olivia opened her mouth wide and laughed. "I've missed you, Fee. I wish you lived nearer."

"Or visited more often. I know, I know. I've heard it all from Bridie." She toyed with her fish and chips before putting her cutlery back on the table with shaky hands. "It's as if I step into a time warp every time I visit. Some things change, some things stay the same. I revert to my teenage self, complete with the old body issues and insecurities. I sense it happening the moment I pass the sign for Ballybeg, yet it's like I'm powerless to stop it."

Olivia speared a chip. "It could be worse. I'm stuck in a trap of my own making and I can't figure a way out."

"Are things that bad at home?"

Olivia shrugged. "Ah, no. You know me. I tend to exaggerate. It can get a bit suffocating at times. Aidan's busy with work, and now his political career. I spend my whole life being Mrs. Aidan Gant, and I have neither the time nor the energy left to be Olivia."

"What about your little brothers? Do you still babysit them a couple of times a week?"

"I collect them from school, yes. Now that they're teenagers, they can look after themselves—allegedly."

Fiona sprinkled malted vinegar on her chips. "If there's an upside to delaying my trip, it's the opportunity to spend more time with you."

"Not to mention the opportunity to set your divorce proceedings in motion," Olivia said wisely. "Aidan might be a pain at times, but he's a damn good lawyer. And I happen to be his personal assistant. Why don't you come by the practice at eleven on Monday morning? Bring

Gavin with you. Maybe there's a way to get an annulment."

"I certainly hope so. The sooner we can sort this out, the better for all of us."

Feeling more cheerful than she had all day—which wasn't saying much—Fiona smiled and ate a vinegar-soaked chip. *Bliss.*

12

Gavin woke to hammering in his head and a dog licking his feet.

"Ugh. Don't wanna get up."

"Rise and shine," said a female voice before yanking the duvet off his bed. "Time to kick the booze and face reality."

He sat up, blinking. Fiona stood at the foot of his bed, Wiggly Poo at her side. She wore black from head to toe, offset by crimson lipstick. The lip ring was back in place, as was the attitude. If she was going for the avenging angel look, it was working. "How did you get in?"

She raised an ebony eyebrow. "Through the front door."

"Smart arse. Did I leave it unlocked?"

"No, Jonas let me in. But it would've made no difference. Bridie has your spare key, remember?"

"What are you doing here?" He rubbed his sleepy eyes. "Where's Jonas?"

"Waking you up. We have an appointment with Aidan Gant in half an hour." She opened his wardrobe and rifled through his clothes. "As for Jonas, he's gone to Cork City with his mother and Luca to shop for school supplies."

When he threw his legs over the side of the bed, Wiggly Poo went into ecstasies of delight, tail wagging, tongue lolling. Gavin scooped him up and scratched under his chin. At least someone was pleased to see him. To his annoyance, it appeared Muireann's claims of labradoodles being hypoallergenic were accurate—at least in his case. He frowned, a memory emerging through his hung-over haze. "How'd you end up with the dog? He was meant to be staying with Mary McDermott."

"Yeah…for the wedding that never happened." Fiona flashed him a sideways grin. "To paraphrase Jonas, Mary evicted Wiggly Poo this morning due to crimes against vegetables."

"He dug up her prize-winning spuds?"

"Yup. And destroyed a pair of designer shoes."

He sighed and petted the dog's soft golden fur. "You have an appetite for expensive clothing, don't you? I guess Mary's another person I'll owe money to."

"Add Bridie to your list. Wiggly Poo smashed a few of her ornaments during a midmorning rampage."

"Aw, shite. How's she doing, anyway? You said something about an operation last night."

Fiona selected trousers and a shirt and hung them on the door to his en suite bathroom. "I said that on Saturday night. Today's Monday. You've been on a two-day bender."

Two days? *Jaysus.* No wonder his head hurt. "Will she be okay?"

"Yeah. The operation is scheduled for this morning. Once we're done with Gant, I'll go by the hospital."

"Run this by me again," he said, returning Wiggly Poo on the floor and grabbing his clothes. "Why are we going to see Aidan Gant?"

"Seriously, Gavin. Have you *no* memory of the past forty-eight hours?"

"I'm hung over, but I'm not that far gone. Even if I was, the wreck of a rental suit reminds me my life has gone from promising and prosperous to a complete fucking fiasco."

"In that case, you'll agree it's in both our interests to sort out this marriage business without delay. Gant's a creep, but he's a good solicitor. He'll know what to do. And if he doesn't, he'll know who to refer us to."

"You're…different today."

It was true. The girl he used to know was awkward with a tendency to hunch. She'd had a quick temper but lacked the ability to stand up for herself effectively. But despite her prickly exterior, she was a sweet kid and fiercely loyal to those she loved. Also smart, funny, and—by the time they'd hit their early twenties—prettier than he cared to contemplate.

The woman who stood before him now was anything but awkward. She'd shed the puppy fat but retained her curvaceous figure. She stood tall, proud, and sexy as hell.

"Perhaps I remember who I've become," she said in a clipped tone. "Not who I was."

"Huh? Sorry, Fiona. I'm not up to solving riddles this morning."

Her expression was inscrutable. "Never mind. Best get moving. I'll wait with the dog in the car."

"You want us to bring Wiggly Poo?"

She cocked an eyebrow. "In the half hour Jonas left me dog-sitting him, he ran riot through Bridie's house. Would you leave him alone?"

Within fifteen minutes, Gavin was showered, shaved, and dosed with headache tablets. Fiona and Wiggly Poo were waiting in her VW Polo.

Gavin eased himself into the passenger seat and put on his seat belt. The meds were starting to clear his head sufficiently for memories of the last couple of days to come flooding back.

He groaned. He should've buried his head under his pillow and stayed in bed. He wasn't ready to face the world and view the wreckage of his previously orderly and peaceful existence. So much for his goal to live a drama-free life. Not even his mother's wildest shenanigans had resulted in this much mayhem.

Fiona parallel parked outside Aidan Gant's offices. She removed the dog carrier from the back seat.

Gavin eyed the puppy with suspicion. Wiggly Poo was snoozing in his cage, looking cute and deceptively innocent. "Is bringing him in wise?"

"Probably not, but it seems cruel to leave him alone in the car."

Aidan Gant's legal practice comprised of three spacious rooms and a small entrance lobby.

Olivia ushered them to a leather sofa in the waiting area and buzzed her husband.

A few minutes later, Aidan Gant emerged from his office. His smarmy smirk was enough to make the acid in Gavin's stomach crawl up his esophagus.

"Gavin." Gant's limp handshake was in stark contrast to Bernard's crushing counterpart. "And Fiona." He held her hand a second longer than strictly necessary. "Let's go into my office."

Gavin lifted the cage containing Wiggly Poo. "What should I do with the dog? He's a little on the wild side."

Gant recoiled and regarded the travel cage as if it contained a rabid beast.

"I'll look after him." Olivia took the cage from Gavin. "You go on in with Aidan."

Gant's office was the largest room on the premises. The white walls were laden with paintings. Gavin was no art expert, but he judged them bad enough to be expensive.

"Take a seat." Gant gestured to two leather armchairs on the other side of his desk. "Olivia will bring the coffee tray shortly. I had a copy of your marriage certificate faxed from Las Vegas." He shuffled the papers on his desk and shoved a printout across the desk.

Gavin stared at his hands. "It's the real deal?"

"Oh, yes. You're definitely legally married." The slick smile was back in place. He might be one of Bernard's cohorts, but he was thoroughly enjoying this situation.

Gavin shifted in his seat. "How do we end the marriage? Can we fly to Vegas for a quickie divorce?"

Gant laughed. "If only it were so simple. You're not

legal residents of Nevada. You'll have to file for divorce here in Ireland."

"That'll take ages," Fiona said. "Is there no way we can get an annulment?"

"Hard to do, I'm afraid. In order to get an Irish court to grant an annulment, you have to prove the marriage is either voidable or void. A voidable marriage is one which can be judged to be no marriage at all because one or both partners suffers from a serious mental illness or is incapable of sexual intercourse. This may be due to impotence or homosexuality." Gant eyed Gavin slyly. "I take it that's not relevant in your case?"

Cheeky sod! Gant was loving seeing him brought low. "No, it is not relevant."

"What about the other type of null marriage?" Fiona asked.

"A void marriage is one that never existed. For example, one or both of the partners was already married, the partners are too closely related to be legally married, or one or both of the partners were incapable of giving their consent at the time of the ceremony."

Gavin's ears pricked up. "Does being drunk off our arses count?"

"Intoxication is one reason to declare a marriage void, but it is rarely accepted in court. Sure, if it were that easy, half of Ireland would be running in with that excuse."

"But we were genuinely drunk at the time of our Vegas wedding," Fiona said. "As was our officiant."

"I believe you, but it won't wash in court. The ceremony took place eight years ago. If you'd come home to Ireland and immediately initiated proceedings to annul the marriage, you'd have stood a chance. You say you first found out the marriage was valid on Saturday morning, but the claim is almost impossible to prove."

Well, screw that.

"If we go for the divorce option, how long will it take?" Gavin asked.

"The law says you need to be living apart for a minimum of four out of the past five years before you can apply for a divorce."

"We've never lived together," they said in unison. Their eyes clashed for a second, reigniting the old spark of awareness.

Gavin massaged his temples. He must be losing the plot. They were sitting in a solicitor's office discussing their divorce and he was remembering her naked.

"The courts won't care you never lived together. Provided we can prove you've maintained separate residences for the past four years, we can start the proceedings." Gant's smirk was seriously getting on Gavin's nerves. "But there's a backlog. Could take a couple of years. I wouldn't go making alternative wedding plans if I were you."

If the lawyer had punched him in the solar plexus, Gavin couldn't have been more winded. "Two years?" he spluttered. "You can't be serious."

Two years of his life in free fall? No flipping way.

"I'll also warn you that it's not only a long process, but an expensive one."

"Whatever it costs, we'll work something out," Fiona said. "Right, Gavin?"

He stared at the geometric design on the carpet. For

flip's sake. He'd have to compile a list of his mounting debts.

Olivia entered the office, bearing a tray laden with freshly baked scones and steaming black coffee. Under normal circumstances, Gavin would have pounced on the scones. This morning, his stomach roiled at the sight of food. He accepted a double espresso and knocked it back in one.

"Now that we've discussed your divorce, I have a small matter to parlay with Gavin." Gant's grin was positively gleeful. This did not bode well.

Fiona took the hint. "I'll wait outside and have my coffee with Olivia."

When the door clicked shut behind them, Gavin met Gant's amused expression. "I assume I'm the latest addition to Ireland's unemployment problem."

Gant steepled his fingers. "Put it this way: Bernard's given me a box containing the contents of your desk. In accordance with your contract of employment, your salary will be paid in full until the end of your period of notice."

Gavin took a ragged breath. *Shite.* Not unexpected, but a crushing blow all the same.

"He's also supplied me with an itemized list of the wedding expenses you owe him." Gant shoved a piece of paper across the desk.

At the sight of the sum written on it, bile surged up Gavin's throat. The cost of the wedding was no surprise, but seeing it in black and white was a stark reminder of how quickly his life had turned into a sewer system.

"Bernard knows you can't afford to pay this amount at

once," Gant continued, "therefore, he has a proposition for you."

Gavin pinched the bridge of his nose. "Go on." Whatever scheme his almost father-in-law had concocted would not be to his benefit. The man's idea of a business proposition generally left the other party a weeping, bloody mess.

"From my understanding, you and Muireann currently split the cost of the mortgage repayments on Clonmore Lodge."

"Yes." And a hefty sum it was, too, regardless of Bernard's supposed bargain sale price on the house.

"If you agree to pay the full mortgage repayments between now and the time you sell the house, Bernard will give you until Christmas to pay the money you owe for the wedding. In addition, he will furnish you with a glowing reference to show prospective employers."

Gavin bit the inside of his cheek until he tasted blood. "Firstly, I'm legally entitled to a reference. Secondly, the law does not require me to reimburse the Byrnes for the wedding. I intend to do so because I feel a personal obligation to Muireann. Finally, how the hell does Bernard expect me to cover the mortgage if I'm out of a job? Glowing reference or not, I'm unlikely to find a new position immediately. My redundancy payment will only go so far, and we all know how hard it is to offload property in Ireland these days."

Gant shrugged. "You're entitled to a reference, true, but not to a glowing one. As for finding the money to pay the mortgage…frankly, that's your problem. If you refuse to sign the deal, you'll have to pay back the full cost of the wedding by the middle of October."

"What if I tell Bernard to go fuck himself?"

The smirk evaporated. "Then you'll be hard pressed to find an architectural job anywhere in the south of Ireland."

In other words, Bernard would pull strings to ensure he had no choice but to emigrate. His hands balled into fists. *The rat bastard.* "This is blackmail. What's to stop me from calling my union rep?"

"Absolutely nothing. Go ahead and call them if you wish." The Cheshire cat smile split his cheeks. "However, Bernard did mention a small matter of missing funds from the shopping center project. He seemed to think you might know something about it and is considering contacting the police."

Gavin's pulse quickened. "That's total bollocks and you know it. I'm the architect. I have nothing to do with the company finances."

"Nevertheless, Bernard believes he has compelling evidence against you. And given that you've just announced to over three hundred people your intention to commit bigamy, I doubt the police will be inclined to believe you're above theft."

He staggered to his feet, his world spinning. "I'll need to think on it."

"You do that." Gant stood to see him out. "But don't think too long. Bernard Byrne is not a patient man."

~

Fiona pounded up the stairs of Cork University Hospital. Her lungs were burning, and her bad leg was aching. Why had she quit going to the gym? Laziness? Lack of time? Both?

"Excuse me." She dodged a white-clad doctor descending from the second floor and took the remaining stairs two at a time.

It was just shy of three o'clock, and visiting hours on St. Ignatius ward were in full swing. A green-faced patient attached to various IVs was wheeled out of the lift, and a man on a stretcher was wheeled in. Visitors crowded the nurses' station inquiring after family members and friends.

Nurse Collins, the friendly nurse from yesterday, was wheeling an elderly man down the corridor.

"Your auntie came through the surgery fine," she said with a cheery smile when Fiona approached. "She's resting in her room."

"Thanks." Fiona struggled to catch her breath after her dash up the stairs. Tomorrow she was buying running shoes. "Is she ready for visitors?"

"Your uncle and cousin were already here. Bridie's a little groggy, but I'm sure she'd love to see you." Nurse Collins's smile stretched wider. She leaned closer to Fiona in a confidential manner. "Your cousin told me what you're doing."

Stealing her man? Wrecking her wedding? Marring Muireann's otherwise perfect existence with her plump-and-pierced presence? The list of possibilities was endless, and none should have put a benevolent smile on Nurse Collins' face.

"What do you mean?"

"She said you've canceled your world trip to look after Bridie."

Whew. Nothing too horrific, thank goodness. "Not canceled. Postponed."

"How wonderful." Nurse Collins patted her arm. "After six months of looking after your aunt and her shop, you'll need the break."

An icy trickle wound its way down her back. "What?"

"If she's lucky, she can return to work in four, but we usually estimate six to be on the safe side."

Her mouth gaped so low she'd start drooling if she didn't haul her jaw into place. *Oh, feck.* What had Muireann done?

Nurse Collins's beeper emitted a piercing sound. "Back to work I go. Stop by the nurses' station on your way out, will you? We need to organize Bridie's stay at the nursing home."

"Nursing home?" *What the feck?*

"She'll need to spend a couple of weeks in a nursing home after we discharge her. She'd have to be there even longer if she didn't have you to look after her at home. Pop by on your way out, and we'll discuss the details."

"Uh...sure."

Nurse Collins and the wheelchair disappeared into a room to the left, leaving Fiona to gather her racing thoughts. This was a joke, right? Were they seriously expecting her to cancel the trip she'd spent five years saving for? She'd taken a sabbatical from teaching to travel, not to play the role of nursemaid and general dogsbody. Would Bridie be out of commission for six whole months?

"Watch out!" An old lady in a motorized wheelchair whizzed past.

Fiona leaped to the side with seconds to spare.

"Sorry, dear. I'm not used to the brakes on this thing yet. Are you okay?"

"I'm grand," Fiona said, waving her on. "No harm done."

The old lady moved off down the hall. Would her aunt need a wheelchair when she got out of hospital? How would she be able to go shopping if no one was with her?

The olive green walls spun, forming a whirling tunnel of echoing voices chastising her for her failures as a niece, as a cousin, as a friend.

She went into Bridie's room. If her aunt had looked poorly on Saturday, today she looked like death—bloodless lips and chalky complexion.

Fiona bent to kiss her.

Bridie opened one blue eye. "Thank feck it's you. I was afraid Muireann and Bernard had come back."

"You're remarkably chipper for a woman described as groggy by one of the nurses."

Her aunt emitted a derisive snort. "Would you want Bernard and Muireann hovering over you if you felt like shite? One bellowing abuse at all and sundry, and the other moaning about her various woes. I had to pretend to be out of it. It was the only way to get them to leave."

"You're dreadful," Fiona said, laughing. "Can I get you anything?"

"No, pet. Sit down and talk to me."

She pulled up a chair. She'd tell Bridie there'd been a miscommunication. Her aunt would understand.

"Bernard says you've canceled your trip to stay and run the Book Mark." Bridie's wan face creased in concern. "Why didn't you tell me? You said you'd postponed until next week."

"No, I..." *Tell her. Tell her now.* "Does Sharon still work part time at the Book Mark?"

"Yes. I don't know what I'd do without her. She's a cheeky minx but a good worker." Bridie slumped further into her pillows. "I'll be honest with you, Fiona. The business is struggling. Those who can afford it have switched over to digital. The rest are suffering from the economic downturn and sticking to used books. I can't afford to pay someone to run the shop for me, and I can't afford to close for however long I'm unable to work."

"Don't worry. I'll get it sorted."

"Are you sure about this, pet? Won't you lose money by canceling at short notice? Bernard was convinced your insurance would cover the cancellation cost, but to the best of my knowledge, that buffoon hasn't traveled farther than the UK."

A buffoon indeed. With a cunning, calculating cow of a daughter. Fiona's fingernails dug into her palms. How dare they try to manipulate her into staying in Ballybeg? Bernard had plenty of money. Why couldn't he hire a nurse to look after his only sister? This trip was a once-in-a-lifetime opportunity. Why should she have to cancel it?

"Fiona?" Bridie prompted. "Are you losing money on this?"

She unclenched her fists. "My travel insurance is comprehensive." *But I'm certain canceling to look after an injured aunt isn't covered in the fine print.*

"You don't have to stay, pet. I don't want you to put your life on hold for a few months because of me." Bridie's eyes searched her face for clues.

Fiona tried to coach her facial muscles into a neutral expression. Unwelcome memories flooded her mind. Her parents' laughter and her brother's smiling face as they drove along the coast road that fateful day. The oncoming tractor, the screech of brakes, the screams of terror.

The next images featured her aunt. Bridie visiting her at the hospital after the car accident. Bridie by her hospital bed when she woke up after each of the three operations on her leg and spine. Bridie at the rehabilitation center. Bridie taking her to live with her at the cottage.

Fiona squeezed her eyes shut, quashing the memories with a mental sledgehammer. "I have the next few months off work. Australia's not going anywhere. Of course I'll stay to help."

13

It was the Wednesday after Gavin's non-wedding day. High time—according to a terse text message from his former fiancée—for him to collect his crap.

Thus he found himself in the passenger seat of Jonas's dad's clapped-out transport van, driving through gale-force wind and torrential rain.

Luca and Wiggly Poo sat in the back, the former holding a running commentary on the make, model, and serial number of every vehicle they passed on the road, and the latter barking wildly at the few cyclists intrepid enough to venture out in this weather.

"Aren't you glad you never found a buyer for the cottage?" Jonas asked, swerving to avoid a pothole. "If you'd sold it, you'd be out on your arse."

"If I'd sold it," he replied dryly, "I'd be in a position to reimburse the Byrnes their share of the wedding costs. As it is, I've no choice but to sell the BMW and hope to goodness we can sell Clonmore Lodge this side of Christmas."

Jonas cocked an eyebrow. "How'll you get around without a car? The public transport system's shite."

"I'll buy a used one. Anything with four wheels will do." Actually, he was gutted at having to sell the Beamer, but he needed cash, and he needed it fast. The wedding had bled his account dry, and the couple of investments that were still worth something after the economic crash were tied up for a few more years.

"I don't understand why you feel obliged to pay back the Byrnes," Jonas said. "Losing the money for the wedding won't make much difference to their coffers."

"No, it won't, but that's not the point. The wedding fiasco was my screwup. I don't have a problem with paying them back the money they lost. Besides, if I don't, Bernard will make damn sure I'm not just unemployed but unemployable."

"That man is a vindictive prick."

"Tell me about it."

Jonas slowed the van to a cruise and turned into the driveway of Clonmore Lodge.

"Whoa," they said in unison.

Gavin stared out the passenger window in mounting horror. He rolled down the window as if a view unimpeded by glass could alter what he was seeing. Muireann had purged Clonmore Lodge of his belongings. She'd chucked his beloved book collection into the koi pond. His clothes, computer equipment, stereo system, and an assortment of miscellaneous items lay heaped on the grass, already muddy from the lashing rain.

"Aw, hell."

With the exception of a toothbrush and a couple of changes of clothes, he'd moved his belongings from the cottage to Clonmore Lodge four months ago. Now they'd been forcibly ejected from the house to the garden.

He pressed his brow to the edge of the car window, transfixed by the sight of twenty thousand euros' worth of his property destroyed.

And that wasn't counting the books. Most could be repurchased, either as a physical copy or a digital edition, but nothing could replace the sentimental value he'd placed on each volume. Creases on pages with passages he found particularly moving. Smells associated with happy hours reading and re-reading. The feel of those particular books in his hands and the escape they represented.

"I know you jilted her at the altar, concealed a secret marriage to her cousin, and humiliated her in front of the entire town...but seriously?"

Gavin shot his friend a sideways scowl.

Jonas wore his "poker face"—studied blankness of expression belied by the glint in his eyes and the twitch at the corners of his mouth. "Next stop the clothes shops?"

"Fuck the clothes." Gavin climbed out of the car, waving his arms in the direction of the pond. "Look what she's done to my books."

He sprinted over to the pond and fished out a soggy volume. It was by a fantasy author—one of his favorite comfort re-reads. Muireann knew he loved this book.

Luca and Wiggly Poo spilled out of the car and surveyed the wreckage. Wiggly Poo found an old cable to attack and applied himself to the task with gusto.

Luca peered into the pond. "That can't be healthy for the fish."

"She's done a thorough job, all right." Jonas flipped through the remains of Gavin's one and only childhood photo album. "Guess your relationship's dunzo."

"No need to sound *quite* so cheerful."

"Nah, I'm just pissed you held out on me about Fiona and Vegas." Jonas wagged a finger at him. "I want a full and unabridged account before Luca and I leave for Dublin."

"Didn't I tell you last Saturday?"

"You told me a lot of things last Saturday, mate," Jonas said with an insouciant grin, "but you were too intoxicated to make sense. Something about a drunk Elvis impersonator marrying you and Fiona, and you paying him off the next morning. Sounded more fantastical than one of my plots."

"Then I *did* tell you what happened. That was the truth."

His friend's jaw dropped. "Well, fuck me. I was sure you were hallucinating."

"Alas, no."

Gavin let the soggy book fall to the ground. His jaw clenched. Yeah, he'd screwed up. Muireann had a right to be angry. She had a right to throw him out, but she did *not* have the right to deliberately destroy his belongings.

He marched up to the front door and pressed the bell for a good ten seconds.

No response.

He pressed it again, longer this time.

An upstairs window opened. His former fiancée glared

down at him through eyes puffy from crying. She'd let her fake tan fade, and the newfound pallor lent her a majestically tragic air. "What do you want? Haven't you done enough to hurt me?"

"I'm sorry for the wedding screwup. I'm sorry I hurt you, but it doesn't entitle you to wreck my stuff."

"Wreck your stuff? You wrecked my life!"

"Come on, Muireann. Quit the dramatics and come downstairs. We need to talk."

"You publicly humiliated me—" her voice broke on a sob, "—in front of everyone. You're the last person I want to talk to."

"You know we need to talk. Preferably in private. If you're not up to it today, I'll call by tomorrow."

Her laugh was forced. "Don't want to have this conversation in front of Jonas and Luca? I'm sure they're dying to know why you're so keen to talk to me."

"Nope," Jonas said. "The only thing I'm dying for is a smoke. Come on, Luca. Let's wait by the van."

"Gavin wants to know whether or not I'm pregnant." The words were loud enough to qualify as a shout.

Jonas's step faltered, but he continued walking, keeping a firm grip on Luca's hand.

Luca turned, his eyes wide with amazement. "She's having a baby?"

"Muireann," Gavin said. "For heaven's sake."

Jonas tugged Luca's hand and propelled him out of earshot. Wiggly Poo bounded after them, not willing to miss the opportunity of another ride in the van.

"No, I am not having a baby."

His shoulders sagged with relief. Thank fuck for that news.

The look she cast him could curdle milk. "Glad I could make your day."

"Surely you agree that having a baby in the current situation would be a disaster."

Defiance faltering, she deflated before his eyes, rage spent. "Tell me the truth. Did you really want to marry me, or were you more interested in signing the deal with my father?"

"Yes, I wanted to marry you." He answered without hesitation, only noticing after that he'd used the past tense.

Her puffy eyes narrowed. "Why?"

"I..." He scrambled for the right words. "We deal well together—or did up until the weekend. We want the same things in life—stability, security, comfort."

"How romantic," she drawled.

He furrowed his brow. "Hearts and flowers have never been important to us. We're not into fake gestures or drama."

Her penetrating stare made him squirm. "And yet you've caused more drama than Ballybeg has seen in many a year. I'm embarrassed to show my face in public."

"You have no reason to feel embarrassed," he said. "This...it's all on me."

"Yes, it is." Her lips formed a hard line. "Which is why you're not going to object to me using our honeymoon tickets to go on holiday with Mona and Brona."

*Their honeymoon...*he'd wanted to go to New Zealand; she'd wanted to go to Mauritius. No prize for guessing who'd won that tussle. "Of course you should go. Your parents paid for the trip. But when you get home, we'll have to decide what to do with Wiggly Poo."

"Daddy gave him to us for a wedding present," she said with a shudder. "I'll always associate him with being jilted at the altar."

"What are you saying?" A ball of annoyance formed in Gavin's stomach, persistent and acidic. "Don't you want to keep him?"

"I was thrilled when Daddy gave him to me. He was to be our dog." Her mouth formed a moue of distaste. "But if there's no us…he's tainted."

"What, exactly, do you expect me to do with him? He's a dog, not a toy."

"Oh, for heaven's sake." She gave an exaggerated sigh. "As far as I'm concerned, the dog's your problem. Keep him, give him away, toss him to the pound. I'm beyond caring."

Unbelievable. She foisted a dog into their lives and expected him to deal with the consequences when she decided she was done being a dog mammy.

The anger he'd been trying to keep under control rose to the surface. He'd treaded gently with her out of a sense of guilt, but he was pissed about his wrecked stuff, irritated by her refusal to speak to him in private, and downright furious at her attitude toward the dog. "For flip's sake, Muireann. You can't treat a dog like a disposable toy. You brought him into our lives. You can't go and abandon him."

"He barely knows me. He's spent more time with you."

"Whose fault is that? You wouldn't answer my calls or return my messages."

"Go to hell, Gavin. I'm done with you. Sort out your own problems."

"What about my stuff? You destroyed over twenty thousand euros' worth of my property."

She rolled her eyes. "Go ahead and sue me. Good-bye, Gavin, and good riddance." With that parting shot, she slammed the window shut and disappeared from sight.

ON THE FIRST day of her temporary career change, Fiona arrived early. Seeing as she had feck all idea how to run a bookshop, she figured she'd better get a head start.

The blustery wind sliced through her thin sweater as she walked down Patrick Street. A typical Irish morning. An image of her sunning herself in Singapore sprang to mind. She swallowed past the lump in her throat. She'd make it to Singapore. She'd make it to Australia. All she had to do was muddle through the next few months, then figure out a way to spend at least a couple of months traveling.

Outside the shop, she rummaged through her bag for the key. Once she'd dealt with the alarm, she slung her bag on the counter and surveyed the premises.

The Book Mark was situated in a gorgeous turquoise building. The ground floor housed the bookshop, and the top floor was divided into two small flats Bridie rented out to augment her income. In addition to selling used and new books, the shop boasted a small café where patrons could enjoy a scone or a slice of traditional Irish brack washed down with a cup of tea or coffee. The café was located at the entrance of the shop and consisted of six small tables, all named after an Irish author of note. This had been Fiona's idea several years ago, and Bridie had loved it.

The ground floor of the building had originally been composed of three rooms plus a small kitchen and a storage area little more than a large cupboard. The two rooms at the back had been converted into one and accommodated the books. The café was effectively housed in a separate room, but the connecting door had been removed, allowing customers in the café ample incentive to be lured into the bookshop by a tantalizing glimpse of the latest bestsellers.

The Book Mark was the one place in Ballybeg that contained no unwelcome blasts from the past. In the months following her brother and parents' deaths and her release from hospital, Fiona had spent many contented hours here, allegedly helping Bridie serve customers but more often than not curled up in the stockroom immersed in a book.

Fiction had been her escape, her grief counselor, and her inspiration, all rolled into one. To this day, there was very little in her life that a good book couldn't help, if not cure.

Moving her head gently from side to side, she felt the tension in her neck ease. She was in need of a good book at the moment. Thankfully, little had changed in the shop's layout in the years since Fiona had left Ballybeg. She found the historical romance section with ease and selected a couple of used Georgette Heyer books to read before bed.

She popped the books into her handbag, but ringing them up on the new cash register defeated her. Thank goodness it was Sharon's day to help. The girl had grumbled when asked to start work an hour earlier than usual, but Fiona needed help getting up to date on suppliers and the accounts. In the meantime, she'd don the yellow rubber gloves she'd found in the stockroom and blitz the place.

An hour later, Fiona was dusty and exhausted, not to mention on the verge of a full-blown panic attack. She glanced at the display on her mobile phone. The bakery delivery van hadn't shown up, and neither had Sharon.

Feck!

She dialed Joe Gillespie's number.

"Gillespie's Baked Goods," rumbled a deep voice on the other end. "How can I help you?"

"Joe?"

"Speaking."

"It's Fiona Byrne. You were supposed to delivery pastries to the Book Mark over an hour ago."

There was a pause on the other end of the line and the scraping sound of a chair being pushed back. "I'm not due to deliver to the Book Mark until next Saturday. Sharon said the thirteenth."

She gritted her teeth. *Bloody Sharon.* Was that why she hadn't come in this morning? "Joe, I need a delivery today."

"I'm sorry, but no can do. We're swamped. I've no time

to go out in the van again. If you can drive over here, I'll see if I can fix you up with a few buns."

A few buns. Fan-fecking-tastic.

"I'm alone in the shop. I can't get to Cobh and back before the first customers arrive."

"Sorry, Fiona. Do you want me to do a delivery tomorrow morning?"

"Yes, please."

After she ended the call, she dialed Sharon's number.

"Whazzup?"

"Whazzup is that you were due at the Book Mark by eight o'clock this morning. Instead, I'm standing here with five minutes till opening time, no baked goods to sell in the café, and no assistant. Where the hell are you?"

"Chill, Fiona." Sharon yawned. "Didja want me in today? Cause it was our Shea's birthday last night, and we were out on the razz. I'm flipping knackered."

Fiona counted to ten in English and in Gaelic. "Sharon, Bridie employs you to help out in the Book Mark on Wednesdays, Thursdays, and Saturdays. Every Wednesday, Thursday, and Saturday. If you want a job, get your arse in here pronto."

"All right, all right. Don't get your dreadlocks in a twist."

Fiona stared at the phone. Her dreadlocks? The cheek of the child. She ran a hand over her wild black curls. The effect of Ballybeg's sea air was to turn her naturally curly hair into a frizzy mess, but deep conditioning treatments kept it in pretty good nick. "If you want to get back into my good graces, stop off at a shop on your way and pick up something we can sell to café customers."

"You'll pay me back, right?"

Fiona tongued her lip ring and prayed for patience. "No, I will not. Consider it payback for screwing up my morning."

"You're going to be hell to work for, aren't you?" Sharon gave an exaggerated sigh.

"A slave driver," Fiona said dryly.

"Hokey dokey. I'll be there in ten."

14

After Muireann's exit from the scene of the crime, Jonas and Gavin gathered what few possessions could be salvaged and loaded them into the van. Jonas dropped Gavin to the cottage and helped him to carry the stuff inside.

"Whew," Jonas said after they'd heaved the last box into Gavin's tiny bedroom. "Done at last. You sure we shouldn't have taken the lot to the dump?"

"If we had, I'd be naked. The books and tech stuff are ruined, but the clothes should wash up decent."

Gavin cast a jaundiced eye over the boxes. After his ex-fiancée's rampage, he didn't have much left. He was pissed about the books, but he had to put a positive spin on the situation. Like his stereo system, his relationship with Muireann was beyond salvation. He should feel devastated at the thought of his would-be wife heading off on their honeymoon without him. He should feel outraged at her dumping the dog on him on a permanent basis. Yet all he felt was numb.

Jonas wiped sweat from his brow and stretched. "I could murder a cup of tea."

"Not a beer?"

"Ah, go on then, but it'll have to be a low-alcohol variety. Luca and I are driving to Dublin straight after I drop the van back to my dad. We have a meeting with Luca's new teacher and teaching assistant tomorrow."

They went through to the cramped-but-cozy kitchen where Luca and Wiggly Poo were enjoying a lemonade and a bowl of water respectively.

Gavin grabbed two beers from the fridge, popped the caps, and handed one to Jonas. He adjusted his jaw and tasted the words on his tongue. Sentimentality went against his nature, but some things needed to be said. "Thanks, mate. For everything."

Jonas grinned. "Ah, don't go maudlin on me. Sure, you'd have done the same if it were me."

"Yeah, I would." And he meant it. He'd been tight with Jonas since his first week at the local secondary school. Most of the boys had given him a wide berth or ribbed him over his odd accent. Jonas hadn't given a shite about his origins. He'd simply accepted Gavin in the here and now and blithely assumed the feeling was mutual. From the moment Jonas sat across from him at the lunch table and asked him to pass the salt, they'd had each other's backs.

"I take it there's no going back with Muireann?" Jonas asked between sips of beer.

Luca was coloring now, a wild kaleidoscope of colors

resembling something that might—with a lot of imagination—be a cow.

"No." Gavin scooped up Wiggly Poo and let him bury his snout into his neck. "I think it's as good as over. She's off to Mauritius with the twins."

"Thank fuck for small mercies," Jonas said, raising his beer bottle in salute. "Here's hoping they emigrate."

"Don't hold back, mate," he said with a dry laugh. "Tell us how you really feel."

Jonas's face crinkled into a smile. "Sure, you know what I think. Fiona did the three of you a favor by crashing the wedding."

"Fiona's beautiful," said Luca solemnly. "Especially her hair. I'm drawing a picture of her."

Gavin ruffled the little boy's dark curls. "You're only saying that because she's got curly hair like you."

"No, I'm not. She's got nice boobs, too. See? I drew them, too."

Jonas roared laughing.

Gavin rolled his eyes. "Like father, like son."

"Nah. He has better taste in women than either of us."

Gavin gazed out across the street to the crashing waves on the beach. "I'll miss you two."

"And we'll miss you. Cheer up, mate. We're coming down to visit the weekend after next. We might need to put in an appearance at the homestead, but we can definitely stay one night with you, if you'll have us."

"Of course I will," Gavin said, smiling at Luca. "I'll have him, at least. He doesn't nick my beers from the fridge."

Jonas drained his bottle and shoved back his chair.

"Right, Luca. We're off. Pack up your coloring stuff and say good-bye to Gavin."

Luca gathered his colored pencils into a pencil case, careful to arrange them according to the color spectrum, and packed everything into his small rucksack.

Gavin walked with them out to the van. The rain had eased up, but the wind had not.

Jonas grabbed him in a bear hug and slapped him between the shoulder blades. "Take care, mate. Do the sensible thing and stay single."

"If I was single in the legal sense, I wouldn't be in this mess."

"Of your two brides, my vote's for Fiona. She's turned into a mighty pretty girl. You're divorcing her, right?"

"What else can I do? If we can't get the marriage annulled, we'll have to go through divorce proceedings."

"Shame." Jonas smirked, bending to pick up Luca's rucksack. "Did more happen between the pair of you in Vegas than you're letting on?"

Gavin's cheeks burned. "Don't be daft. We're just pals."

"Pals don't get married." Jonas tossed the rucksack onto the backseat of the van. "See you in a couple of weeks. In the meantime, don't do anything I wouldn't do."

"That doesn't leave much to the imagination."

Jonas grinned broadly and strapped Luca into his car seat.

Gavin bent to give the little boy a kiss on the forehead. "Take care, mate. Look after your dad."

Luca's small face creased in determination. "I will."

Gavin stood at the gate, watching the van dwindle out of sight. Right now, he was *persona non grata* in Ballybeg.

While Muireann and her parents weren't exactly popular in the town, they were wealthy, and therefore influential. He was unemployed and unemployable, at least in the environs of the town.

In a few short months, he'd gone from solvent and mortgage-free to the reluctant co-owner of a heavily mortgaged monstrosity. But he'd turn it around. He had no choice. Both financial necessity and ambition wouldn't allow him to give up without putting up a damn good fight.

A wet tongue slobbered on his neck. "Woof!"

He stroked the dog's golden fur. Now it was just him and Wiggly Poo.

~

THIRTY MINUTES after Fiona told Sharon to get her arse over to the Book Mark, the bell above the door jangled.

Fiona looked up from the cash register where she was struggling to serve a customer. Her jaw dropped.

Sharon MacCarthy strutted into the shop wearing a canary yellow sequined top that displayed a generous amount of what the rag mags referred to as "side cleavage." Her skinny jeans were ripped in strategic places, and her chunky heels added a good six inches to her lanky frame.

"Howya, Fiona. Howya, Missus Keogh." Sharon flashed the briefest of smiles at Fiona and the customer, then continued to chomp on her gum. "I picked up a pack of them jammy biscuits from the Spar and more instant coffee cause we're nearly out."

Jammy biscuits? Instant coffee? What the actual feck?

Fiona gave Mrs. Keogh her change and bagged her romance novels.

"Give my regards to Bridie when you see her," said Mrs. Keogh as she bumped her wheelie trolley out of the shop.

"Will do," Fiona said. "Happy reading."

No sooner had the door shut behind Mrs. Keogh then Sharon snorted with mirth. "Happy reading? Old Missus K.'s in here every Saturday filling her trolley with crappy books. I don't know how she manages to get through so many in a week."

"Mrs. Keogh is a customer." *And one of the few regulars the Book Mark still had if this morning's trade was anything to go by.* "Treat her with respect."

Sharon slung her shopping bag on the counter and unpacked its contents. "Sorry about the cock-up this morning. I was convinced you'd said next Saturday."

"You're here now." Fiona eyed the biscuits and instant coffee with suspicion, and jerked a thumb at the old coffee machine on the counter. "What's wrong with the machine?"

"Banjaxed," Sharon said cheerfully. "It's been out of order as long as I've worked here."

"Please don't tell me you've been serving the customers instant coffee regularly?"

Sharon nodded. "Or tea." She pointed to the box of tea bags perched on a wall shelf.

Fiona peered at the box. Was that dust? She took it down and inspected the use-by date. Her shoulders slumped. Great. Instant coffee and stale tea bags. No wonder business was slow. "Put a plate of biscuits on each table. If we've nothing better to offer our customers today, they're on the house."

Sharon opened the packets of biscuits and emptied them onto plates, then fired said plates onto the café's six tables. "There," she said, puffing out her sequin-enhanced chest. "We're all set."

Fiona raked her underling from head to toe. "Does Bridie let you wear these clothes to work?"

Sharon flashed her an impish grin. "Lord, no. She's always on at me to put on a cardi."

Fiona folded her arms. "Then put one on. This is a bookshop, not a night club."

"You're a hard woman, Fiona." Sharon's grin was as wide as the Atlantic. "I think we'll get on great."

"Hmm…that remains to be seen. When you've put on your cardigan, can you check what's wrong with the cash register? In the meantime, I'll see if I can rustle up a coffeemaker from somewhere."

She pulled her mobile phone out of her handbag and flicked through her contact numbers. She had few friends left in Ballybeg and fewer still who wouldn't be at work by this time on a Wednesday morning.

Her thumb hovered over the entry for "Eejit." It was a new addition to her contact list, input in a fit of pique at Aidan Gant's office on Monday morning. She hit dial.

"Hullo?" If Gavin's voice were a weather forecast, it would have heralded an overcast day with a threat of thunder.

"It's Fiona."

Silence.

"Fiona *Byrne*."

More silence.

Fiona dropped her voice to a whisper. "Your lawfully wedded wife, you eejit."

He cleared his throat. "I recognized your voice. Just took me a moment to gather my thoughts."

"Are your thoughts sufficiently gathered for you to do me a favor? After the Drew Draper screwup, I figure you owe me."

"I owe a lot of people at the moment, Fiona," he said with a low laugh. "Yeah, okay. I'm in the middle of writing job applications, but I was about to take a break. What do you need?"

"A coffeemaker for the Book Mark's café. A machine, a French press, a stovetop espresso maker. Frankly, anything that makes real coffee will do."

"Bridie's instant powder not doing it for you?"

"Heartless sod," she said. "How can you laugh at my predicament? We caffeine addicts need our fix."

"Tell you what. As long as you'll let me come by for my morning coffee, I'll loan you my machine until you get a new one."

The church bells were chiming eleven o'clock when Gavin Maguire strode into the Book Mark, larger than life and sexier than sin.

In the time since she'd last seen him, he'd smartened up. Which was to say he was no longer sporting a two-day beard, bed head, and rumpled clothing. He was clean-shaven and wore formfitting jeans and a red-checked shirt. He looked good. More than good.

He caught her staring, and his amused half smile made her cheeks burn. "Morning, ladies."

Gavin maneuvered his way past Fiona, his hip brushing her side for a millisecond. Her tummy did a funny flip, and her cheeks grew hotter.

Sharon, seemingly oblivious to Fiona's discomfiture, went into full flirt mode. "How are ya, Gavin? Surviving life as a single man?" She sashayed across the bookshop and posed her canary yellow bosom directly under Gavin's nose.

"I'm grand, Sharon." He retreated from her sequined glory. "And yourself?"

He deposited the large box he was carrying on the counter and took out a modern coffee machine and an assortment of colored capsules.

Sharon fluttered her eyelashes. "I've a raging hangover but the sight of you and real coffee is making me feel much better."

Fiona crossed her arms. The flaming cheek of the girl. She'd had no complaint about the caffeine situation before Gavin the Coffee Hero rode to the rescue.

The bell above the shop door jangled, indicating the arrival of another customer. An elderly man in tweeds came into the shop, and nodded at them.

Gavin flashed Fiona a knowing smile, adding fuel to her rapidly rising temper. "Looks like both you ladies could do with a coffee. Why don't I show Fiona how to work the machine while you serve Mr. Delaney?"

Sharon shrugged in the nonchalant manner of a woman confident that if this specimen of manhood didn't succumb to her sex appeal, the next one would. "Right-o," she said and strutted off to wow the hapless Mr. Delaney with her charms.

Gavin filled the machine's water tank and inserted the plug. For a large man, he had surprisingly slender fingers. Long, supple, graceful. Concert pianist fingers, as Fiona's mother used to say.

He toyed with the colored capsules, each touch like a caress. His azure blue gaze pinned her in place. "How do you like yours, Fiona?"

She blinked, gave herself a mental shake. What the feck was she doing fantasizing about Gavin Maguire? If it wasn't for his fuckwittery, she'd be lounging by a pool in Singapore.

"Hard," she said hoarsely. "No, I mean strong." *Get a grip, Fiona.*

He arched a dark blond eyebrow, an amused curve to his sensual lips. "A ristretto?"

"Yeah," she muttered, ignoring the throb in her unmentionables. "That's what I meant."

The curve of his lips grew wider. He was enjoying this, the prick. Enjoying seeing her blush and stammer like the green schoolgirl she'd once been. Well, feck him. She left that girl behind years ago.

"I can make my own coffee." Her fingers closed over his. The two of them were close now. Close enough for her to smell the spicy scent of his cologne and the minty tang of his sharply exhaled breath.

They stood there a moment, fingers frozen in an unwitting caress.

A shiver of awareness made her tremble. She released his hand and stood back. "Ristretto's fine."

15

"What's the rush?" Olivia asked as Fiona dragged her into the lift of Debenham's department store and hit the button for the second floor. "I thought you borrowed a coffee machine from Gavin."

"I did. That's the problem. The deal included him dropping by the Book Mark for his morning coffee."

Olivia tossed her glossy red hair over her shoulder. "Okay, let me get this straight. Gavin brought the machine round yesterday. You lasted *one morning* of him stopping by the shop?"

"Having him about is…unsettling." *What an understatement.* She'd been hyper aware of his presence the entire ten minutes and forty-five seconds he'd spent in the café, conscious of his every move and every breath. If she had to live in Ballybeg for the next few months, the last thing she needed was Gavin Maguire underfoot and under her skin.

"Do you see a lot of each other now you're living next door?" asked Olivia in a coy tone.

Fiona rolled her eyes. "Stop with the matchmaking, Liv. Never gonna happen."

"Never gonna happen *again*, you mean?"

"You're loving this, aren't you?"

Olivia choked back a laugh. "Not loving your predicament, but I'll admit your aunt Deirdre's face was a sight to behold."

The lift shuddered to a halt, and the doors slid open to reveal the kitchen electronics department.

"Come on," Fiona said, stepping out of the lift. "Let's find a kickass coffee machine. Preferably one loud enough to drown out Sharon's constant chatter."

"You must be finding Gavin's presence very unsettling if you left Sharon in charge when you made a dash for Cork City." Olivia sent her a quizzical look. "That smacks of desperation."

Fiona exhaled through her teeth. The thought of the mayhem her hapless assistant could cause in a few short hours was giving her hives, but the idea of a daily encounter with Gavin galvanized her into action.

"Put it this way. The shop's heavily in the red and likely to sink further into debt the longer I'm forced to serve stale buns in the café. Sharon's antics can't alienate customers we don't have."

Olivia's deep blue eyes twinkled. "The terms 'Sharon MacCarthy' and 'customer service' don't belong in the same sentence."

"She's cheekier than my students. Why hasn't Bridie fired her? She's a nice girl, and she's a decent worker when given clear instructions, but she positively delights in winding people up."

"Ah, you know Bridie," Olivia said. "She's always had a soft spot for wounded birds."

Fiona eyebrows shot north. "Sharon wounded? The girl's as tough as fiberglass."

"If she's driving you mad, why don't *you* fire her?"

Fiona shoved a stray curl behind her ear. "Because Bridie specifically forbade me to. I'm allowed to change whatever else I want in the shop, but Sharon stays."

"Her family's dodgy as feck. Ruairí is the first MacCarthy to do something with his life that didn't result in a mug shot."

"Provided Sharon doesn't do anything illegal in the shop, she can plaster her bedroom walls with mug shots as far as I'm concerned." Fiona stopped at the kitchen electronics aisle and eyed the multitude of coffee machines on display. "Right. I need a robust machine capable of making decent espressos, cappuccinos, and regular coffees."

"Do you want a frother?" Olivia asked. "If so, don't go for a machine with one of those nozzle yokes. They're a bitch to clean. You'll save time and stress if you spend a bit more and get a proper frother."

"Okay." She scanned the shelves packed with machines—small, large, and every size between. "There are so many to choose from. Any recs?"

"This is the model we have at home." Olivia pointed to a large machine with an array of buttons and a digital display. "It was pricey, but I love it."

Fiona glanced at the price tag and recoiled. “Is it hard to use?”

“Nah.” Olivia tossed her glossy red ponytail over her shoulder. “Dead easy. If you get this one I can run you through it.”

“Speaking of running me through things…I have a proposition for you.”

“Oh?”

“Remember how you planned to open a café?”

“Yeah. Those were the days.” Olivia’s laugh rang hollow. “Instead, I’m a secretary and general dogsbody in my husband’s legal practice. Not quite where I pictured myself ten years ago.”

“Long story short, I’m not happy with Gillespie’s baked goods. Today’s delivery was stale. I’m having no luck finding an alternative supplier at short notice, and I’m reaching the point of despair.”

“How can I help?”

“You can bake,” she said bluntly. “I’m offering you a bit of extra cash in return for some of your delicious muffins and scones.”

Olivia beamed. “Yeah, all right, but I can only manage a couple of hours a few evenings a week. Why don’t I show you how to prepare a few basic recipes yourself, and I’ll do the rest? Bridie has a decent oven at the cottage, if I recall correctly.”

Fiona nodded. “Yeah. It’s one of the rare modern appliances she owns.”

“Excellent,” Olivia said. “We’ll have a few batches of fairy cakes and sticky buns baked within a couple of hours. We’ll stop off and buy the ingredients on our way back to Ballybeg. I'll show you how to soak the ingredients to make tea brack and fruit cake, then we'll make them tomorrow evening."

"You make it sound simple."

"It is. Don't worry, Fee. We'll have you serving excellent coffee and yummy baked goods in no time."

"That would be fantastic. Seriously, I have to do something to lure more customers into the shop, and the café seems to be my best bet."

"Are things that bad at the Book Mark?"

"Unfortunately, yes. I don't want to do the bare minimum to keep the shop afloat. If I'm to work at the Book Mark for the next few months, I want to make it profitable."

"Do you have any ideas?" Olivia asked. "Apart from firing Gillespie's?"

"I've jotted down a few, yeah." Fiona rummaged through her bag and extracted a small notebook. "A monthly book club. A children's story hour. An official stand at the Ballybeg Christmas Bazaar."

"Wow. Sounds like a lot of work."

"Better to be busy than bored." Fiona shoved the notebook back into her bag. "I'd best pay for this machine before we get chucked out by store security for loitering."

THE FADING AUTUMN sunlight bathed Gavin's home office in a warm orange. He yawned and stretched, pushed the chair back from his desk, and contemplated having another cup of coffee.

It had been a productive day. He'd arranged appointments with a couple of potential buyers for Clonmore Lodge, bought a new computer (essential in his line of work), and applied for a few architecture jobs. In the two and a half weeks since his unengagement and unemployment, he'd applied for every suitable position he could find advertised. At the moment, he was concentrating on the area around Cork City, but he'd likely need to cast his net wider once the rejections started rolling in.

Bernard Byrne's influence in the building trade in Cork was considerable but waned the farther away from Cork one got. Staying in Cork was his goal, but he might not have a choice. Whatever happened, he only had a couple more weeks to decide whether or not to sign Bernard's agreement. He was screwed whatever he did. If he refused to sign, he'd never work in the Irish building trade as long as Bernard held sway. If he signed, he'd have to keep Bernard sweet until the day he retired.

"Woof!" Wiggly Poo sat by his side, panting.

"You can't possibly want more food." Gavin gave him a vigorous scratch.

The dog wagged his tail in delight.

Ah, he was screwed. He hadn't wanted a dog in his life—still didn't—but the little fella was growing on him. He knew what it felt like to be unwanted. It was a raw ache that faded with time but never disappeared. He couldn't inflict that on another creature, not even a dog.

Given that he hadn't so much as sneezed in Wiggly Poo's presence, it was safe to assume his allergies did not extend to labradoodles. "Come on, mate. Let's see what we can find in the kitchen."

Gavin padded into his cozy kitchen, opened a tin of dog food for Wiggly Poo, and fixed himself a coffee. Wiggly Poo devoured his meal faster than the time it took Gavin to down his ristretto.

He leaned against the kitchen counter and regarded his small home with affection. The converted fisherman's cottage was a snug, four-room affair. He'd loved it from the moment he'd first walked through the low front door fifteen years ago. His mother had inherited the cottage from a relative, but it had been too small to accommodate her growing family with her new husband.

As far as Gavin was concerned, it was perfect. When his mother and stepfather had moved to Wexford, Gavin had stayed on in the cottage. The instant he'd had the cash, he'd bought them out of their share of the house and done the place up.

He'd taken up the worn carpets to reveal the solid stone floors underneath and polished them to the nth degree before decorating them with patterned rugs. He'd replaced the peeling wallpaper with brightly colored paint. The walls in each room were a different color, offset by a white ceiling. He'd been obliged to follow the Ballybeg tradition of painting the outside of the cottage a vivid hue but had bent the rules somewhat by opting for black and white stripes.

When the piercing doorbell rang, he jumped, almost spilling his coffee. Frowning, he set the cup on the smooth granite counter. He wasn't expecting any callers.

In the hallway, his visitor's feminine form was visible through the door's stained glass inlay.

Fiona stood on his doorstep. She had flour on her

nose. He had a sudden urge to lick it off. What the flip was wrong with him? Was he losing what was left of his mind?

"Hello, Gavin."

"Hey, Fiona. What's up?"

She was wearing one of Bridie's old aprons, floral with a lace trim. "Olivia and I are trying out recipes, but my aunt's kitchen scales are broken. Can we borrow yours?"

The words came out in an unpunctuated rush. She blushed and teased her lip ring with her tongue, sending an unexpected surge of longing to his loins.

"Uh, sure," he said slowly, doing a mental inventory of the contents of his kitchen cupboards. "I think I have scales somewhere. Tell you what, I'll have a rummage and call over when I've found them."

"Thanks. I'll be…" She jerked a thumb over the hedge dividing his front garden from Bridie's, then legged it.

"Right," he said into the empty air. "I'll be right over."

He rooted through several kitchen cupboards before he found an ancient pair of kitchen scales. He blew dust off them. "I think a quick scrub is called for, don't you, Wiggly Poo?"

The puppy woofed his enthusiastic agreement.

When the scales were clean and dried, Gavin slipped out his front door. The dog squeezed between his legs and shot out into the garden and out the gate.

"Steady on, mate," Gavin said, racing after him. "I doubt you're welcome next door after the porcelain-smashing fiasco."

"I'd say he's smashed all there is to smash," said Fiona, opening Bridie's front door. She'd tied her curly hair up in a bun now, but the sexy streak of flour on her nose remained.

His eyes met hers and held them for a second. A soft patter began in his chest. Had she always had eyes that shade of green-blue, or was it the light?

His gaze dropped to the flour on her nose. He should tell her. *Nah.* She'd only go and rub it off.

She caught him staring. "What? Oh!" Her hand flew to her face and rubbed off the flour, revealing a smattering of freckles underneath. She smiled, drawing his attention once again to her platinum lip ring.

He'd never kissed a woman with piercings before. She hadn't had them when they'd slept together in Vegas. Did she also have a...*Jaysus. Get a grip, Maguire.*

He hauled his thoughts out of the gutter and shoved the scales at her. "Here you go. They're clean and everything."

"Thanks. We need to get the measurements accurate for the fairy cakes."

"I haven't had fairy cakes in years," he said, still fixated on the lip ring. They'd barely spoken since the day he'd dropped the coffee machine round to the café. He'd reneged on his promise to call by each morning for a coffee fix, somehow sensing his presence unsettled both of them. Yet when she'd sent Sharon to return his machine to him, he'd been disappointed.

"The scales might be banjaxed. I haven't used them in ages." He was babbling, hovering on her doorstep for no rational reason.

He'd messed up her life, all because he'd not had his wits about him that morning in Vegas, not made sure

Draper had shredded the documents in front of him before forking over the money. He'd screwed up, and now they were all paying for it.

Wiggly Poo chose that moment to charge at Fiona, squeeze past her legs, and bound into Bridie's house.

Oh, shite.

A screech from the kitchen indicated Wiggly Poo was up to his old tricks.

"The sticky buns," Fiona cried and ran to the kitchen.

Olivia stood in the middle of the kitchen, an expression of horror on her face. Wiggly Poo had leaped onto the table and was helping himself to a cooling tray of freshly baked buns.

Stunned silence reigned until Fiona let out a crack of laughter. "There goes an hour of hard work."

"I'm sorry," he heard himself say. "The dog is a menace. I've signed us up for obedience school, but it doesn't start for another couple of weeks."

"Naughty dog," Fiona said, scooping him up and lifting him far away from the tray of buns. "I'm no expert, but I'd wager those are not part of your puppy diet plan."

Wiggly Poo licked her face.

Gavin's loins tightened. He shifted uncomfortably and tried to think of ice-cold plunge pools. *Aw, man.* He was a hopeless case. How could he be envious of a dog?

Olivia picked through the remaining sticky buns. "We can salvage a few," she said dubiously.

"No, we cannot," Fiona said. "I'm not serving puppy-slobbered-on buns to my customers."

"Sure, how will they know?"

"Olivia, business is tight enough without an outbreak

of food poisoning on the premises." Fiona laughed and extracted butter from the fridge. "No, I'll start from scratch. It'll give me a chance to practice for when you're not available to help me bake."

"You're planning on baking your own stuff to sell in the Book Mark café?" Gavin asked.

"Yeah." She tipped flour onto the scales. "I'm not impressed by Gillespie's."

"Gillespie's buns are bland," Gavin said. "I'm not a fan."

"You should call by and try out our wares. I'll give you a bun on the house as a thank-you for lending me your coffee machine." Her apron fit snugly around her backside. The same splendid backside he'd seen bared in all its glory a couple of weeks before.

His focus on ice-cold water deserted him, and the swell of his arousal strained the zipper of his jeans. Bloody hell. He had to get out of here before he disgraced himself. "Come on, Wiggly Poo. Let's get you home before you cause more mayhem."

The little dog wriggled in Fiona's arms until she set him free. He bounded up to Gavin with the enthusiasm of a dog that hadn't seen his master in a month.

Gavin picked him up and settled him under his arm. "I'll come by the Book Mark with Luca at the weekend. He's always up for a new book and a sticky bun."

"You're babysitting him again?" Olivia asked in a caustic tone. "Does Jonas actually live in Dublin? He seems to spend most of his time plaguing us with his presence."

Gavin swallowed a laugh. Olivia and Jonas irritated the hell out of one another and had done from the time they'd been spotty teenagers. Time and alleged maturity had done nothing to change the situation. "Jonas and Luca are coming to keep me company in my splendid isolation."

Fiona snorted with laughter. "Join the club. I suspect my tainted presence is part of the reason trade is slow at the Book Mark. My aunt and uncle aren't speaking to me, and neither are their friends and acolytes."

"It'll pass," Olivia said with confidence. "Once people find something new to trigger their outrage radar."

Fiona packed a couple of fairy cakes into a paper bag and handed it to Gavin. "You can be my taste tester. Just keep them away from Wiggly Poo."

"Thanks," he said, careful not to touch her when he took the bag. "See you Saturday."

He waved good-bye and took Wiggly Poo back to his cottage, trying hard to eradicate visions of Fiona's luscious arse from his mind.

16

It was Saturday and the bookshop was hopping. Thanks to Sharon and Olivia, word of the new coffee machine and edible baked goods had spread.

Fiona mopped sweat from her forehead. The fickle Irish weather had turned from mild to frigid in a matter of days. Which was to say the temperature was hovering around four degrees Celsius—low enough to give the Irish hypothermia.

Unfortunately for the staff of the Book Mark, the heating was on the blink. It recognized two settings: off or on at a level fit to give heatstroke.

And no, the bookshop was not equipped with air-conditioning.

"It's bleeding savage out there," Sharon said, lugging a box of books into the small stockroom. "But it's worse in here. I ought to get danger pay for working in this heat."

She suppressed a smile. "How does a glass of iced tea sound?"

"It won't buy me a one-way ticket to Ibiza, but I'll take it all the same."

Fiona poured two large glasses of iced tea and added a slice of lemon. "The electrician's coming by on Monday. We'll have to put up with the heat until then. In the meantime, keeping the windows open is the best we can do."

Mrs. Keogh heaped her pile of books on the counter.

"How are ya, Missus K.?" Sharon asked in a voice that projected around the shop. "More romances, I see. Did you ever try that *Fifty Shades of Whatsit*? There's loads of sex in that one. I'm sure you'd love it."

Poor Mrs. Keogh blushed to the roots of her snowy white hair.

Fiona shot her assistant a warning look. "Here, Mrs. Keogh. Let me help you load up your trolley. Would you like a sticky bun to enjoy at home? It's on the house."

"Oh, that's very kind of you, dear." Mrs. Keogh examined the glass display on the café counter, her hands aflutter. "May I have one with sprinkles on top? They remind me of the buns my mother baked when I was a child."

"No problem." Fiona put the bun in a paper bag and placed it at the top of Mrs. Keogh's trolley. "Happy reading." When Mrs. Keogh had left, Fiona faced her cheeky assistant. "Seriously, Sharon. You can't speak to the customers like that."

"Missus K.'s well used to me," Sharon said, shoveling a fairy cake into her face. "She'll be grand."

"The next time she's in here, I want you to make a point of being nice to her."

"Huh?" Sharon's heavily made-up eyes widened. "Aren't I always friendly?"

"There's friendly, and there's cheeky, and you don't appear to know the difference."

"Do you think I offended her?"

Fiona gave a mental eye roll. "Sharon, the poor woman was scarlet. You embarrassed her."

Her assistant chewed on her cake thoughtfully. "Yeah, all right. I'll tone it down. She's a nice old biddy, actually."

"When you're done eating the stock, I want you to unload the dishwasher. We're out of cups."

With Sharon occupied and the café patrons served, Fiona seized the opportunity to slip into the tiny stockroom at the back of the shop where two boxes of used books required sorting and price-tagging.

She'd barely begun tackling the contents of the first box when the familiar jangle of the door indicated the arrival of another customer. The second she heard his deep, rumbling voice, she knew who it was. Unfortunately, her body was also acutely aware of his presence. A rush of heat coursed through her, and her hands flew to her wild hair.

It was Gavin. And he wasn't alone. A high child's voice accompanied him. Her heart hammered in her chest. She was daft to have this reaction to his presence. Besides, she was still pissed with him over his idiocy in Vegas. Although, truth be told, she was more annoyed with herself for not checking.

Flustered, she smoothed down her creased shirt and fiddled with her hair in an effort to put it in some semblance of order. She caught a glimpse of her reflection in the small bathroom mirror at the back of the stockroom. *Holy hell.* The heat was making her curls even frizzier than usual. Giving her hair up as a lost cause, she took a deep breath and ventured out into the shop.

She spotted him immediately—not that it would be difficult, given his size and the smallness of the shop. "Hey."

The top of his shamrock tattoo peeked out from beneath his shirt collar. Before he turned around to face her, the back of his neck stiffened.

God, he was gorgeous. Her knees turned to jelly. She'd avoided staring at him since she'd gotten back to Ballybeg and was making up for lost time now. Despite his height, he carried himself well and gave the impression of speed as well as bulk. His dark blond hair shone in the autumn sunlight streaming through the shop window. When he was a teenager, his face had been angelic-looking. Age and experience had made it rugged, lending it a comfortable, lived-in appearance.

His sensual mouth curved into a smile. Fiona was sure she was blushing from head to toe. "Hey, yourself."

His deep voice did things to the lower part of her anatomy she was sure weren't appropriate in a public place.

Fiona shifted her attention to the small, dark-haired boy at Gavin's side who was examining a book on dinosaurs with a stern expression on his tanned face. "You must be Luca."

"Luca," Gavin prompted.

The little boy wrenched his attention away from the dinosaur book. "You're the pretty lady who lives in Bridie's house."

"He takes after his dad," Gavin said, grinning. "Has an eye for the ladies."

Luca squinted at Fiona. "Did that hurt?" he asked, pointing to her lip ring.

"At first, but not anymore. My tattoos hurt more." Fiona shoved a stray curl behind her ear. "Can I offer you two something to eat?"

Luca made a dash for the W.B. Yeats table.

Fiona and Gavin exchanged smiles. "I'll take that to be a yes," she said. "What'll you have?"

"An espresso for me and a lemonade for Luca." He went over to examine the display of sweet treats. "And two berry scones."

Fiona placed two scones on a large plate. She added two small ramekins, one filled with clotted cream and the other with Bridie's homemade strawberry jam, and set the plate on their table.

"Say, Fiona…"

Her heart skipped a beat. "Yeah?"

"You always had great taste in books. I find myself… lacking a library at present."

"Muireann chucked his books in the pond," said Luca through a mouthful of scone, "but she's not pregnant."

The customers at the next table ceased their conversation and swiveled in their chairs to gawk at Gavin.

He turned the color of Bridie's jam.

"Yes," Fiona said, scrambling for something—anything—appropriate to say. "Under the circumstances, that would have been awkward."

Gavin shot her a look from beneath his lashes.

Her tummy muscles began to spasm.

"Oh, go on," he said dryly. "You know you want to laugh."

"Out of the mouths of babes," she said with a giggle.

"Ah, yes. Luca can be relied upon for his attention to detail. Now, about those books…"

"To spare your blushes, I'm willing to roll with a change of subject. Do you still like sci-fi and fantasy? I remember you buying a lot of those when I used to work here years ago."

"Yeah, I do. Also crime fiction. No need to give me any of Jonas's books. He's already given me replacement copies for the entire series."

She raised a teasing eyebrow. "Signed, I hope?"

"Of course."

At the sight of his sexy half smile, the butterflies in her stomach came to life. "I'll pick out a few books and leave them at the counter. How does that sound?"

"Like excellent customer service." His upper lip was covered in cream from his scone. He licked it off with his pink tongue, and she noticed his tongue piercing for the first time. A jolt of sexual longing hit her groin. She swallowed, shifted position, and moved into the book room to search for his books.

Every once in a while, she stole a surreptitious glance in their direction, her green eyes darting away the instant they met Gavin's blue ones. She selected six books for him —two fantasy, three sci-fi, and one techno thriller—and set them beside the cash register.

"He's a bit of a ride, isn't he," Sharon said in a voice loud enough to shatter glass. "And the chemistry between you two is flaming sizzling. I can totally see why you got married."

"Sharon," Fiona said between gritted teeth, "could you keep the volume down please?"

Her assistant chomped on her gum and stared at Fiona through eyelashes thick with jet-black mascara. "I don't think he heard me. Sure, look. His back's turned."

Fiona felt heat creep up her cheeks. Unless Gavin was deaf as a post, there was no way he hadn't heard Sharon's bellowing.

Shite. Her life was devolving into a slapstick comedy with her as the unwitting star of the show.

Luca and Gavin finished their scones and beverages, and Gavin paid what he owed, adding a generous tip. Armed with his new dino book, Luca looked very pleased with himself.

On their way out of the shop, Gavin paused. "Luca, can you wait for a sec? I need to have a word with Fiona."

Oh, crap on a cracker. He was going to mention what Sharon had said. How mortifying. Fiona buried her curls in an account book and tried to look absorbed.

"Fiona, I've been thinking," he began. "It's probably a daft idea, but you wouldn't consider moving to the UK, would you?"

What the feck? She blinked at him, uncomprehending. "Why would I want to move to the UK?"

"I've been doing some research. If you and I were to live in the UK for a while, we could file for divorce there."

Fiona's belly cramped. "You want us to move to the UK to speed up the divorce process?"

"Yeah." He flashed that bone-melting smile of his. All

she felt was ice in her veins. "I don't want to leave Ballybeg permanently, but I could cope with living abroad for a couple of years. The divorce would be done and dusted in half the time it'd take in Ireland."

"Right," she said faintly. "And I'm to do what, exactly, during our time in the UK?"

He beamed at her. "You could teach. I looked it up on the net. Your Irish teaching qualification should be accepted in the UK."

"Let me get this straight. You want me to give up my job in Dublin, postpone my travel plans yet again, and move *my entire life* so you can get back with Muireann sooner?"

The smile faltered. "I don't know that Muireann would have me back. I just thought a quicker divorce would allow both of us to get on with our lives faster."

"I'll sum up our present situations, shall I?" Her mounting anger was making her cheeks burn. "*You* are unemployed and unlikely to find a job in this area as long as my uncle wields influence over the building trade whereas *I* have a permanent teaching position and a home in Dublin—not to mention plans to travel once Bridie is well enough to take over the shop."

He blinked. "Bridie mentioned something about you going to Australia. Is that what you mean?"

"Yes, you self-absorbed twat. The same trip I've had to postpone to stay here and help Bridie. You're not the only one whose life plans got screwed."

"Steady on." As if realizing he'd raised his voice, Gavin's gaze darted around the shop. "I didn't know the ins and outs of your trip."

"Why would you?" she snapped, losing the battle to keep her temper in check. "You're too caught up with your own woes to spare a thought for mine. There's a sense of *déjà vu* about all this. You thought only of yourself the morning after our Vegas wedding, and you're just as selfish now."

"Calm down, Fiona." He held his palms up in a gesture of peace. "I didn't mean to insult you."

"No? You never mean to insult or hurt anyone, Gavin, you just bloody do." She slammed the accounts book shut. "You never even asked me if I was okay with you paying Drew Draper not to register our marriage. You'd decided you'd made a mistake and to hell with what I thought."

His mouth gaped. "You wanted us to stay married?"

Yes, she had—with every atom of her being. Watching him walk out that hotel room door and out of her life smashed her heart to smithereens.

She took a shuddery breath. "I'm not bloody well moving to the UK for your convenience. How dare you suggest I uproot my entire life to suit your agenda?"

"I'm sorry, Fee," he said, taking a step back. "Forget I mentioned it. It was a stupid idea."

"Too right it was a stupid idea. The only person you care about is yourself. What happened to you, Gavin? Back when we were teenagers, you used to have a personality. You used to have dreams. Now you're yet another Celtic Tiger cliché—selfish, entitled, and mercenary."

He flinched as though she'd struck him. He opened his mouth as if to say something, then obviously thought the better of it. "I'd better go. We'll talk another time, yeah?"

She glared at him, piercing him with her gaze. "You

have Aidan Gant's number. Call him if you want to arrange another meeting."

After Gavin and Luca left the shop, she noticed the pile of books she'd selected for him by the cash register. *Feck.*

Sharon sidled up to Fiona. "You handled that well, boss. Sarcasm intended."

"Sarcasm unwelcome. Keep your snout out of my business."

"Keep your granny pants on," Sharon said. "I was only going to share a few words of wisdom."

"Wisdom?" Fiona looked her assistant up and down. "How old are you, anyway? Twenty? Twenty-One?"

She stuck her chest out. "I'm a mature nineteen."

"When I was a mature twenty-one—" Fiona made quotation marks with her fingers, "—I married the eejit who just exited the shop."

Sharon cocked a painted-on eyebrow. "And the moral of the story is...?"

"Stay the feck away from Las Vegas."

17

fter closing the shop, Fiona headed for Cork University Hospital. She drove faster than she should, foot to the metal.

Damn the man!

One minute he was Mr. Nice Guy, his maple-syrup smiles making her forget every morsel of common sense she possessed. The next, he'd reverted to selfish mode, the change swift and brutal, like battery acid on an open wound.

Well, feck him. She'd just dumped one selfish manhole. She was damned if she'd let another screw her around, lawfully wedded husband or not.

When she arrived at the hospital, visiting hours were drawing to an end. St. Ignatius ward was the quietest she'd ever seen it. Bridie's room was half empty with only a couple of beds occupied. Her aunt was propped up in hers, lounging on pillows and leafing through a magazine.

Fiona kissed her plump cheek.

Her aunt peered over her spectacles. "How's my shop? Still standing, I hope?"

"The shop's grand," Fiona said with a little too much force to come off natural. "Don't worry about a thing."

"How are you getting on with Sharon?" One corner of the woman's mouth quirked.

"Sharon is…an interesting employee."

Bridie guffawed with laughter. "That's one way of putting it. She's a good girl at heart, though, and she hasn't had the easiest of lives. She deserves a chance."

Fiona's smile froze. "Sure."

Bridie sighed and lowered her magazine. "You'll have seen the numbers by now. Business is bad."

"Yeah." Fiona pulled up a chair and sat down. "But if I'm going to be in Ballybeg for a while, I might as well make myself useful. I've come up with few ideas to attract more customers into the café."

Her aunt's cheery look faded. "I can't afford a major investment at this time, and the bank won't loan me any more money."

"Don't worry about the money. None of my plans require a major cash-out. For starters, I've bought a new coffee machine for the shop." Bridie started to protest, but she cut her off. "Consider it a get-well-soon gift. Besides, it was an act of self-preservation. If I'm to work at the Book Mark for the next few months, I need decent coffee."

Bridie's eyes welled with tears. She blinked them away as if they'd never existed. "You're a good girl. I don't know what I'd do without you. Truth be told, I should've had this operation months ago, but I couldn't afford to pay someone to run the shop in my absence, and the business would fold if I closed it while I'm out sick."

Fiona ached at the sight of her usually hale and healthy aunt so poorly. "Concentrate and get back on your feet—literally and figuratively. I'll keep the shop afloat." *And Sharon in line.*

"I feel awful you've had to cancel your trip, love."

"Don't worry about it. I'll spend a few weeks traveling once you're back on your feet." She squeezed her hand. "That's what family's for."

"I wish Bernard shared your feelings," Bridie said with a sniff. "If that bastard hadn't ripped us off, I wouldn't be in this mess, and you'd have money in the bank."

Fiona stiffened. "What are you talking about?"

Her aunt opened her mouth to respond, then shut it again when a nurse arrived with the tea tray.

The tea was black to the point of being stewed. Fiona dumped a lump of sugar into her cup and added a splash of milk to Bridie's. Once tea was served, she focused on her aunt's pale face. "What's all this about Bernard ripping us off?" She lowered her voice so the woman in the next bed wouldn't overhear.

Her aunt sighed and took a sip of tea. "Don't mind me, love. I should've kept my trap shut. I've no proof."

"Ah, come on. You can't leave me hanging."

"All right. But what I'm about to tell you stays between us." She lowered her voice to a whisper. "The last thing I need is Bernard suing me for slander."

Fiona's fingers tightened around her cup. "Surely he wouldn't sue you. You're his sister."

"Sister or not, I wouldn't put anything past Bernard."

Bridie cradled her cup of tea, and the grooves on her forehead deepened. "My father did pretty well for himself. The farm was large and prosperous, and he invested in property back when prices were low. When he died, I inherited the cottage and the house on Patrick Street. Your father inherited the house you lived in until your parents died, and Bernard got the house in Cobh that he now rents out to holidaymakers. The farm and the surrounding land were left to Mammy.

"Mammy always said she'd split the farm house and land between me, Michael, and Bernard when she died. We all knew Bernard was her favorite, but she was a fair woman, and I can't imagine her cutting me and Michael out of her will."

"Yet that's what happened," finished Fiona.

"Yet that's what happened," Bridie said with a sigh. "Your father predeceased her, making you the rightful heir of his share of the farm. Only when my mother died and her will was read out, she'd left everything she owned —house, land, family photos—to Bernard."

Fiona exhaled sharply. "I knew the land had been unfairly divided between the siblings, but I had no idea you thought there was something fishy about the will. What makes you think something was amiss?"

"Put it this way—the will was dated two months before Mammy died, and the witnesses were Deirdre and a woman called Ann Dunne, one of the nurses at the nursing home where she lived for the last year of her life. I don't know what her previous will said, but I'd bet my porcelain dog collection that it was a three-way split."

Fiona thought of Wiggly Poo's ornament-smashing

rampage and made a mental note to get cracking on finding replacements before Bridie got home.

"Soon after Mammy died, Bernard sold the farm and much of the land surrounding it and bought Clonmore House with the proceeds. I'm not saying he's not a shrewd business man, but I've always felt there was dirty dealing going on." Bridie put her mug of tea on her bedside table and looked out the window. "But I've no proof. And even if I did, Bernard has so many politicians in his pocket that I'd have no chance of getting justice. It's not what you know in this country. It's who you know and who you've paid off."

"Ain't that the truth." Fiona's mind was racing, weighing her aunt's words and their implications. Bernard was a loathsome toad. She'd never liked him, not even as a child. But would he stoop to defrauding his only sister and his orphaned niece of their inheritance? She had her answer before her brain formed the question. She sensed the truth in her gut, in all its acidic glory. "What about the land he's using to build the shopping center? Was that part of my grandparents' estate?"

Her aunt nodded. "That's the only parcel of land he didn't sell right after our mother died. He's clung to it all these years, biding his time until he had the money and planning permission to build the center."

Fiona visualized the vast stretch of land spreading out from her grandparents' old farmhouse. Theirs had once been one of the largest farms in the area, back when farming was still a reasonably profitable endeavor. She thought of Bridie's precarious financial situation and her own years of studying and working in order to scrimp and save to put a down payment on a one-bedroom apartment in Dublin, then of her struggle to put money aside for her world trip. In contrast, Muireann had never needed to do more than play at working as an interior designer and got to swan off to London, Paris, or New York on shopping trips. It was hard not to indulge her inner green-eyed monster.

A thought coalesced, faint at first, then gaining clarity. "Wait. Isn't that where the fairy tree is?"

"Oh, aye," Bridie said, shaking her head sadly. "They want to cut it down."

The words lashed Fiona like a whip. "Bernard can't do that. Felling a fairy tree brings bad luck to anyone associated with its destruction."

"Bernard pays no heed to the old beliefs. His only concern is increasing his bank account."

"Is there no way to stop him?"

"There's talk of a protest, but I doubt anything will come of it. Everyone who's anyone in Ballybeg has a stake in that shopping center."

Fiona tapped the side of her cup in thought. "We could stop him if we could prove he tampered with Nana's will."

"You'd go to all that trouble to save the tree?"

"Hell, no. If my uncle cheated us, I want to know. And believe me when I say I'll make the bastard pay."

Her aunt gripped her arm. "Dwelling on what might have been is a mug's game. Believe me, I've been there. I never should have brought it up."

"If there's nothing to prove Bernard did wrong with the will, there's nothing we can do," Fiona said. "But one way or another, I intend to look into it."

"Be sensible, love, and leave well alone." Bridie released her grip. "I'm sorry for getting maudlin. I rarely think about it these days, but it's hard not to at the moment with Bernard gloating over his building project and me struggling to keep the shop going."

"Don't worry about it now. Concentrate on getting better." Fiona rearranged her aunt's pillows. "Are you comfortable? Or at least as comfortable as you can get?"

"I'm grand, pet." Bridie gave her a wan smile. "You go off home, and please don't do anything rash."

18

Gavin awoke to sunlight streaming through his bedroom window and a dog farting in his face. "Ugh!" He shoved the dog off him and sat up in the bed.

The room spun. It was Sunday morning. He'd been out for a few drinks with Jonas the night before. Clearly, he'd had one too many. He'd have to rein in the drinking, and fast. He had enough problems at the moment without adding another to the list.

"Woof!" Wiggly Poo leaped off the duvet and pawed at the bedroom door. "Woof!"

Gavin rubbed sleep from his eyes. "How the hell did you get in here?" Memories of a whining puppy outside his bedroom door broke through his uncaffeinated haze. "Feck. Did I let you sleep in my room again?" He groaned and hauled himself out of bed. "All right, all right. Let me get dressed and we'll go out."

He grabbed an old T-shirt and shorts from his

wardrobe and pulled them on. His reflection in the full-length mirror was not a pretty sight. Thick stubble lined his jaw, and his hair stood up in wild tufts. A shave and a hairbrush would take care of them, but there wasn't much he could do about the dark bags underneath his eyes. He wasn't sleeping well, and it showed.

The puppy dropped one of his running shoes on his toes.

"Thanks," he said dryly. He laced the shoes and clipped Wiggly Poo's lead to his dog collar. "Come on. Let's face the world."

The dog raced out the cottage door and down the garden path, dragging Gavin in his wake.

"Wait up, mate. I'm supposed to be taking *you* for a walk, not the other way around."

Someone snorted from the neighboring garden. "Haven't you realized he's in charge?" Fiona was leaning against the gate to Bridie's cottage. Her dark curls were pulled back in a ponytail, and she wore workout gear. Her green eyes flashed with annoyance at the sight of him.

His stomach lurched. He'd put his size twelves in it yesterday. He ran a nervous hand through his short hair and took a step toward her. "Listen, about what I said yesterday—"

"It's grand," she said, bending to stroke Wiggly Poo's curly fur. "Forget about it."

"It's not grand. I was an eejit. And selfish. You're absolutely right on that score. I hadn't thought it through."

She sighed. "I wish I hadn't said anything about our marriage. I wish I'd ignored that piece of paper, not let Olivia look us up in the online registry."

Gavin took a step closer. This time, she didn't move. "But you'd have known," he said softly and stroked her cheek. "You'd have known I was committing bigamy. Plus you were giving me the choice of what to do. You weren't to know Bernard would barge in right at that moment."

She looked up, paralyzing him with her electrifying green gaze. She wore no makeup, and her freckles stood out more than usual against her pale skin. "What would you have done?" she whispered. "If Bernard hadn't barged in?"

He took a ragged breath and stepped away from her. He looked out over the beach below. "I don't know. My mind was in turmoil, bouncing from one decision to another. In hindsight, I hope I would have done the right thing and told Muireann the truth."

"Fair enough." She fell silent a moment, then said, "I have something for you. Wait a sec."

She darted inside Bridie's cottage and reemerged with a plastic bag. "You forgot these," she said, handing him the bag, careful to avoid touching him. The sleeve of her workout shirt slid up to reveal a beautiful vine tattoo.

He peeked inside the bag. It contained several books—the ones she'd picked out for him yesterday. "Thanks, Fiona. I'm looking forward to reading them. What do I owe you?"

"On the house. Consider them reimbursement for letting us borrow your coffee machine." She tugged down her sleeve, concealing her ink. He wondered how far up her arm it extended.

"That's a gorgeous tattoo," he said. "I'd like to get

another one, but Muireann was always on at me to get rid of the two I've got."

"I'm glad you didn't. They suit you." She blushed and her eyes dropped to her scuffed running shoes.

Wiggly Poo whined and tugged at his lead.

"Were you planning to go for a run on the beach?" He yanked on Wiggly Poo's lead as the dog tried to trot across the road to the stone steps leading to the beach.

She bent down to give the puppy another scratch, giving Gavin an excellent view of her Lycra-clad legs. "I was thinking about it. But it'd be more of a power walk in my case. Jogging's not ideal with my leg. Plus I'm out of shape." She motioned to his cottage. "Jonas and Luca not staying with you?"

"No. They stayed over with Jonas's parents last night. Luca is going through a phase of having night terrors. Nuala—his grandmother—is great at calming him back to sleep. So what about that power walk?"

Her face split into a small smile that evaporated into uncertainty a second later.

"Come on," he urged. "Come with us. Wiggly Poo will put us both through our paces."

She was still for a beat, then nodded. "Yeah, okay. As long as you promise not to drive me to the point of collapse."

They took the route west, out toward the caves at Craggy Point. The caves were perennially popular hangouts for local teenagers and the site of many a secret tryst. Depending on the tides, they were partially submerged, but the water rarely got so deep as to be dangerous. Gavin and Jonas had enjoyed plenty of cookouts in the caves during their youth.

"I haven't been out to Craggy Point in years." Fiona bent to catch her breath. "Not since I was in my teens."

"Am I going too fast for you?"

"Compared to Wiggly Poo," she panted, "We're both snails."

"How's your leg?" he asked, indicating her right leg. "To be honest, I'd forgotten all about it until you mentioned it earlier."

Her soft lips curved. "I usually forget myself. It bothers me in colder weather or if I run without warming up. Other than that, it's fine."

"Here." Gavin tossed her his water bottle.

She caught it and straightened, then took a long drink. "I remember this cave." She pointed at narrow entrance just visible beyond the next boulder. "It was always my favorite."

He grinned at her. "What did you get up to in there? Or is it too scandalous to share?"

"Don't be daft." She swatted him with the water bottle. "The most I ever did in the caves was share a drunken snog."

"So why's it your favorite? I don't remember anything special about it in comparison to the others."

Indecision flickered across her face. Finally, she shrugged. "Come on. I'll show you."

They clambered over fallen rocks and made their way to the cave's entrance. The tide wasn't long out, and the cave floor was slick with seaweed and seawater.

"It's toward the back." She stepped gingerly over a clump of seaweed.

He followed her in, Wiggly Poo dancing at his heels. Why couldn't he find something to focus on other than her backside? Ever since the dress-splitting incident, he associated Fiona with fabulous female buttocks. He blinked and shifted his focus to his feet. If he didn't watch his step, he'd be the one flat on his face with his arse in the air.

"Here." She stopped in front of a section of cave wall and smoothed her palms over rough rock. "Do you have a torch?"

"Yeah." He fished his torch out of his back pocket and handed it to her.

Fiona switched the light on and shone the torch at the wall. "Look," she said, pointing at two faded names carved into the cave wall. "Michael and Cathy Forever. August 1980. My parents."

"Wow," Gavin said. "They knew each other way back then?"

"Yeah. They met in primary school and were a couple by the end of secondary school." Her voice broke on the last words of the sentence.

"You must miss them very much," he said gently, giving her shoulder a tentative pat.

She bit her lip, and her eyes shifted to the carving on the wall. "I miss them every day. My little brother, too. They say time heals, but I don't agree. I've reached the point where I don't burst into tears every time something reminds me of what I've lost. It's easier in Dublin. No shared memories. But it's hard not to think of them when I'm in Ballybeg."

"I can understand that." His touch on her shoulder turned into a caress. "You're very brave, you know. Much braver than I'd have been in your position."

She shook her head. "I'm not brave, Gavin. I only wish I were. I wish I were confident and able to take on the world with a smile, no matter how crappy I was feeling."

"You, not confident? If you're not, you're very good at faking it. Besides, you've done pretty well for yourself, from what I can see."

"I was daft enough to marry you."

"True." They fell into an awkward silence, neither knowing how to break the ice. The mention of their Vegas madness put a dampener on every conversation.

"Come on," he said finally. "Let's get out of here before we freeze. And I'd better get home. I need to make a few calls about jobs."

"Any luck with getting interviews?" she asked, navigating the slippery ground with care.

He grimaced. "None so far. Nor have I found a buyer for Clonmore Lodge. Bernard's tentacles extend far and wide."

Not to mention the looming deadline. Aidan Gant had left several messages on his voice mail. The first few were amiable, asking if he'd decided what to do about the agreement. The latest message saw Gant's cordiality slip several notches. He was curt and to the point: Gavin was to be at his office at five o'clock on Friday the 17th of October. Bernard had 'graciously' extended Gavin's deadline to accommodate Gant's busy schedule. This wasn't an invitation. It was a bloody order. One way or the other, Bernard Byrne intended to bleed him dry, and there wasn't a damn thing Gavin could do to stop him. He ground his teeth in frustration.

"Oh!" Fiona gasped, slipping on a piece of damp seaweed. Gavin caught her in the nick of time, breaking her fall. Her face was millimeter from his, those adorable freckles visible even in the faint light of the cave.

He should draw back, cut the cord of temptation. His heart slammed against his ribs, and her ragged breathing mirrored his own.

His focus was riveted on her nose. That adorable, freckle-smudged nose he'd been so keen to lick just a few days ago.

He kissed it, then drew back and heard her intake of breath. Her lips parted, revealing very white teeth and the tip of her very pink tongue. As if drawn to the magnet of her lip ring, he touched her lips with his.

The kiss was tender at first—tender and tentative. Then she leaned into him and took control. Her tongue sought his. She kissed him as if their lives depended on it, shoving his back against the cool cave wall. He felt his pulse quicken and his erection harden. Every sensible thought of why this was a *very* bad idea went on hiatus, leaving his hormones in the driving seat. *Jaysus.* This woman would be his undoing.

He hadn't kissed like this since school. Back in those long-gone days when a kiss was all a boy could expect from a date and he made damn sure to maximize its potential. A lost art…one he wanted to practice more often. He drew her closer, matched her intensity, beat for passionate beat. And then it was over, as abruptly as it had begun. She pulled back, stumbling.

They stood there a moment, staring at one another, breathing heavily.

"I'm sorry," she said, drawing a ragged breath. "I shouldn't have done that."

"No." He pulled her close and nuzzled her hair. "I kissed you first. And I'm not in the least sorry. Maybe I should be, but I'm not."

"Woof!" Wiggly Poo inserted his hairy snout between them.

Fiona laughed and scratched his neck. "Looks like someone's bored with the cave."

"Yeah." Gavin took a deep, shuddery breath. "We'd better get going."

"Please make it a more sedate pace this time," she said. "I've got a stitch in my side."

"Wimp. I'll bet you can jog if you try alternating it with a minute's walking."

"Sadist. If I collapse in an undignified heap, you're responsible for carrying me home." She gestured to her figure. "And in case you haven't noticed, I'm no lightweight."

He pressed his tongue into the roof of his mouth and let his gaze roam over her curves. Yeah, he was doomed. "I think I could manage to lug you for a bit."

19

Fiona crunched up the gravel drive to Fatima House, the nursing home where Bridie had been transferred two weeks previously.

September had faded into October, bringing an abrupt end to the horde of holidaymakers in Ballybeg. Tourists, she'd discovered, were good news for the Book Mark. They popped in for a coffee and a freshly baked scone and stocked up on reading material for the beach. Now it was time to implement her plans to lure extra locals into the shop. The first Children's Story Hour was scheduled for next Wednesday afternoon, and the inaugural meeting of the Ballybeg Book Club would take place at the end of the month.

Despite throwing herself into Plan Save the Book Mark body and soul, she couldn't stop thinking about Gavin Maguire.

That kiss...that crazy, impulsive, hormone-altering kiss. If she hadn't pulled away, what would've happened?

Would he have called a halt? Stopped them from ripping each other's clothes off and making love on the cold cave floor? And if he hadn't, would the sex have been as soul-searing as it had been all those years ago in Vegas?

She fanned herself, exhaled in a whoosh. Her body temperature increased by a few degrees merely thinking about it.

Since the day in the cave, she'd been avoiding him and ignoring his texts. It was the cowardly route. She knew this, but her head was spinning. This wasn't mere sexual attraction—on her side, at least. The feelings that had lain dormant were showing signs of life. Over the years, she'd had several boyfriends, but none had impacted her the way he had. She'd had better sex since their night in Vegas and longer relationships. But no one had come close to penetrating her heart.

She parked the car in the last available space and took the short flight of stone steps leading to the entrance of the nursing home. Inside, the marble-floored lobby was quiet.

"Is Bridie Byrne back from physiotherapy?" she asked the gray-haired lady sitting at the reception desk.

The woman smiled. "Wait a moment. I'll call and see." A couple of minutes later, she replaced the receiver. "You can go on upstairs. Bridie's finished her lunch."

Her aunt was reading in an armchair by the window of the small room she shared with two other women. She glanced up when Fiona came in. "How's my shop?"

"Still standing," Fiona said with a smile.

"You and Sharon haven't come to blows?"

She laughed. "Not yet. Ask me after we get through next week's Children's Story Hour."

Bridie lowered her book and removed her spectacles. "How are you coping with life in Ballybeg?"

A muscle in Fiona's cheek pulsed. "Ah, you know," she replied with a shrug. "Not what I signed up for, but I'm surviving. It's nice to be able to see Olivia regularly."

"Your aunt Deirdre was in to see me yesterday."

"Oh, yeah? Does she still have the pitchforks out for me?"

"She said Muireann extended her holiday. She's spending a few weeks with a friend in Brisbane."

A pang of envy pierced Fiona's solar plexus. "Muireann's in Australia?"

"Apparently. According to Deirdre, you got Muireann's man, and Muireann got your Australian jaunt."

"Only I don't actually *have* her man."

The line between Bridie's brows deepened. "Any news on the divorce?"

"Nothing to report. Aidan Gant started the proceedings, but it'll take years to go through."

Bridie patted her hand. "It'll be grand, pet. Don't you worry. Did I tell you Gavin came to see me?"

"He did? When?" Her pulse became a rhythmic pummel in her wrist.

"Oh, he's been in several times. To the nursing home and to the hospital." There was a sly glint in Bridie's eye. "Did I not mention it to you?"

"No, you did not," Fiona said, eyeing her askance, "as you perfectly well know."

Bridie's mouth settled into a smug smile. "He's a good

lad, is Gavin, and a good neighbor. He's been a great help to me over the years."

"He was always the helpful sort." Fiona's racing pulse eased.

"Aye. After selling his BMW, he bought an old SUV from a friend. Plenty of leg room, he says. He's offered to drive me home when they spring me from here."

Which would mean she'd be driving to the nursing home with him. Fiona shifted her weight from one foot to the other. "Do you know when you'll be discharged?"

"The doctor says next week or the week after."

"How are you finding it in here? Apart from the boredom?"

"I'm surviving. It will be a relief to get home though."

Fiona scanned the room. It was old and old-fashioned but painted an inviting cream color that was a lot more hospitable than the gross olive green of St. Ignatius ward. "This isn't a bad place. For a nursing home, I mean."

Bridie nodded. "This is where your grandmother was before she died. You won't remember it, of course. You were in hospital after..." She trailed off.

"After the accident," finished Fiona. "It's fine, Bridie. The mention of it doesn't upset me anymore. It was a long time ago." She unzipped her rucksack and took out a couple of books and a box of Cadbury's Roses. "Before I forget, here are the books you asked me to bring. The chocs are from Sharon."

"Tell her thanks."

"Will do." She glanced at her watch. "I'd better get back to the shop. I told Sharon I'd look in before closing time."

"Will you come by over the weekend? I get bored with

only those two biddies for company." Bridie jerked a thumb at the two gray heads in the neighboring beds.

Fiona struggled not to laugh. "Of course." She bent to kiss her aunt on the cheek. "Take care of yourself."

"And you too, love."

On the way out, Fiona paused in the lobby. So Fatima House was the place her grandmother had allegedly signed her last will and testament, witnessed by Deirdre and a member of staff. What was the nurse's name? Ann Something-or-other…Dunne!

She strode toward the reception desk, noting the slight limp that plagued her when the weather cooled. The gray-haired receptionist was on the phone. She smiled at Fiona and gestured for her to wait a moment. Fiona scanned her nametag. Carol Murphy.

A few minutes later, Carol finished her call and replaced the receiver. "How can I help you?"

Fiona flashed her an ingratiating smile. "My grandmother was in this nursing home fifteen years ago, shortly before she died." The story sprang from her tongue easily, proving the old adage that the most effective lies stick close to the truth. "Nana mentioned a nurse she was fond of. Ann Dunne, I think she was called. I know it's been a while, but do you know if she still works here?"

"The name doesn't ring a bell," said Carol, creasing her brow in contemplation. "But I started working here ten years ago. I'm guessing she was before my time."

Damn. Unfortunate, but not surprising. There would have been a lot of turnover in staff after fifteen years. "What a shame. I was hoping to have a word with her. She was such a lovely woman." Laying it on a bit thick, but what the hell.

"Hmm." Carol looked pensive, then perked up. "I know who we could ask. Jack!" she called. "Do you have a minute?"

An elderly porter materialized from the other side of the lobby. "Yeah?" He regarded Fiona with a dubious expression.

"This girl is looking for a nurse who used to work here years ago. Ann Dunne."

The porter's friendly demeanor turned wary. "Ann Dunne, you say? What would you be wanting with her?"

If his tone was anything to go by, Fiona's description of Ann as a "lovely woman" might have been a tad shy of the mark. "Ann nursed my grandmother during her final illness. I'd like to get in touch. Do you know where she's living now?"

The porter snorted. "Ann's long gone from Fatima House. Good riddance, I say."

Feck. How was she to respond to that? "I take it you didn't like her?"

He curled his lip. "No one liked Ann. Except the patients, of course. Oh, yeah. The patients were fond of her—or so she'd have us believe."

Oh, dear. This did not sound good. "How do you mean?"

"Ann was always getting gifts from elderly patients. Valuable trinkets and the like. There was never a question of her stealing the stuff, but she was a dab hand at cozying up to the old folks and getting them to leave her presents in their wills."

"Isn't that unethical?" she asked. "Is it even allowed?"

The porter shrugged. "A tighter watch is kept over such shenanigans nowadays. Back then, if there was no hint of a crime, the nursing home bosses tolerated it."

No hint of a crime..."When did Ann leave?"

"Long time ago now. I can't remember precisely. Said she'd won the lottery, would you believe?" He shook his head. "Swanned out of here like Lady Muck."

"You have no idea where she went?"

"Nah. I doubt anyone else who worked here back then knows either. Like I said, Ann wasn't popular among the staff."

"Thanks for your time, Jack." Fiona smiled at him and Carol and took her leave.

Back in the car, she stared out the windshield at the tall trees swaying in the wind and drummed the steering wheel. The anger that had been simmering since the day Bridie had told her the story of the will was reaching volcanic proportions. If the porter's tale was true, Ann Dunne was a con artist with a penchant for exploiting her patients. In other words, exactly the sort of person who—with sufficient financial incentive—could be persuaded to sign a fake will.

Bernard was a selfish bastard. If she'd questioned his ability to rip off his sister and niece when Bridie first told her the story, it was because she didn't want to believe it. But believe it she did. It was time to put Olivia's Google-fu skills to use once more. Hopefully, this time they wouldn't result in mayhem.

Fiona clicked her seatbelt into place and reached for the ignition.

Her mobile buzzed, loud and insistent. She moved her hand from the car key to her phone. "Sharon? What's wrong?"

"Hey, boss," her assistant roared down the phone. "You've got a fella waiting for you in the café."

Fiona held the phone away from her ear to preserve her sense of hearing. Whoever he was, he couldn't be Gavin. Sharon would've mentioned him by name. "Does this fella have a name?"

"Ah, yeah. Pete, I think. Wait a sec and I'll check." There was a clatter at the end of the phone as if something metallic had hit the floor. Fiona gripped the phone tighter. Whatever had gone flying in the Book Mark, ignorance was bliss. "Oy. You in the hat," Sharon shouted in the background. "What's your name?"

A muffled male voice responded.

"Fiona? You still there?"

"Yes, Sharon," she said with exaggerated patience. "I and my bleeding ears are still here."

"Your man says he's called Philip. Know him?"

Know him? *Oh, feck.* What the hell was her faithless, feckless ex doing in Ballybeg? Her pulse accelerated. "I don't care what you have to do, just get rid of him."

"Eh?"

"Get rid of him. I'll pay you time-and-a-half if you do."

Sharon chomped her gum and considered. "Make it double and you have yourself a deal."

"You're utterly merciless."

"I prefer the term opportunistic myself."

"I'll be at the shop within a half hour. Have him gone before I get there."

Sharon gave a cackle of laughter. "Yes, boss."

Fiona disconnected and gunned the engine. The moment she thought her life couldn't possibly get more complicated, flaming Philip showed up.

IF AIDAN GANT'S slick smile stretched any wider, Gavin would become reacquainted with his lunch.

"You made the right decision," the solicitor said with honeyed insincerity.

"I made the only decision that wouldn't force me to emigrate." Gavin stuffed his copy of the contract into his briefcase and snapped the clasp. "We both know this is a dirty deal."

"Don't be so negative. See this as a fresh start."

A fresh start? Yeah, right. Fresh as a decaying corpse. He'd signed a deal with the Devil. And if Bernard was the Devil, Aidan was the Devil's advocate. Literally.

"I'll see myself out." He was already through the door before Gant could say farewell.

Olivia was seated at her desk, frowning at her computer monitor. She glanced up when he passed. "See you, Gavin." Her deep blue eyes held concern.

He averted his gaze and muttered a good-bye. He didn't want sympathy. Sympathy wouldn't get him out of this bloody mess. His sole chance of escaping Bernard's sphere of influence before bankruptcy was to sell Clonmore Lodge or the cottage as quickly as possible. In the current economic climate, it seemed impossible.

He'd gone over his options a million times. Finding the

cash to reimburse the Byrnes for their share of the wedding costs was never going to happen before the middle of October. Bernard knew that when he'd suggested it as a potential solution. Unless Gavin wanted to leave Ballybeg—and Ireland—contractually binding himself to pay the full mortgage on Clonmore Lodge was the only option. Not to mention the prick's threats to accuse him of embezzlement. He clenched his fists and exhaled through gritted teeth.

As if to mirror his mood, the weather gods had gone all out. Thunder rumbled in the distance, and hailstones pelted from the heavens. The moment he stepped off the premises, he was soaked and getting wetter by the second.

Right now, he didn't give a fuck.

"Gavin? Are you okay?"

The voice cut through his consciousness. Her Cork accent was flavored with a dash of Dublin. He hadn't noticed it before—the lowered vowels and the nasal tinge—but he heard it now, clear as day.

Fiona stood in front of him, blinking through the rain. She was armed with an umbrella and wearing an unflattering raincoat. Hailstones danced at her Doc-clad feet, and rain ran down the bridge of her nose in a defiant rivulet.

She was adorable.

"I'm grand," he lied.

"Bollocks. You look like shite."

"Queen of the compliments, aren't you?" He smiled, despite himself. Her dry humor always had this effect on him. She was direct, forthright, and no nonsense. She was, he thought in a moment of crystalline clarity, the most genuine person he knew.

She angled her umbrella to ward off the wind, but it was a useless endeavor. Her gaze flickered toward Gant's nameplate. "What did you want with Gant? Something to do with the divorce?"

"No," he said quickly. "Of course not. We agreed to deal with the divorce together."

"So…if not the divorce, what?" She gestured for him to elaborate.

He sighed. "This town's too small for secrets. You'll hear soon enough. I've signed an agreement with Bernard."

"You prefer your business partners with cloven hooves?"

He roared laughing. "Are you a mind reader? I was thinking the same thing when I walked out of the office."

She swiped rain from her nose, her gaze never leaving his face. "Are you here on foot?"

"Yeah."

Hesitation flickered across her face, then hardened into a decision. "Come on. I'll give you a lift."

"Ah, no. It's a ten-minute walk."

"A walk with hailstones the size of my thumb pelting you from above. Don't be daft." Her mouth formed a half smile. "I've to look in on the Book Mark for a sec, but I'll drive you home right after."

"Ah, no. No need to trouble yourself."

"Shut up, Maguire, and do what you're told."

"You're a bossy woman."

The half smile became whole. "So my students tell me."

The street separating them from the Book Mark was fast turning into a river.

"I hope you can swim," she said.

He laughed. "I'll have you know I'm a qualified diving instructor."

"Good. Because if this keeps up, we'll have to dive to find my car."

She yanked him into the quagmire, and they waded across the street to the bookshop.

"Shite," he said. "The weather's wild this evening."

"Not as wild as my life," Fiona said and pushed open the shop door.

"Fiona!" Sharon MacCarthy leaned over the café counter, exposing a generous amount of cleavage. "And Gavin Maguire. Don't the pair of you make the picture of marital bliss?"

"Cut the shite. Where is he?" Fiona's body tensed, her eyes darting around the shop.

"Your actor fella?" Sharon toyed with her chewing gum. "He fecked off a half hour ago. Said he had to get to Cork City for an audition."

Fiona's posture slumped in relief. "Did he say if he'd be back?"

Sharon took out a nail file and began tending to her talons. "Nah. All he said was to pass on his regards, and he'd be 'seeing you.' Whatever that means."

Fiona teased her lip ring. "Thanks. You'll close the shop, yeah?"

"No problem." Sharon waved her nail file in the air. "Everything's under control."

Outside, Fiona's car was covered in hailstones.

"Who's the actor fella?" Gavin asked, struggling with his seatbelt.

"Pull it hard," she said. "The seatbelt's wonky."

He yanked, finally getting sufficient length to click the fastener into place. "Your body language didn't exactly indicate a person thrilled by the prospect of his presence."

She gunned the engine and eased the vehicle into the busy evening traffic. "Philip's my ex. He said he'd look me up if he was in the area. I guess news spread that I'd post-poned my trip."

Her ex, eh? And an actor. Gavin was predisposed to hate the guy on principle. "There must be a reason he's your ex and not your current."

"Must be." She didn't elaborate, and he didn't push.

Within a few minutes, they were pulling into Bridie's designated parking space on Beach Road.

For a moment, they sat silent in the stationary vehicle. The air was electric with unspoken words.

"Want to come in?" she said finally. "I have leftover spag bol we can reheat. Nothing fancy, but it tastes good."

His fickle stomach rumbled. "Sounds delicious."

He followed her inside Bridie's cottage. While she reheated the food, he set the table.

"Wine?" she asked. "I've a half-full bottle of Pinot Noir if you're interested."

"Sure," he said. "Why not?" Actually, he could think of a million reasons why not, and not merely about the wine. He shouldn't be here. She was too…tempting. Unsettling. Muireann (when she wasn't trashing his belongings) was cool, calm, and reserved. Fiona was impetuous and volatile and displayed her emotions with every gesture.

She dished out the food. They ate in wary silence, each hyperaware of the other's presence.

"How's Bridie? She said you were going to see her today."

"Bored." She smiled at him, warming him from the inside out.

He took a hasty gulp of wine. He should eat and leave, before they did something they'd both regret.

She ran a finger round the rim of her wineglass. "Want to tell me what deal you signed with my uncle? Knowing Bernard, it was nothing good."

"No," he said grimly. "Not for me, at any rate. Bernard set me an ultimatum. Either I ponied up his share of the wedding expenses by the middle of October, or I signed an agreement to keep paying the full mortgage on Clonmore Lodge until Muireann and I find a buyer. According to the written terms of the agreement, I have until Christmas to repay the wedding expenses."

"What about the unwritten terms of the agreement?" she asked shrewdly.

"Bernard doesn't bring charges of financial fraud against me."

She sucked in a breath. "The prick."

"The charges are a load of shite, but Bernard has too many connections for me to believe justice would be served. He knows he has me by the short and curlies. I don't have the cash to reimburse him for the money he invested in the wedding. If I'd refused to sign the agreement, he'd have blacklisted me. The construction trade's tight these days. If Bernard told his cronies not to hire me, my career in architecture would be finished."

Her lips thinned. "That's blackmail, pure and simple."

"Yeah, but what can I do? He holds all the power cards. And he knows it."

She leaned across the table and took his hand. "You'll be fine, Gavin. You're a talented architect. You'll find a way out of this mess."

He slid his fingers over her thumb. Her hands were incredibly soft and smooth. And the skin on her wrists…

She inhaled sharply and withdrew her hand.

"Sorry, Fiona. I don't know what came over me." He thought of Muireann and her cold perfection and the life he should've, would've, could've had. And then he remembered the callous way Muireann had severed her connection with Wiggly Poo, who at this very moment was likely running wild at Jonas's parents' house.

Their eyes locked. She leaned across the table, close enough for him to smell the fresh scent of her perfume and the wine on her breath.

"Kiss me," she whispered.

20

K*iss me.* Was she out of her mind? What had she been smoking when she'd invited him round for dinner?

Gavin's mouth touched hers, eradicating any hope of her forming a coherent thought for the foreseeable future. His kiss was gentle, soft. The tenderness broke her. She stood, trembling, her mind and body at war.

He also stood, breathing heavily. "Fiona, I—"

"Don't say it," she said. "Don't say we shouldn't have done that. I'm sick of us kissing and regretting it afterward."

His blue eyes were cloudy with an emotion she couldn't pinpoint. "Speak for yourself. I regret a lot of things, but kissing you isn't one. Did you kiss me and regret it?"

"No," she said with an assurance that surprised her. "Never. What I regretted was your reaction."

"I called you," he said. "I left messages. You never replied."

"No." Her voice broke on a treacherous quaver. "You walked away."

She both felt and heard his intake of breath. "You're talking about Vegas. I was talking about the cave. Fiona, I didn't walk away after the cave. You did."

She swallowed past the lump in her throat but didn't break eye contact. She couldn't, even if she'd wanted to. What should she do now? Ignore the weirdness between them and bid him goodnight? Or throw caution to the wind and screw him senseless?

Her decision, when it came, was swift and decisive. She closed the space between them, wrapped her arms around his neck, and pulled him close. His heart beat against her chest, and his rapid breathing warmed her throat, her ears, her neck.

She deepened the kiss, matching his tongue move for move.

He slid his arms down her torso, molding each curve with the palms of his hands. When he reached her backside, he cupped her buttocks and lifted her onto the hard granite surface of the kitchen counter. She moaned—a primal, instinctual reaction from a place deep inside.

"Are you sure?" His words tickled her neck.

"Yes," she said. "I'm sure. Are you?"

"Yeah." He looked her in the eye. "This time, I am."

She slipped her hand into his. "Let's go into my bedroom. I can't shag someone with a statue of the Virgin Mary looming over me."

He roared laughing. "That's what I always liked about you, Fiona. Your sense of humor."

"Oh, yeah?" she cocked an eyebrow cheekily. "Here was me thinking it was my breathtaking beauty and killer curves."

"Those too." He pulled her into her bedroom and kicked the door shut.

"The shades are open—" Her protest fell on deaf ears. The kiss increased in intensity, and she forgot about potential indecent exposure. Hell, the whole of Ballybeg could come for a gawk if it meant he wouldn't stop.

Gavin's hands slipped under the thin fabric of her skirt and skimmed her thighs. The tender flesh of her inner thighs shivered at his touch, sending tiny electric shocks shooting through her body. He slid his hands higher, finding her knickers. Hooking his fingers in the sides of the panties, he slid them off.

"You're gorgeous," he said. The words kneaded her like an erotic massage. "But I'm pretty sure Mrs. Cotter's curtain twitched. Time for privacy." He closed the curtains and shoved her onto the bed with a playful push.

She landed on the soft mattress with a laugh. "No fair," she said, propping herself up on her elbows. "I'm half-naked and you're still fully dressed. If you want me to take my bra off, you'd better give me an incentive."

He grinned, and his gaze roamed over her body. "Good thing I'm a dab hand at getting my shirt off in five seconds."

His fingers flew over the buttons, revealing a couple more centimeters of male chest with each movement. A light sprinkling of blond hair snaked to his navel. His hands strayed to the zipper of his jeans. Her breath caught, and her eyes widened.

"Go, on," she said hoarsely.

"Isn't it your turn?"

"Oh, no. You owe me, Maguire. Consider this payback." She leaned against the pillows to enjoy the show.

He undid the button and eased the zipper over the bulge in his underwear. He tugged the jeans over his hips and down his legs. He kicked them to the side.

His erection was clearly visible through the stretchy material of his underwear. The wetness between her legs increased. She wanted him. She wanted this. And she wanted it now.

As if reading her mind, he slid his underpants to the floor.

Whoa. He was rock hard and bigger than she remembered.

She sat up on the bed and unhooked her bra. She let the straps slide over her shoulders, watching him the whole while. Slowly and deliberately, she tugged her breasts free from the cups and attempted to toss the bra to the side. It ruined her sleekly seductive strip tease by catching on her wrist. She made a few vain attempts to shake it free. "Well, feck."

He laughed and came to the bed. "Here," he said and freed her hand. He kept his thumb on her wrist and stroked, dancing his fingertips across her pulse then up her arm along her vine tattoo. The pressure in her groin was building.

"Touch me," she demanded.

He grinned. "I am touching you."

"Lower," she said. "I mean, higher."

Running one hand across her breasts, he used the other to caress her inner thighs. "You mean both." He kissed her shoulder and trailed kisses over her breasts, down her belly, between her legs. He stroked her, teasing the sensitive flesh around her clitoris, exploring her clit ring. "So you *are* pierced down there."

"Had you wondered?" she asked with a laugh.

Gavin's grin was wolfish. "Oh, yeah."

He increased the pace. Jolts of electric ecstasy flowed through her. She didn't want this to stop. She didn't want him to stop.

"Faster," she gasped. "With more pressure."

"Show me." He pulled her hand down and placed it over his. "Show me exactly how you want it."

Fiona guided his fingers, applied the right pressure in the right places. Meanwhile, his other hand strayed to her breasts, teasing her nipples, pinching hard.

She groaned, sensed her peak near. "I want you inside me."

"Your wish, my lady, is my command." He got off the bed and pulled his wallet out of his jeans.

She watched him lazily while he rooted for a condom wrapper. When he returned to the bed, she tickled the silky-smooth skin of his penis. "Can I put it on?"

"Of course."

She rolled the condom over his shaft, teasing his balls with every movement.

Flipping her onto her back, he positioned himself

between her legs. He nuzzled her neck and nipped her earlobe. She guided him inside.

The first thrust was a shock. She gasped sharply and felt him fill her.

He stilled for a moment, then began to move. She wrapped her legs around his waist, digging her heels into his buttocks. The thrusts were gentle at first, soon increasing in power and intensity. Fiona's hands roamed over his muscular torso and traced the lines of the shamrock tattoo at the base of his neck.

The sensation of skin against skin was electric. He trailed angel kisses along her neck and across her shoulders. When he nipped her earlobe for the second time, she cried out.

"Not good?" His words were a hot rumble against her neck.

"Too good," she whispered. "Do it again."

He laughed, the sensation reverberating on her shoulder. He increased his speed, each thrust bringing her one step closer to release. She went with it, relished the slow build to ecstasy.

Finally, he shuddered and came with a guttural groan, propelling her to her own climax.

She swallowed a scream when it hit and clung harder to his muscular body.

When it was over, she collapsed against the cushions and let the aftershocks ripple through her. "Damn, that was good."

He wound one of her dark curls around his hand. "I hope I didn't wear you out."

"No. Why?"

"Because that was round one."

She laughed. "How many rounds are in this game?"

"As many as I can manage." He smiled. "Sadly, I'm not eighteen anymore."

She reached for him and drew him close. "No," she said. "Nor am I."

Their tongues were enjoying a mutual exploration match when her phone rang.

"Ignore it," he murmured. "Let it go to voice mail."

When the insistent buzz started for the third time in five minutes, she groped for her phone. "It's from an unknown caller. I hope Bridie's okay."

"Fiona?" Sharon's usual chipper tone when Fiona hit the answer button was absent, replaced by panic.

Fiona threw her legs over the side of the bed. "What's wrong?"

"The police are after coming round to my house. They didn't have your mobile number, and Bridie's is switched off."

"Sharon, calm down and tell me what's happened."

"Someone's vandalized the Book Mark," Sharon said, sniveling. "And the police have gone and arrested me."

21

"What a mess." Gavin cast his gaze over the wreckage. He and Fiona were standing in the Book Mark with Liam O'Mahony, Jonas's father. Liam ran a small building firm and had agreed to help with the repairs.

And a number of repairs were needed. Shattered glass lay strewn across the café floor, leaving the wind howling through the empty window frame. A couple of chairs were broken, and the front door was busted.

Fiona sucked in a breath. "Who would do this to Bridie?"

"We don't know the vandalism was specifically aimed at Bridie," he said, putting an arm round her shoulders. "It might have been kids messing."

"On a night like this?" She shook her head. "I don't buy it."

Neither did Gavin, but he was at a loss to come up with another explanation. Bridie was popular in Ballybeg.

Yeah, she'd pissed off a few of the old biddies with her sharp tongue, but he couldn't imagine the likes of Nora Fitzgerald smashing windows and breaking locks in an act of vengeance.

He picked his way carefully over the shards of glass and the scattered books from the window display. "Damn lucky most of the books are kept in the back two rooms, or you would have lost a lot of stock."

"I'm going to check the book rooms and the stockroom." Fiona pulled a pen and notepad out of her handbag. "I'll make a note of anything missing. You okay to deal with Liam?"

"No worries," he said, grabbing a sweeping brush from the café kitchen. "Let me know if you need a hand."

Liam was standing before the broken shop front, busy with his measuring tape. He was an older, gruffer version of Jonas, but a few centimeters shorter and wider than his son. Despite being in his midfifties, his barely lined face and stray silver hairs made him look a decade younger. "I have plywood in my workshop," he said when Gavin approached. "Once I've measured this out, I'll go home and cut it to size."

"It's not too much work for you?" Gavin swept the debris into a pile.

"Nah, it's no trouble." Liam pulled a pen from behind his ear and scribbled figures on a notepad. He jerked a calloused thumb at the window frame. "I'd tell you to put up a few bin bags until I get the plywood, but with wind this strong, there's no point."

"How long will it take to get a replacement window?"

"Couple of days," the older man mused, creasing his

tanned brow. "Three at most. One of my men will come by in the morning to fix the lock on the door."

"Thanks. I appreciate you coming out so late."

"No problem. Glad to do Bridie a favor. She's a fine woman, is Bridie Byrne." Liam glanced in the direction of the book room and lowered his voice. "Shame I can't say the same of her bastard of a brother."

Gavin had to smile. In the eight years he'd been with Muireann, Liam had never said a word about his infamous falling out with her father. Now they were no longer engaged, it appeared the gloves were off. "There was a dispute about payment, right?"

Liam scowled and slipped his measuring tape back into his coat pocket. "He stiffed me on a bill."

"What happened?"

"Bernard hired me and my men to deliver and install windows for his holiday home in Cobh. After the job was done, he claimed we'd done shoddy work and he was only prepared to pay half the sum we'd agreed." He snorted. "Bollocks. There was nothing wrong with those windows, but what could I do?"

"Take him to court?"

Liam gave a bitter laugh. "You, of all people, should know what Bernard Byrne is like. If I'd tried to sue him, his fancy lawyers would've crushed me. To top it off, he'd have blacklisted me across the county. It was cheaper for me to suck up the loss."

Gavin's jaw tensed. Flaming Bernard. The man had no moral code. "Let me guess. He told you he was interested in hiring you as a contractor for his company, but he wanted to try you out on a smaller job first."

Liam grimaced. "That's about the size of it."

"I'm sorry you were taken in. You're not the first person Bernard's fecked over, and I daresay *I* won't be the last."

The older man hunched his shoulders and pulled his raincoat tight around his broad torso. "I'd better get to work on the plywood. I should be back within the hour. I'll bring Wiggly Poo with me."

"I hope he hasn't given you and Nuala any trouble."

Liam grinned. "He's an active pup."

After Liam left, Gavin went in search of the Book Mark's cleaning supplies. He'd a hunch he'd once seen Bridie take a mop out of the small room at the back of the shop. He flipped the light switch in the stockroom. Yes, here they were. Mop, brush, and pan, and a variety of cleaning cloths and fluids. He grabbed the broom and returned to the main room of the shop.

He brushed the broken glass into one pile and the soggy books into another. Better leave the books for Fiona to sort through. They were beyond salvation, but she'd need to make a note of the titles destroyed. He fetched the brush and pan and scooped the broken glass into bin bags, careful not to cut himself or miss stray shards on the floor.

Visions of Fiona's lush curves and soft moans replaced the mess on the floor.

They'd had sex. They'd had amazing sex. Sleeping with her had to rank right up there with one of his crazier life decisions, along with their drunken Vegas wedding. So he *should* regret it. Yet he didn't. Not for a millisecond. Fiona made him laugh, made him forget his worries. He felt good when he was in her presence. She saw him for who he was, flaws and all, and not for who he had the potential to become. And yeah, the fantastic sex was a definite bonus.

Spending time with her was a sharp contrast to the life he'd almost had. The stable, secure, stress-free life with Muireann as his wife. And the sharp realization that what bothered him most about his engagement wasn't the fact that it ended, but *how* it ended. He'd never been so financially screwed in his entire adult life, but neither had he felt so emotionally free.

"Nothing was taken from the book rooms." Fiona stood on the threshold that marked the divide between the café and the shop proper, a thin worry line showing between her brows. "Not that I'd expected to find anything missing. Who'd be desperate enough break in to nick a few books?"

He gestured to the cash register. "You're sure no money was stolen?"

She shook her damp curls. In spite of her raincoat, she'd gotten soaked on their sprint from the car to the shop. The moisture weighed down her hair. He hadn't realized how long it was. He yearned to touch it, itched to tug at one of her curls and stretch it to its fullest length.

"We only keep a few rolls of coins in there," she said. "I always drop the day's takings off at the bank. There's no excuse not to—I pass the night safe on my way home."

"Do you want me to drive you to the police station? We can come back here and finish tidying once Liam's fitted the plywood and we're not downwind of a gale."

A small smile broke through her tense expression.

"Yeah, I'd appreciate a lift. I need to talk to the police about Sharon and fill in whatever paperwork they need for the break-in."

~

THE STORM HAD INCREASED in intensity over the course of the evening, and heavy sheets of rain pounded the car. Lightning zigzagged through the sky, illuminating the overflowing potholes in the road.

"I appreciate this. I don't fancy driving my Polo in these conditions." Fiona snuck a glance at Gavin, noticing the light stubble dusting his jaw. A mere hour ago, that stubble had been teasing her skin.

"Not a problem." He slowed his car when they drove through a heavily flooded crossing. "And you can stop thanking me. I'm glad to help out."

She twisted her fingers in an anxious knot, then laughed. "I'm babbling, aren't I?"

"Just a tad." He gave her an amused sideways smile.

The easy camaraderie they'd established over the past few hours had hit a post-coital speed bump. What should she say? What should she do? They needed to define what had happened between them and establish boundaries. Was this a friends-with-benefits situation? Or a hormone-spiked one-off?

The car jolted over the uneven surface of the road and sloshed through a puddle. "Not far now," Gavin said. "Have you seen the new station yet? It's the absolute pits—a three-room hovel with peeling paint and a leaking roof. I'd say they're having fun in this weather."

The mundane conversation was a welcome distraction from the jumble of confusion performing somersaults in her head. "Why did they close the old station? I remember they used to be in a quaint building off Patrick Street. Funny I didn't notice its absence on my recent walks through the town."

"Police cuts." Gavin shook his head. "They razed the old place to build houses during the boom years and intended to erect a small building to house the station. It never happened. The local Guards are still stuck in their so-called interim solution, with the staff cut to half and their jurisdiction increased threefold. It's a flipping disaster. Frankly, it's a wonder any crimes get solved in these parts." He flipped on the indicator and slowed the car. "Here we are. You'll get to see it for yourself."

They eased to a halt outside a small building with an old-fashioned tin roof.

She peered out the rain-splattered window. "I see Ruairí's car is already here."

"Bailing his little sister out, no doubt." Gavin drummed his fingers on the steering wheel. "And not for the first time."

"Sharon's no saint, but I can't see her doing this. She's cheeky and irreverent, but she's careful with the money and has a quick head for numbers. Besides, why would she want to risk losing her job? It doesn't make sense."

"I'm inclined to agree with you, but let's see what the police have to say on the matter." He cut the engine. "Do you want me to come in with you?"

"I can handle it. Thanks for the lift, Gav." She fidgeted with her umbrella before leaning sideways and brushing his cheek with her mouth. His stubble tickled her lips, and his spicy scent sent her erogenous zones into overdrive.

They stayed like that for a moment, each frozen in an awkward silence. Finally, he cleared his throat. "I'll stay here until you're ready to go home."

"Okay, I won't be long," she said and stepped out of the car straight into a puddle. *Feck.* She could add wet feet to her list of woes. The wind rendered her umbrella more a hindrance than a help. She pulled up her hood and made a run for it.

A young man in a Guard's uniform held open the station door.

"Thanks," she said, shaking out her umbrella.

"Terrible weather," the young man said in a Donegal accent. "Outside and in." He pointed to the array of strategically placed buckets catching the leaks around the station. "I'm Garda Brian Glenn." He pumped her hand hard enough to crush her bones.

"Fiona Byrne," she said and shrugged off her wet coat. "I'm here about Sharon MacCarthy. She's suspected of vandalizing my aunt's bookshop."

"Oh, aye." Garda Glenn said in a tone flavored with irony. "Sharon's a frequent visitor—as is the rest of her family. If there's a crime committed in these parts, ten to one it's either the MacCarthys or the Tinkers."

"Oy," said a deep voice. "Cheeky pup. You've never arrested me."

Ruairí MacCarthy was sitting on a chair in what passed for the reception area, thumbing through a newspaper. His faded Rugby shirt was strained at the shoulders, making him look even more bear-like than usual.

"Hey." Fiona nodded at him. "Are they seriously going to make you post bail? I can't imagine Sharon trashing the Book Mark. It doesn't make sense."

"She says she didn't do it," Ruairí said gruffly. "And I believe her."

"Let me out of this fucking room!" Sharon's screech penetrated the hard wooden door separating the neighboring room from the reception area.

"Stop your caterwauling," said Garda Glenn. "I'll let you out if you promise to behave. I'm not having you trashing the place again."

"She'll behave," said her brother in a voice that brooked no argument. "Won't you, Sharon?"

An answering sob came from behind the door.

"Sharon, I know you didn't vandalize the Book Mark," Fiona said softly. "Will you please tell us what happened?"

"Okay." Her assistant sniveled and hiccupped.

Garda Glenn sighed and extracted a key from his pocket. He unlocked the door, and Sharon launched herself out of her prison and into Fiona's arms.

Fiona patted her peroxide hair. "There, there, pet. It'll be grand."

Sharon released her and fished a tissue out of her pocket. "I dunno who did it," she said between sobs, "but it wasn't me. I swear."

"I believe you. Tell me what happened."

The girl dabbed at her mascara-streaked face and honked into her tissue. "I was walking along Patrick Street on my way to the bus stop. When I passed the Book Mark, the alarm was blaring and I noticed the smashed windows. I went inside to check if anything was nicked. I was about to call you when that buffoon showed up and put me in handcuffs."

"One of the tenants above the Book Mark reported a break-in in the bookshop," Garda Glenn said, eyeing Sharon with distaste. Obviously there was no love lost between this pair.

"When I arrived," he continued, "I found Sharon inside. She'd busted open the cash register and was rooting through it. What was I supposed to think?" He crossed his beefy arms and tried to look stern and authoritative.

"Bollocks," Fiona said. "Sharon knows we don't keep any money on the premises. Besides, why would she bust the till open when she knows the code?"

The policeman's thick lips parted, but no words came out. "I'm sure we'd find her fingerprints all over the place if we checked."

Jaysus. If Brian Glenn was representative of up-and-coming policemen, Ireland was fucked.

She gave a hiss of impatience. "Of course you'd find Sharon's fingerprints all over the shop. She works there. You'd also find my fingerprints, Bridie's fingerprints, and the fingerprints of goodness knows how many customers."

"We done here?" Ruairí tossed his newspaper aside. "Because it doesn't sound like you've got anything to warrant keeping my sister in custody."

Garda Glenn muttered something under his breath. "Fine. Take her home. I might have more questions, mind, depending on what I turn up."

By Fiona's guestimate, Garda Glenn was going to "turn

up" sweet shag all. "I'll continue going through the shop this evening," she told him. "I'll make a list of anything missing. So far, though, everything looks to be present and correct."

"Okay," he said. "I'll call round the shop sometime tomorrow morning."

Fiona said good-bye to Ruairí and Sharon on the station steps before heading back to the SUV. Inside the car, Gavin was listening to nineties rock on the radio. She slid into the passenger seat and slammed the door shut.

"How'd it go?" he asked, his eyes creasing in concern. "I take it the police have no leads other than Sharon?"

She snorted. "Leads? That fella Brian Glenn couldn't win a game of *Cluedo*, never mind solve a real case."

"Did he let Sharon go?"

"Yeah. Ruairí's driving her home."

"By the way, Liam called while you were inside. He's going to meet us at the Book Mark with the plywood and Wiggly Poo."

"How soon will he be able to replace the glass?"

"Couple of days." Gavin reached across and took her hand. "Listen, we need to talk about what happened."

Heat crept up her cheeks. "I know we do. It was a one-off, right?"

"Do you want it to be a one-off?" he asked softly. "Seriously?"

She took a steadying breath. His hand on hers was warm, comforting. "Gavin, we're getting divorced. Up until a few weeks ago, you were set to marry my cousin. How can this be anything other than casual sex?"

His laugh tickled her neck. "Casual sex isn't synonymous with a one-off."

"You want a repeat?"

"Hell, yeah. Don't you?"

"Yes...," she said slowly.

"But?"

"How can you even ask that? Our situation is beyond screwed up."

He stroked her hand, sending electric shocks skittering over her skin. "Then let's establish a few ground rules—assuming we both want this to continue. We're friends who happen to be sleeping together. If either of us wants to change the status back to friendship alone, there'll be no hard feelings."

She stared out the window but could see nothing through the rivulets of rain running down the glass. "I'm only in Ballybeg for a few months. Once Bridie's back on her feet, I'll leave."

He was staring at her earnestly, his blue eyes gray in the dim light. His hair had grown since the wedding and was starting to curl over his ears. He wasn't paying the scrupulous attention to his appearance that he had while living with Muireann. "I realize your life is elsewhere," he said. "I just thought...we get on, you and I, despite our crazy circumstances. We can at least be friends—with or without benefits."

"Okay," she said slowly. "But any benefits will have to be enjoyed before Bridie comes home. When I have to balance looking after her with running the Book Mark, I'll be too busy for distractions."

A grin suffused his face. "So if I were to offer you a...

distraction...after we collect Wiggly Poo from the Book Mark, would you accept?"

The electric sensation on her skin shot straight to her groin. She stared at his supple lips and the masculine curve of his jawline. Her hesitation stretched into a few charged seconds. Finally, she leaned over and kissed his cheek. "Yes, I'll stay over—on one condition."

His eyebrows formed a question. "What?"

"Wiggly Poo is *not* sharing our bed."

22

Fiona snuggled closer to her warm bed companion, enjoying his wet kisses, curly fur, and dog breath.

Wait a sec. Dog breath? What the...?

Her eyes flew open. Two brown doggie orbs stared back in blatant adoration. Definitely not the male she'd been dreaming about.

Wiggly Poo licked her face and nuzzled her playfully.

"How did you get in here, you naughty boy?" She scratched his belly.

"Sorry, did he wake you?" Gavin emerged from the bathroom, a towel slung around his hips. He could have dispensed with the towel. Over the past week, she'd become well acquainted with what lay underneath.

She propped herself up on her elbows. "What was that I said about not sharing your bed with Wiggly Poo?"

Gavin grinned at her and rooted through his

wardrobe. "Sure, wasn't he very well behaved the last few nights?"

"Then why is he in the room with us this morning?"

"Because, my dear, you sleep like a stone. Did you not hear him howling outside the door last night?"

"I was—" warmth crept up her cheeks, "—rather tired."

"I'd love the opportunity to tire you further, but it's after eight o'clock and we're due to collect Bridie at the nursing home at nine."

"Feck!" She threw off the duvet and leaped out of bed. Naked and blind without her contacts, she scrambled around the floor of Gavin's bedroom, locating various discarded items of clothing. A sock, a second sock, her bra. *Crap.* Where were her knickers?

"Looking for these?" Gavin dangled a pair of lacy Brazilian-cut underpants out of her reach.

"Give me those." She snatched the knickers and quickly put them on. His grin grew wider. "I'm going next door for a shower and clean clothes," she said. "I'll meet you at the car in twenty minutes, yeah?"

"Fine." He zipped up his jeans. She tried—with a modicum of success—not to fantasize about pulling them off. "I can't wait to see your hair after your blitz shower. It'll be frizz central."

She stuck her tongue out at him and closed the door behind her.

They'd developed an oddly comfortable routine over the last few days. She'd spend the night (always at his place—it didn't seem right having him stay over at Bridie's). The next morning, they'd have breakfast together before she headed to the Book Mark, and he continued the job search/interview hamster wheel.

Liam O'Mahony had been as good as his word. He'd installed the new window on the Tuesday after the break-in. Apart from the storm-stained walls in the café, the shop looked its old self. Fiona had provided Garda Glenn and the insurance company with a detailed list of the damages. Thankfully, Liam was prepared to wait on his payment until the insurance money came through. Had he not been so accommodating, she'd have been in a serious financial tight spot.

By the time she was showered and dressed, Gavin was waiting for her in his SUV.

She clicked in her seatbelt. "Do you know Muireann's due home in a few days?" They'd avoided mentioning her cousin, distracting one another with jokes when dressed and sex when not, but they couldn't avoid the topic indefinitely.

"I heard." He started the engine and pointed the car in the direction of the nursing home.

"Will you call her when she gets back?" The words stumbled out in an awkward jumble.

He shrugged. "Eventually. We have to find a buyer for Clonmore Lodge—assuming she doesn't want to buy me out of my share, which I doubt."

"How do you feel about seeing her again?" Her stomach twisted into knots in anticipation of his answer. She was being daft. They'd already decided their fling was short term. Whether or not he intended to get back with Muireann was none of her business.

"Frankly, I'd rather avoid her indefinitely," he said, "but there's no chance of that in a town this size."

She took a deep breath. "You don't want to try to patch things up with her?"

"That ship hasn't only sailed, it's been shipwrecked." He gave a bitter laugh. "No, we have no future together. I see that now."

They passed the rest of the car journey with meaningless chitchat. When they reached Fatima House, Bridie was waiting in the lobby, packed and impatient to get going. "I haven't felt this itchy to get out of a place since my days at boarding school," she said, giving Fiona a kiss on the cheek.

"I'll take your suitcase," Gavin said.

"Thanks, Gavin. You're a good lad."

He grinned. "Not really. Just mighty fond of your shepherd's pie."

He carried the case in one hand and looped his other arm through Bridie's. She no longer needed to use a walker, but she loathed her crutches and took every opportunity to avoid using them.

Fiona helped her aunt into the car while Gavin stowed her suitcase in the car boot. Out of the corner of her eye, she spied a familiar white-haired figure ascending the steps to the main entrance. "Can you give me a sec? I forgot to ask the nurse something." She closed the car door before Bridie could react and raced up the steps and into the lobby.

She spotted him immediately. Jack, the elderly porter, was carrying a sweeping brush and chatting to the receptionist. Not Carol this time, but a younger woman. "Excuse me."

"Yes?" He peered at her through the thick lenses of his bifocals.

"We spoke a couple of weeks ago. I asked you about Ann Dunne."

"Aye." He nodded. "I remember."

"It occurred to me to ask if you remember what time of year Ann won the lottery. I know it seems a strange question, but—"

"Oh, I remember all right." He leaned on his sweeping brush and narrowed his eyes. "It was before Christmas. We always have a staff Christmas party around the middle of December. Everyone chips in whatever they can afford. Ann was telling people she'd won a fortune in the lottery a few days before we collected everyone's contribution. She contributed a fiver, the same amount she gave every year. Typical."

"Do you remember what year it was?"

He shook his head. "Sorry, I can't recall the year, but it was a long while ago. Twelve years at least."

"Thanks. I appreciate your time."

"Why are you interested in Ann, anyway?"

"I'd rather not get into specifics. It has to do with a will."

"A will, eh?" Jack raised a white eyebrow. "Sounds like Ann, all right. Can I give you a piece of advice?"

The hairs on Fiona's nape sprang to attention. "Go on."

"If you manage to find her, watch your step."

~

On the Friday after Bridie's homecoming, Fiona woke with a splitting headache. This was the third she'd had in the past five days—a record, even for her migraine-prone self.

Juggling Bridie and the shop was wearing her out, not to mention the weird guilt-excitement-stress combo over sleeping with Gavin. Not they'd managed more than a quickie since Bridie's return.

In theory, the time apart should have given her the opportunity to come to her senses, to put a stop to whatever was going on between them. In reality, he was on her mind way more than she cared to admit. He'd gotten under her skin, just as he had all those years ago. It would end. She knew that. His life was here, and hers was anywhere but Ballybeg. It was a fleeting moment of madness, stretched by circumstance.

"What's up with you, missy? Your face is more changeable than the Irish weather. Can't you decide whether you're in a good or a bad mood?" Bridie lowered her morning newspaper and regarded her niece with concern.

"A headache," she said, slipping into the seat opposite her aunt. "I'll be grand once I have breakfast."

She grabbed a triangle of toast from the rack on the table and slathered it with butter and marmalade. The rain outside the kitchen window was relentless. If she'd left for her trip on schedule, she'd be in sunny Perth right now. She bit her lip and tasted the bittersweet tang of regret.

"Harrumph!" Bridie said. "I didn't come down in the last shower. Man trouble is what you have, and I'm betting the man causing the trouble is Gavin Maguire. Come on, spill."

She jerked to attention. So much for hoping her aunt wouldn't notice. "There's nothing to say." She helped herself to tea from the pot on the table and warmed her hands around the mug.

"I might be old," Bridie said, "but I'm not senile. I've seen the way you and Gavin look at each other. Not to mention Ruth Cotter from across the road, telling me you and Gavin were up to all sorts of shenanigans while I was at the nursing home."

So the twitching curtain they'd spotted hadn't been the wind. She squeezed her eyes shut. Damn nosey neighbors. Anonymity was something she loved about Dublin. She didn't know her neighbors' names, never mind their sexual partners'. "Mrs. Cotter ought to mind her own business."

Her aunt sighed. "I'm fond of the lad, Fiona, but he's the last person you should be getting involved with."

"Point taken. Can we move on? Do you need anything from the shops when I come home for lunch?"

"No." Bridie grudgingly allowed her to change the subject. "Is everything organized for the book club?"

"Yeah, we're good to go."

The inaugural meeting of the Ballybeg Book Club would take place at the Book Mark at seven o'clock that evening. Fiona had chosen a prize-winning novel by an Irish author and regretted her choice after the first paragraph.

"How many people did you say signed up?"

"Fifteen." She smiled over the rim of her mug. "Stop

micromanaging. I have it under control. Olivia's helping with the refreshments, and the Major will collect you an hour before the event."

The Major, Olivia's grandfather, was the Earl of Clonmore but rarely used his title. When he'd returned to Ireland after several years in the British army, the locals had nicknamed him the Major, even though no one was certain what rank he'd held, and he hadn't seen fit to enlighten them. The name had stuck.

"At least the Major finished the book." Bridie shook out her newspaper and turned to the crossword. "What were you thinking, Fiona? No one wants to read such shite, no matter how many awards it's won. Most readers round these parts are more into Richard and Judy Book Club picks than Man Booker Prize winners."

"It was a poor choice, I admit, but it's too late to change it now." She yawned and glanced at the kitchen clock. "Time to get to work. If you need anything, let me know, and if it's urgent, call Mrs. Cotter."

The cool morning breeze on her walk to the Book Mark helped her headache, but the pain returned in full force when she turned onto Patrick Street and saw what—or rather who—awaited her outside the shop.

On instinct, she slowed her gait, buying a little extra time to prepare for the inevitable.

Muireann was leaning against the bookshop door, smoking one of her trademark Marlboro Reds and flicking ash carelessly onto the pavement. Despite the bitter winter wind, she wore a thin pink jacket and matching linen trousers. They complemented the deep tan she'd acquired in Australia.

Australia…the place *she* was supposed to be right now.

A pang of envy twisted her gut, but she gave herself a mental shake. Moping was a waste of time and emotion.

Her cousin's eyes narrowed to slits at her approach. She wore the sapphire ring her parents had given her for her eighteenth birthday in the place of her engagement ring. "Good morning, cuz." She sneered and blew smoke in Fiona's direction. "Or should I say Mrs. Maguire?"

Fiona took a deep breath and willed herself to remain calm. "I'm guessing this isn't a social call?"

Her cousin's disdainful gaze raked her ensemble. In contrast to Muireann's colorful outfit, Fiona's was black, warm, and practical. "I wouldn't come near this dump unless I had to."

She checked the smart response hovering on the tip of her tongue. Arguing with Muireann had never gotten her anywhere, and she didn't suppose the weeks since their last encounter had changed the situation. "Look, get to the point. Why are you here? Let's not pretend we're about to kiss and make up."

Muireann tossed her cigarette butt on the pavement and ground it out with her heel. "I'm here about the Christmas Bazaar. Mummy says you're organizing the bookstall this year."

"Yes." Fiona eyed her cousin warily. "What about the bazaar?"

Muireann tossed the straight blond hair Fiona had spent her childhood coveting over her shoulder. "I've helped Bridie with the bookstall for the past five years."

Fiona had the sneaking suspicion this conversation was not going to end on a positive note. "I hardly think—"

"And I intend to help out this year. Mummy and Daddy are known for their charitable work, and I try to do my bit. Everyone will expect to see me at the bazaar."

"Can't you find another stall? Don't they sell cakes you could flog?"

"Everyone knows I work the bookstall. If I don't, they'll talk." Muireann pursed her lips. "I'm sick of them talking about me behind my back."

"Feck everyone," Fiona said. "Let them talk."

Her cousin sniffed. "Easy for you to say. You don't live in Ballybeg. Besides, it's your fault I'm the target of gossip. You owe me the chance to put it right."

"So what are you saying? We should work the bookstall together? You are joking, right? We'd tear each other's hair out within the hour."

"Speak for yourself," Muireann said coldly. "You're the hotheaded one."

Fiona crossed her arms across her chest. "So says the woman who trashed her ex-fiancé's belongings and chucked his books in a fish pond."

Muireann stiffened. "Gavin jilted me at the altar. He deserves all he gets."

They regarded one another in stony silence, neither willing to capitulate. When they were growing up, Muireann had been the undisputed beauty of the family, and Fiona the smart one. Her cousin's long blond hair was straight and tame in comparison to Fiona's unruly dark mane. Muireann was petite, whereas Fiona was tall and gangly. By the time she'd hit puberty, Muireann had boys eating out of the palm of her hand. Fiona, on the other hand, was the quintessential geek. She was more likely to be found curled up with a book in the library than snogging boys in dark alleys. By the time she'd left school, the pinnacle of her dating experience had been accompanying Charlie Hutchinson to his orthodontic appointment.

"Why don't we let Bridie decide?" Her cousin said smoothly. "The stall represents *her* shop."

"Fine," Fiona said. "If you want Bridie to decide, talk to her yourself. Meanwhile, I have to do the job your oh-so-charitably-minded self landed me with."

"In that case, I'll leave you to it. Have fun." Muireann smirked, and pivoted on her heel.

Fiona had barely opened the Book Mark's door when Aidan Gant's sleek Mercedes slid to a halt outside.

Fanfeckingtastic. Please don't let him start on about the divorce.

Olivia climbed out of the passenger's side and waved. Thank goodness. "Morning, Fee."

"What are you doing here this early? Won't Aidan kill you if you don't get to work?"

"Feck Aidan." Olivia waved a dismissive hand in the direction of the car. "I come bearing gifts." She handed Fiona a plastic container. "I went on a mad PMS-induced baking spree last night. I figured you could sell the extra banana-walnut muffins in the café."

Fiona peeked inside the box. They looked divine. "Thanks, Liv. These smell delicious. Listen, would you have time to call into the café later today? Sharon will be here in the afternoon, and we can have a quick chat. There's something I've been meaning to ask you."

Aidan leaned on the horn. Olivia spun round and flipped him the finger.

They were the picture of marital bliss.

"Yeah, fine," her friend said. "I'll pop over during my afternoon coffee break."

When the bell above the shop door jangled indicating the first customer of the day, Fiona was behind the counter writing a to-do list and eating one of Olivia's muffins. She wiped crumbs off her jumper and plastered a smile across her face.

However, the sight of the person standing in the doorframe made her smile wither and die.

23

"Philip?" Her pen fell to the counter with a clatter.

"Hey, babe!" He slouched into the shop, wearing an oversized Abercrombie & Fitch hoodie and jeans. His wavy russet hair was in desperate need of a cut, and he'd acquired a scraggly goatee since she'd last seen him. In short, he was his usual incongruous mix of unkempt yet fashionable. How had she ever found him attractive?

"What are you doing in Ballybeg?" she asked without inflection. Philip was a Dublin boy through and through. He deemed anyone from outside the city to be a bogger. Indeed, anyone beyond South County Dublin was treated with suspicion and derision. That he'd deigned to venture beyond the perimeters of Dublin's fair city was a surprise. In the four years they'd been together, he'd never once visited Ballybeg. Not, she thought with a twinge of guilt, that she'd visited often herself.

He shrugged, as easygoing as ever and most probably stoned. "I came down for an audition. A panto in Cork City."

"You in a pantomime?" Times must be tough if he was considering such a job.

He flushed. "It's work, isn't it?" He shoved his hands in his jeans pockets. "I need something to put on my acting resume. It's not like I'm having much luck in Dublin. Not since my soap opera character was killed off."

"Which panto is it?"

He fixed his gaze on the polished wooden floor. "*Snow White and the Seven Dwarfs*."

"And your role would be...?"

Philip winced. "Dopey."

"Oh, no." She choked back laughter. "Not Dopey!"

The role would fit Philip to a tee. Sad thing was, the irony was probably lost on him. He was good-natured but obtuse, and ambitious but lazy. What he possessed in IQ (he was smart enough to get a decent degree from Trinity) he lacked in emotional intelligence. For a man who was remarkably good at channeling emotions on stage, he was useless at recognizing them in real life.

"Yeah," he grunted. "Have a good laugh, why don't you? Sure, weren't you always telling me I ought to branch out and go for less serious roles?"

"Gosh, I hope the pay is decent."

He gave a noncommittal shrug—a half-hearted, one-shouldered twitch. "It'll do."

Two elderly ladies entered the shop and nodded to Fiona before heading into the book room. At least her crappy morning had the potential to be offset by paying customers.

She retrieved her pen from the counter and started to doodle. "So what brings you to Ballybeg?"

"You said we could stay friends, didn't you?"

She had said that, but she hadn't meant it. It was one of those platitudes one said when breaking up with someone, particularly when the parting wasn't mutual. "Yeah, but I didn't expect to see you here." She glanced at the clock pointedly. "Especially this early in the morning."

"Actually, I'm staying in Ballybeg. At a little hotel."

Her heart plummeted. It was one thing to have him call in to the café on a one-off, but quite another to have him staying in the town. "Let me guess—Glebe Country House Hotel?"

"That's the name." He shoved his hands in his pockets and bounced on the balls of his feet. Philip found it impossible to stay still. It was a trait that had driven Fiona batty when they were together.

"Why didn't you find a place to stay in Cork City? Surely it would be more convenient."

He gave another lazy half shrug. "I left it too late to book a decent hotel in Cork City, and Ballybeg isn't far to commute." He flashed her what was meant to be a charmingly irresistible smile. "Plus I figured I could catch up with you."

Fiona chose to ignore the last comment. She was under no illusion that Philip was in love with her. Otherwise, he couldn't have done what he did. The familiar mix of hurt and anger churned in her stomach. The hurt was the sting of the woman betrayed. The anger was directed at herself. Why had she put up with him for so long? How could she not have seen what the world and her aunt had recognized immediately? No, his reappearance in her life most likely indicated he was broke and his parents were refusing to bankroll him.

She eyed him warily, took in the expensive clothes. Philip always managed to find the cash to buy nice clothes, drugs, and cigarettes, yet he rarely saw the necessity to pay back the people foolish enough to loan him money. No way in hell was she falling back into that trap.

"You couldn't have stayed in a youth hostel in Cork?" she asked archly. "Or were they also booked out?"

His features crumpled. "A youth hostel? Me? You can't be serious."

Dear old Philip, ever the snob. Her doodles were becoming more aggressive, her pen stabbing through the paper. If it weren't for the customers listening to their conversation with rapt interest, she'd throw him out on his arse. Hell, if he continued to piss her off, she still might.

He looked around the shop with a contemptuous expression. He wandered into the book room, critically surveying their wares. She steeled herself for the inevitable condescension.

"So this is your aunt's shop?" he said, picking up a book from the front window display. "Not exactly Waterstones, is it?"

"Did you expect it to be? It's a little new-and-used bookshop in a small Irish town."

"You have to admit it's not what you're used to."

Not what *he* was used to, more like. "I grew up in

Ballybeg. I knew what the shop was like when I agreed to help Bridie."

"Why would you cancel your trip because some old biddy falls and hurts herself? I couldn't believe it when Rachel told me."

Rachel. Her grip around the pen tightened. "Bridie's my aunt, not some old biddy. I did it because it was the right thing to do." Okay, plus her cousin's manipulations and a generous dose of guilt combined to force her hand.

"I don't get why you left Dublin for this dump. You always said you hated Ballybeg."

What Philip didn't "get" was why she'd left him. As far as she was concerned, he could remain in blissful ignorance.

"I owe Bridie. After everything she's done for me over the years, it's the least I can do."

"What about your world trip? You're not seriously going to spend your entire sabbatical year playing nurse and bookseller?"

If he didn't leave soon, she'd strangle him with his straggly russet hair. "Did you come in here to piss me off? Is this your idea of catching up?"

"Steady on, FeeFee." He put his palms up in a gesture of mock surrender. "I was just making conversation."

"Cut the crap. Why are you really in Cork?"

He quickly averted his gaze, shifting his weight from one foot to the other. *Whatever he's done, please don't let it involve a brush with the law.* After the vandalism drama, she'd had enough of the police to last her a lifetime.

"My father kicked me out of the house," he said at last. "Says I have to get a proper job. He'd accept me if I'd followed his footsteps and become a barrister. He doesn't understand the theater, nor anything cultural. He buys paintings as an investment, for goodness sake, not because he actually likes them."

"Maybe he'd be more supportive of your art if you were able to *support* yourself from it."

"I'm trying. I've got an agent. I go for auditions. I get roles but there are gaps between them and I need money to tide me over."

She dug her pen into the paper viciously, slashing red in jagged lines. "Get a part-time job. That's what other actors do."

"As what?" His voice rose to a whine. "I'm not prepared to demean myself by working in a restaurant or a pub."

"So sign up with a temp agency," she said through gritted teeth.

"Spend my days photocopying crap for overpaid managers? No way."

Fiona massaged her temples. Her headache was getting worse. Dealing with Philip and his nonsense was not helping. "You know what, Philip? No. Just no. We had this convo a million times when we were together. I make obvious suggestions how you could earn money between acting jobs, and you reject every single one." She tossed the pen to the side and straightened. "It wasn't my responsibility to organize your life then, and it sure as feck isn't my responsibility now."

His lips curled into a sulky pout. "Neither you nor my father appreciate my talent."

She didn't try to hide her eye-roll. "I've seen you on

stage. I know you can act, but it's not all about acting, is it? You certainly don't present yourself in a professional manner." She indicated his scruffy appearance.

"What do you mean?" he demanded in outrage.

"Don't you think you should at least brush your hair before your audition?"

"Sure, won't I be wearing a wig if I get the role?"

Give up, and give up now, Fiona's inner wise woman told her. Reasoning with her ex was a lost cause. He was the youngest child of an eminent Dublin barrister and his society wife. His mother indulged him while his father berated him for not living up to the family's expectations. Philip had displayed his rebellious tendencies early by eschewing law in favor of theater studies at university. His father had never forgiven him. His mother, on the other hand, gave him cash handouts on a regular basis, and Philip had never needed to find work between acting jobs. Now it seemed both his parents had finally had enough of bankrolling him and were forcing him to stand on his own two feet. It would either be the best thing to ever happen to him or the worst. Thank goodness she no longer had to deal with the fallout.

The doorbell jangled, indicating the arrival of more customers. Fiona's mood plummeted when she saw Gavin and Ruairí enter the shop.

Feck.

She'd have to forewarn Gavin about Muireann working at the bazaar, but she sure as hell wasn't starting that conversation with Philip hovering.

"Philip," she said pointedly. "I have customers. Besides, don't you have an audition to get to?"

He raised his eyes to the blackboard on the wall behind the counter and perused the menu. Her heart sank. "I think I'll have a coffee before I catch the bus to Cork." His smile was forced. "Seeing as I'm here and all."

She ground her teeth. Looked like she was stuck spending more time with Philip before he buggered off out of her life once more.

He sloped over to James Joyce and flopped into a chair. Gavin and Ruairí nodded to him when he passed them by, but he ignored them.

Yet another difference between Dublin and Ballybeg. Everyone greeted one another here, and strangers earned a passing nod. Obviously, Philip didn't know this—or if he did, he didn't care.

Ruairí sat at Oscar Wilde, the table opposite Philip's. Gavin approached the counter.

"Morning Fiona," he said with a friendly grin. In stark contrast to Philip's practiced smile, Gavin's unaffected but infectious grin warmed her from the inside out. "A double espresso for Ruairí, please, and a regular coffee for me."

"Would you like something to eat with your coffee?

"No, thanks."

"Okay, I'll be right over with your order."

She turned her back on the men and busied herself with the coffee machine. She served Philip first. He'd grabbed a copy of today's issue of *The Irish Times* from the magazine rack and was pretending to read. He didn't look up when she placed his coffee cup in front of him.

Please, please, let him leave! Between Muireann and Philip, she'd been obliged to deal with two people she'd rather not have anything to do with, and both on the same morning. And now Gavin was thrown into the mix. All this stress early on a Monday was doing nothing to alleviate her headache. Quite the contrary.

"Thanks," Gavin said when she served their coffee. He and Ruairí were studying something on a laptop. Floor plans, by the look of things.

After what seemed like an eternity but was barely ten minutes, Philip stood to leave. He tossed a couple of coins onto the table without bothering to check his bill. "I'll be seeing you, FeeFee," he said loudly enough for Gavin and Ruairí to glance up from what they were doing.

She prickled at his use of the nickname. She loathed FeeFee, and he knew it. "Won't you be going back to Dublin after the audition?"

He shrugged, a belligerent jut to his jaw. "I'll see. Maybe I'll stick around for a couple of days. It's not like I've got anything else to do."

With that parting shot, Philip exited the shop—but not, alas, her life.

24

Gavin watched the man Fiona had called Philip leave the shop and cross the road toward the bus stop. This must be the actor ex. He was being daft, but he'd hated the guy on sight.

He approached the counter. Fiona was lost in contemplation, the cute little worry line between her brows visible. He had a sudden urge to touch it. He cleared his throat. "Your ex?"

"Yeah. He lives in Dublin." She didn't elaborate.

He smiled. "So I gathered from his plummy accent."

"What were you and Ruairí staring at with such intensity?" She flicked a tea towel over her shoulder and began to clear up used cups and plates.

Keen to change the subject—interesting. His hunch that this Philip guy had had a significant impact on Fiona's life couldn't be too far off the mark.

"Ruairí's offered me a job."

Her eyes widened in surprise. "Is he renovating the pub?"

"Yeah, but that's only part of it." He flashed her a rueful smile. "You're looking at Ballybeg's newest temporary barman."

"Seriously?" She bent over to load the dishwasher, reminding him—and his groin—of how horny her backside made him.

"Why not? I need the money, and he needs someone to help with the Christmas rush. I paid my way through uni working in bars."

"I'm impressed. I would have thought you'd consider a job in a pub to be beneath you."

He laughed, hearing a tinge of bitterness in its echo. "A man with as much debt as I have can't afford to be picky. I've had an offer of a few teaching hours at the university starting next semester. Until then, I need something to tide me over. It's not like I've got job offers flowing in, nor has anyone expressed interest in buying Clonmore Lodge."

"So you're staying in Ballybeg?"

"For the time being. I'm not ready to give up yet. There's still the possibility I'll find a buyer for the cottage."

"Gosh," she said. "Do you want to sell the cottage? You love living there."

He shrugged, his gaze moving to his feet. "If things don't go my way within the next few months, I'll have no choice."

"Hey, Fiona." Ruairí approached the counter, used cup in hand. "Heard anything from the police about the break-in?"

"No, and I doubt I will. As far as Garda Glenn is concerned, if he can't pin it on Sharon, it must've been random kids."

"Aye," he said with a frown. "That's Glenn's attitude, all right."

"Listen, Gavin," Fiona said. "You know how you said you'd help me haul boxes for the Christmas Bazaar?"

"Yeah."

"Muireann will be working the bookstall, too."

He sucked in a breath.

"If it'll be an issue for you, don't worry about helping out. We can manage between the two of us."

He burst into laughter. "Muireann haul boxes? That'll be the day. Trust me, she'll stick you with all the heavy lifting. I'll come by here at about a quarter to twelve, and I can collect you and the boxes."

Her eyes creased in concern. "Are you sure it's no trouble?"

"I'm sure." On instinct, he reached for her hand. "Don't worry about it. I was bound to run across Muireann eventually."

Behind him, Ruairí snorted. Gavin shot him a warning look.

His new boss looked from him to Fiona, then back again. "Ah," Ruairí said. "So it's like that then. I had my suspicions." He clapped Gavin on the back. Coming from a man as strong as Ruairí, a friendly clap on the back was sufficient to dislocate shoulders. "Bye, Fiona. Later, Gavin." He winked and exited the shop.

"The damage in here is worse than I'd hoped." Gavin indicated the rain-stained walls.

"Yeah," Fiona said. "I'm going to paint them over the Christmas holidays. We can't afford to close for a couple of days this time of year, but the walls need to be repainted soon."

"Do you have experience painting walls?"

"Well…no."

"Then let me help you. Get Bridie to pick out the color, and I'll borrow the supplies we need from Liam O'Mahony."

"Are you sure?" She frowned. "It'll be a lot of work."

"Work that will go faster with the two of us doing it."

Her old wary expression was back. "Why are you doing this, Gavin? Why do you want to spend so much time with me? It's not like you lack for friends."

"Because I like you," he said honestly. "And because I owe you."

He regretted his word choice as soon as they were uttered. She stiffened, and the wariness developed hostile overtones. "The only thing you owe me is a divorce. And we both know that will take years."

The last remaining customer approached the cash register. Fiona plastered a smile on her face and rang up the customer's order. She was a terrible actress. Her every gesture projected her moods, and her attempts to hide them were comically stilted.

After the woman left, Gavin flipped the open sign to closed and locked the door.

"Hey," she said. "What are you doing? I can't take a break."

"I'm sorry. Once again, I've been an eejit and said the wrong thing." He took her into his arms. She was stiff as a board but soon relaxed into the embrace.

"I might have overreacted," she said. "It's been one hell of a morning."

"I meant that I feel I owe you because I've wronged you. It was my screwup that led to the mess we're now in. I didn't mean I'm spending time with you out of a sense of duty. I like you, Fiona. I always have. You make me laugh." He stroked her hair and let the silky curl slip through his fingers. "And you're genuine. I don't feel I have to pretend with you."

She snuggled into his chest. "You realize, Maguire, that daylight snuggling might lead us into dangerous territory?"

He nibbled her ear. "Why don't we head into the stockroom for a few minutes?"

"You're a terrible influence," she said, laughing into his chest. "I'm supposed to be a responsible shop manager. I can't shut midmorning."

"Come on. Just for a few minutes." He took her arm and kissed her wrist the way he knew she liked. He slid her shirt up her arm and feathered kisses all the way to the crook of her elbow.

"Gavin…people can see in the window."

"Why do you think I suggested we go into the stockroom?"

"Oh, all right," she said. "But we'll have to make it quick."

"I can do quick. I can do slow. I can do it any speed you like." He grabbed her hand. "But for what I've got in mind, let me take the lead."

"Intriguing," she said as he pulled her into the tiny stockroom and closed the door. "Should I be worried?"

He laughed. "Extremely." He unzipped her jeans and tugged them down, quickly followed by her knickers.

Holy Moses, she was gorgeous.

He leaned between her legs and kissed her.

"What the…Gavin!"

"Shh," he whispered. "I'm taking the lead, remember? You're supposed to at least pretend to be docile for a few minutes."

"I am never docile."

He grinned and silenced her by toying with her clit ring, alternating tugging and massaging the soft skin. From this vantage point, he couldn't see Fiona, but he could hear her breathing change, hear the soft gasps as she neared orgasm.

He felt her pulse around his tongue when she came, pressing her back into the wall. She let out a muffled moan, then collapsed.

"Was I quick enough for you?" he asked as he pulled up her knickers and jeans.

"Uh-huh," she replied, breathing heavily. Her eyes were glassy, and her face was deliciously flushed.

"Excellent." He kissed her hard. "In that case, I'll be on my merry way."

~

FIONA SAGGED against the stockroom wall, basking in the heady afterglow.

Holy feck. What an orgasm!

"Fiona? Are you here?"

She yanked her clothes into place and checked her appearance in the small mirror. Her cheeks were pink-tinged with a healthy glow. Her hair was wild. She pulled a brush through it before venturing back into the shop.

Olivia stood before the counter dressed in a chic black-and-white suit. She'd removed her coat and was hanging it on the coat stand.

"Hmm," she said when she caught sight of Fiona. "You look delightfully flushed. What were you reading in the stockroom?"

"What are you doing here? Didn't you say you wouldn't be able to get away until the afternoon?"

"So I did, but Aidan's buggered off with a golfing crony, and I decided to switch on the voice mail and take a break." Olivia sat down at the James Joyce table and perused the menu. "I'd love to know what's tickled you pink."

"You can wonder all you like," Fiona said. "You're getting nothing out of me."

"Such a bore," her friend said with an exaggerated sigh. "I'm dying for a decent gossip."

"You might be in luck." She made two cappuccinos and set them on the table. "As long as I've no customers, I can talk."

"Oh, yes," Olivia said eagerly. "You said you had something to tell me."

"Yes, but you have to promise to keep it quiet."

"Fee," Olivia said in mock sincerity, "I am the soul of discretion."

"When you like the person confiding in you," Fiona said with a laugh.

"You know you qualify." Her friend dumped two sugars into her coffee and stirred. "So spill."

"Were you aware that Aidan was my grandmother's solicitor?"

"Yeah," Olivia said, licking foam from her lips, "but that was way before my time at the practice."

"Do you know if he kept her file?"

"I'd imagine so. It would be in the archives by now." Olivia narrowed her eyes. "What are you getting at? Do you think there was something amiss with how the estate was handled?"

"I don't know. I recently learned my grandmother always told her children they'd each receive a third of her estate after her death."

"But—"

"When she died, her will left everything to Bernard."

"Families can be odd, Fee. Who knows what she was thinking when she cut your dad and Bridie out of her will."

"Until Bridie mentioned it to me, I'd never questioned the division of the estate. To be honest, I had no idea my grandparents had owned so much land. I assumed Bernard had bought most of his property by himself."

Olivia stirred her cappuccino. "You're not mercenary, Fee, and I'm not stupid. I'm guessing you have reason to believe there was something other than a vindictive old lady behind the will."

"That's just it. My grandmother was the gentlest soul

you could meet. There wasn't a vindictive bone in her body."

"So what's made you suddenly question the validity of her will? What exactly did Bridie say?"

"She said my grandmother's will was written a couple of months before she died. The witnesses were my aunt Deirdre and a nursing home carergiver named Ann Dunne."

"Deirdre?" Olivia blinked in surprise. "Didn't your grandmother loathe her?"

"Exactly. That's what's so odd about it. Plus, I did a little sleuthing at the nursing home and found a porter who remembered Ann Dunne, the second witness. He implied Ann was known for coaxing monetary gifts out of patients, and she left the job after having supposedly won the lottery."

Olivia shrugged. "It happens. Just not to me, alas."

"All the same," Fiona said, "it's odd."

"How can I help you?"

"Would you be able to check if Bridie's description of the will is accurate? The division of the property and the names of the witnesses?" Fiona wrinkled her nose and lowered her voice. "I know I could ask Aidan directly, but he's still Bernard's solicitor."

The bell jangled, and two women came into the shop. Fiona stood hastily and cleared away their coffee cups.

When Olivia had put on her coat, she approached the counter. "I'll have a look and let you know what I find."

25

On the morning of the Christmas Bazaar, the town hall was a hive of activity.

The hall was located in a building dating from the middle of the nineteenth century. Fiona remembered the hall vaguely, but it had been many years since she'd been inside. The floors were a rich polished wood. High ceilings made the room appear larger than it was. An enormous Christmas tree stood in one corner of the hall, and the walls were festooned with decorations. Speakers played Christmas carols in the background although the songs were barely audible above the hum created by the hall's occupants. If it hadn't been for the prospect of spending the day with Muireann, Fiona would have looked forward to the bazaar.

Why had she agreed to go along with her cousin's plan? A weird sense of owing her a favor? But what kind of favor was this? Another chance for Muireann to humiliate her? *Just a few hours,* she reminded herself, *and I'm off for a drink with Olivia.*

Two teenage boys placed a large table next to her pile of book boxes. "Thanks, lads," she said with a smile. "Which one of you is which? I never could remember."

"I'm Kyle," said the slightly taller one.

"And I'm Ronan," said the other.

Both boys sported shocks of red hair and cheeky grins. Olivia's little brothers weren't so little anymore. At some point during Fiona's eight-year absence from Ballybeg, they'd grown from freckled urchins into gangly young men—something her own little brother never had the chance to do. She swallowed past the hard lump in her throat. Grief hit her at unexpected moments. Not as often as it had a few years ago, but when the emotion hit, it had the power to wrench her out of the present.

"Kyle! Ronan!" Nuala O'Mahony, the official organizer of the bazaar, bore down upon them, her lips pursed into a line of disapproval. "What's taking you so long? Hurry up and help Ruairí MacCarthy carry drink crates in from the van."

"We're on it." The boys winked at Fiona and scurried off to do Nuala's bidding.

"Honestly," Nuala said, a frown marring her smooth forehead. "Those two are as foolish as their father."

"That's rather harsh." Fiona had never warmed to Nuala, although she admired her dedication to honoring her late son's memory by raising funds for cystic fibrosis research. Despite a few extra lines etched around her eyes, she was exactly as Fiona remembered. She favored floral-print dresses and brown leather brogues and held her long, dark hair in place with a hair band. The girlish appearance was deceptive, hiding the personality of a termagant.

She was rescued from further conversation with Nuala by the timely arrival of Gavin and Jonas with the last of her book boxes. "Thanks a million, lads. I appreciate it." She smiled at Jonas. "I didn't know you were down for the weekend."

He grinned. "I daren't miss the bazaar. Mum would kill me."

"Jonas," snapped his mother. "Why aren't you helping Susanne set up the drinks stand? Go on, boy. What are you waiting for? There's work to be done around here, and everyone needs to pitch in."

If Jonas was less than thrilled to be commandeered in such a manner, he hid it well. He aimed a mock salute at his mother and headed across the room to a blond woman who was unloading crates of beer and fizzy drinks.

Nuala soon found someone else to criticize. Before another moment could pass, she was advancing toward a group of hapless schoolchildren who were attempting to hang colorful Christmas decorations on the walls. "No! Not there. Oh, for heaven's sake. Do I have to do everything myself?"

Gavin observed Nuala's retreating back in amusement. "Don't worry," he whispered as he deposited more boxes on the ground behind Fiona's designated tables. "Her bark is worse than her bite. She wants everything to be absolutely perfect, and of course it rarely turns out that way. She always gets stressed about the bazaar."

"She'd better not snap at me."

"I doubt she'd dare." His voice was a deep burr. She caught a whiff of his aftershave as he set another book box on the floor. Adrenaline kicked into action, as did her hormones. X-rated memories of their encounter in the stockroom flooded her mind and brought a blush to her cheeks.

He glanced around the hall. "Muireann not here yet?"

"No," Fiona said crisply. "She's late."

She'd sensed Gavin's tension the moment he'd met her at the Book Mark that morning to collect the boxes. It rolled off him in waves. They'd gone through the motions of pretending the easy camaraderie and flirtation of the past couple of months was unaffected, that today held no more significance for either of them than it did for anyone else present at the bazaar.

But they both knew it for a lie.

Muireann would be there—the woman Gavin could've, would've, should've married. In spite of her current gaunt state, Muireann was stunning. Fiona scrubbed up nicely enough, but she paled into insignificance next to her beautiful cousin.

And that was what this was about, wasn't it? It had come to Fiona last night in a moment of clarity. Muireann intended to pose them, put them on display beside one another and show Gavin what he'd lost through his colossal cock-up.

He sneezed a few times in succession. No wonder his voice sounded even deeper than it usually did.

"Do you have a cold?"

He took a clean tissue from his pocket. "I guess so. It came on me last night. I was hoping it wouldn't develop into anything beyond a sinus headache, but I was obviously bang out of luck."

"Perhaps a glass of mulled wine will help."

Gavin laughed. "Yeah, especially after taking a painkiller. I'd be out for the count for the rest of the day."

"The Major is larruping into the rum punch," Fiona said, nodding toward Olivia's grandfather. "So you'd be in exalted company."

"I can just imagine what Nuala would have to say about that. Besides, I'm meant to be serving buns and cakes to the good folk of Ballybeg. It wouldn't do to go dropping a cream cake on the floor, would it?"

"You'd probably have a few crying children to deal with if you did."

He grimaced and blew his nose. "I'd better head over and help Nora Fitzgerald with the cakes. If I dawdle, she'll go nuts. She's already pissed with me over the wedding suit."

"Speaking of suits, what have you done with Wiggly Poo?"

"Did Bridie not tell you?" He cocked an eyebrow. "She offered to look after him."

Fiona laughed. "Poor Bridie's in for a fun morning."

"Gavin," screeched Nora Fitzgerald from across the hall. "Are you helping me or not?"

He grinned at Fiona through watery eyes. "I'd better get going."

"Thanks again for hauling boxes."

She watched him stride across the hall. So this was it, then. He'd see Muireann and come to his senses. He'd decide to win her back. She swallowed past the lump in her throat. Did she really believe he was so fickle? And if she did, what did it say about her self-esteem?

Her mind racing, she unloaded the various boxes of used books, old annuals, and magazines. They took up two of the large tables provided by the town hall, and she had surplus supplies in reserve for later.

She'd finished arranging her wares to her satisfaction when Muireann made her entrance. Her cousin swanned into the hall, stopping to air-kiss everyone she passed.

"Hello, Fiona," she said when she reached the bookstall. "You're looking festive." She smirked at Fiona's red pullover.

"It's warm," Fiona said tersely, "and the town hall is not."

Muireann's peach cashmere pullover and light gray slacks looked perfect on her slender frame.

"You're late." She didn't bother to disguise her impatience.

"Only by a few minutes." Her cousin rooted through a box of old magazines.

"Here's a calculator, in case you need it. The cash box is here. It should never be left unattended. If one of us needs to leave the stall, the other has to be here. Understood?"

Muireann nodded absently, flicking through a magazine.

Fabulous. She must have had a moment of insanity when she agreed to work with her cousin. "Look, either get to work or leave. I'm not shouldering your share of the work in addition to mine."

Muireann arched an overly plucked eyebrow. "From

what I can see, you've set everything up. Why can't I read a magazine until the bazaar starts?"

Fiona bit back a retort. She itched to slap the smug expression off her pretty face. The only thing keeping the impulse in check was the knowledge it was exactly what her cousin wanted her to do. She gritted her teeth and willed patience.

When the bazaar opened at two o'clock, there was a crowd of people waiting at the doors. Over the next couple of hours, they were run off their feet, which kept Fiona from dwelling on her guilt and resentment toward her cousin and her deepening feelings for Gavin.

Muireann proved to be a surprisingly good worker. She was a natural with the customers, particularly the men. To Fiona's amazement, she'd read a number of the more popular authors and was happy to chat with customers about their favorite books. She'd never work her cousin out. The woman was an enigma.

"Is it okay if I go on a break?" Muireann asked when the throng had eased.

"Yeah, go on," Fiona said, wrestling with a stubborn roll of two-euro coins. "Be back in fifteen minutes, then I'll take my break."

Her cousin sauntered across the hall in the direction of the cake stand.

A cacophony of barking drew Fiona's attention away from the unfolding drama of Gavin and Muireann's first post-non-honeymoon encounter to the hall entrance.

Oh, no.

Aunt Deirdre, Bridie, and their respective canine companions stood underneath the mistletoe, glaring at one another. Deirdre carried Mitzi and Bitzi in an oversized handbag while Bridie had Wiggly Poo on a lead.

Fiona exhaled a sigh. This was all she needed.

Aunt Deirdre tottered through the hall on her stilettos, giving a regal nod to people she deemed worthy and the cut direct to those she did not. She halted in front of the bookstall and gave Fiona a haughty once-over. Mitzi and Bitzi stared at Fiona through their beady eyes. "Fiona," her aunt trilled. "What a lovely pullover. It's amazing what bargains one can find these days at Oxfam."

Fiona exhaled slowly. If suggesting she'd found her pullover at a charity shop was the worst insult Deirdre was going to throw at her, she could cope.

Deirdre leaned closer, presenting Fiona with a close-up of her artificially frozen forehead. "I know why you've always needed to compete with Muireann. You have an inferiority complex. Understandable, given your history."

"I miss my parents, but rest assured I don't envy Muireann you as a mother."

Her aunt's thin lips twisted. "The police told Bernard what happened. We know Eamonn's death was your fault."

The words hit Fiona like a punch to the solar plexus. "It wasn't my fault."

"I'm sure you tell yourself that, my dear, but Eamonn wouldn't have died if he'd been wearing his seatbelt. According to Bernard's police contact, he took it off because he was fighting with you in the back of the car."

Hot tears stung Fiona's eyes. She blinked them back. What a bitch. What a complete and utter cow.

"So tell me…how do you live with yourself?"

"Stop it." Her tears were falling as fast as her rapid breathing. "Just stop it. I know you hate me for what happened at the wedding, but don't drag Eamonn into this. His death was not my fault."

Deirdre sneered. "If it wasn't your fault, why do you feel guilty?"

"Shut your miserable gob and leave Fiona alone." Bridie and Wiggly Poo stood side-by-side, united in indignation. The puppy growled at Deirdre and his arch-enemies, Mitzi and Bitzi.

"Get that rabid beast away from my babies," snapped Deirdre. "He ought to be put down."

"The only one who ought to be put down is you," Bridie said. "How dare you spout such vicious lies? I know you're bitter about the broken engagement, but Gavin and Muireann were never a good fit. In a few years time, they'll consider this a blessing."

"What would you know?" retorted Deirdre. "You're a miserable old spinster whose tepid love interest is a man even more ancient than yourself."

"I clearly know more about your daughter's feelings than you do," Bridie said, bristling. "You direct all your attention to those fecking Chewbaccas."

Through her tears, Fiona choked back a laugh.

Deirdre's frozen forehead struggled to emote, but it was a losing battle. "My what?"

Fiona blew her nose. "She's referring to those bloody rat dogs you cart around with you everywhere."

At that moment, Mitzi and Bitzi made a leap for freedom and scampered across the hall.

Wiggly Poo gave a delighted bark and yanked on his

lead. Determined to rid Ballybeg of vermin once and for all, he took off in rapid pursuit.

26

Gavin's day had gone from bad to worse. His throat felt like he'd swallowed razorblades, and his swollen sinuses were making his head throb.

Muireann was here. This was no surprise. He was grateful to Fiona for forewarning him, but foreknowledge hadn't lessened the impact of seeing her in the flesh. She'd lost a lot of weight and looked peaky in spite of her tan.

Here was the woman he'd intended to marry standing next to the woman he had married, albeit unwittingly. Muireann was wealthy, connected, and effortlessly beautiful. Fiona, in contrast, was everything Muireann was not: funny, sharp, sexy, and irreverent. She was neither wealthy nor connected, nor—in the traditional sense—beautiful. Yet she had the power to truly reach him, to awaken a depth of emotion he hadn't thought himself capable of.

"Oy." Jonas grabbed a cream bun from the tray in his

arms. "Do you want to trade places? Your dripping nose is putting people off the cakes."

"Really?" Gavin laughed. "More like you want to escape your significant other."

"Come on, man, please?" His friend mimed a hangman's noose. "I'm desperate. You know I'd do it for you."

"Yeah, okay. It makes no difference to me whether I serve food or drink. Your mother won't be impressed, though."

"You mean because her oh-so-subtle attempt at encouraging harmony between me and Susanne backfired? Seriously, Gav, if I don't get away from her soon, there'll be a public fight. Definitely *not* what my mother wants at the bazaar."

Gavin moved over to the drinks stand, where Susanne was occupied filling plastic cups with Coke. She was the blandly attractive type with dyed blond hair and clothes two sizes too small for her figure. Her smile of greeting was tight and unwelcoming. "You look like hell," she said, giving him a wide berth. "Why aren't you home in bed?"

"I promised Nuala I'd help out. I didn't want to let her down."

"So instead you decided to share your germs with us?"

"I didn't feel this bad when I woke up. It's gotten worse over the past few hours."

"You should go home. You don't want to be ill for Christmas, do you?"

"Why don't I stick around for another half hour? The rush should be over by then."

She nodded, already turning her attention back to the line of thirsty customers.

Gavin poured himself a glass of lemonade. He needed something to quench his thirst and give him an energy boost. He'd just taken a large gulp of his drink when Muireann appeared before him.

"Hello, Gavin." Up close, her complexion was green beneath her tan, and dark shadows formed bags beneath her eyes.

"Hey. How are you?" He looked over at Susanne in the hope of salvation, but she was busy serving customers. Resigned, he faced his ex-fiancée. "What do you want to drink?"

"I'll have a diet cola." She peered closer at him. "Are you sick?"

"I could ask you the same question. Are you coming down with something?"

"Jet lag and a cold. You?"

"Also a cold." He eyed her warily. What should he say next? Continue the charade of meaningless small talk? They'd been a couple for years yet could find nothing better to talk about now than their respective winter ailments?

He handed her the cola. Her fingers were cold as icicles.

"You should be home in bed," he said. "Not stuck here in a draughty hall."

"I wanted to get this over and done with. The whole town is staring at us, waiting to see what we'll do."

She was right. He sensed the collective gaze of the crowd boring into his flesh.

"I'm done hiding in the house," she said. "The sooner

we're seen together in public, the sooner they'll find something else to gossip about."

She wasn't far off the mark. He loathed being the center of attention, especially as the result of personal drama. He'd been there, done that a thousand times during his childhood, courtesy of his mother and her numerous break-ups.

He opened his mouth to say something, but he was parched. Grabbing his glass of lemonade, he took a gulp.

A scream worthy of a banshee stopped him mid-swallow.

Holy hell. Mitzi and Bitzi streaked across the floor with Wiggly Poo in hot pursuit. Deirdre was by the bookstall, framed by an ashen-faced Fiona and a puce Bridie.

"Someone stop that dog," cried Deirdre. "Save my babies." Then she resumed her banshee wail.

Bridie stepped forward and walloped her sister-in-law across the face. "Stop your caterwauling, Deirdre. You've only yourself to blame for bringing those rats to the bazaar."

"Aw, shite." So much for not being the center of a public scene. He leaped over the drinks stand and legged it after his naughty pet.

Over by the Christmas tree, Aidan Gant was holding court with a sullen-faced Olivia at his side and a few of his political cronies as his audience. The Chihuahuas shot between his legs and hid beneath the tree.

"Aidan, do something," shouted Deirdre, tottering across the hall. "Hold them up out of Wiggly Poo's way."

Aidan rearranged his facial features from slack-jawed to smarmy. "Don't worry. I'll have them out in a jiffy."

Gavin caught Wiggly Poo by the collar just as Aidan was crawling beneath the Christmas tree to forcibly remove the Chihuahuas.

Out of the safety of their carrier bag and the cooing ministrations of their mistress, Mitzi and Bitzi were in no mood to be manhandled by Ballybeg's up-and-coming politician. Aidan, clearly clueless when it came to dogs, chose that moment to stage a cheesy campaign photo. "Will you take a snap of us, Gavin?"

"What, now?" Was the man totally mad or completely self-absorbed and oblivious to the chaos around him?

"I'll do it," Olivia said and took her mobile phone out of her coat pocket.

The flash sent the Chihuahuas wild. One sank its jaws into Aidan's nose, while the other attacked his cheek.

Aidan spun around yowling, the dogs clinging to his blood-streaked face.

27

Fiona wrapped the last of the pre-packaged gift sets in cheery Christmas paper. In the week since the mayhem of the Christmas Bazaar, the festive shopping frenzy had begun in earnest. Good news for the Book Mark's coffers but bad news for her feet.

Unfortunately, her hectic days didn't prevent her mind from dwelling on her relationship with Gavin.

After much soul-searching, she'd reached to a decision. She was going to end their fling. It wasn't just the awkwardness of having Muireann back in Ballybeg. Nor was it the ridiculousness of their non-marriage and impending divorce. She'd fallen in love with him all over again. Her heart skipped a beat whenever she saw him. She got butterflies in her stomach whenever she thought about him, and his barest touch turned her into a molten mess. She had to get out before she lost her mind as well as her heart.

"Ow!"

She looked up to see her aunt hauling a box of books into the book room. "Bridie! Let me." She wrested the box out of her aunt's determined grasp. "Why on earth did you decide to help out today? You know what the doctor said."

Bridie glared at her, hands on her broad hips. "I'm sixty-four years old, missy, not four," she retorted. "I can judge for myself whether or not I'm fit to work."

She shook her head in defeat. "You're impossible."

"If you're not going to buy something or help out, you can shoo!" Bridie growled at Olivia, who was perched on a stool behind the counter, flipping through a glossy magazine. Aidan was away at a conference, and Olivia had volunteered to help out at the Book Mark for a couple of hours each afternoon.

"Oh, give over," Olivia teased. "Sure, aren't I adding deco to the place?"

Bridie snorted. "Some deco. Cleavage is what that is, young lady. In my day, young women were taught to dress modestly." She shook her head in disapproval. "Nowadays, every female over the age of twelve is going around with bare bellies and bosoms on display."

"Now, Bridie," Olivia said with a wicked grin. "Surely not *every* female over the age of twelve. I'm sure the ladies of the Ballybeg House and Crafts Society would be scandalized to learn one of their leading members was displaying her blubber to the world. Are you planning on starting a trend?"

A chortle resounded in Bridie's throat. "Blubber? Why, I'll give you blubber!" She pulled up her plus-size blouse and grabbed a substantial handful of flesh from around her midriff. "This, here, is what a genuine Irish woman looks like. If you two had eaten a decent meal of meat and potatoes every day when you were growing up, you wouldn't be the scrawny beanpoles you are today."

A strangled gasp sounded from behind them. A man—and potential customer—hovered on the doorstep. He gaped in horror at the sight of Bridie's bare belly before beating a hasty retreat.

Fiona and Olivia erupted into laughter.

Bridie let the hem of her blouse drop. "Well!" she said indignantly. "He's obviously not a real Irish man if he's overcome by the sight of bare female flesh. Sure, he's a scrawny little fella. He could do with a good feeding—and perhaps a slice of brack."

Fiona cocked an eyebrow. "Subtle as ever, Bridie. Fine, I'll cut us a couple of slices." She squeezed past her friend and filled up the kettle at the small sink in the café's minute kitchen. "Anyone for a cup of tea?"

"As long as it's Barry's and not those shite PG Tips. The Brits might think they've got a monopoly on tea, but none of their weak-kneed stuff beats a good, strong cup of Barry's."

She smothered a laugh. "You do realize tea doesn't grow in Ireland? I'm sure Barry's get their tea in places like India and Sri Lanka—just as PGs do."

"Harrumph! Those Brits can't make decent tea-in-a-bag. And I won't touch those leaves. If I wanted bits of foliage floating round in my tea, I'd grab a bunch off a bush and be done with."

Olivia lowered her magazine and looked at Bridie with a wicked glint in her eyes. "In case you've forgotten, 'those

Brits' include my grandfather. Who, as I recall, is your particular friend."

Bridie blushed an unbecoming puce. "There's nothing untoward between me and the Major," she said primly. "He's merely an unattached gentleman with whom I occasionally play a round of cards."

Fiona exchanged an amused glance with Olivia. Until recently, she'd have said her sixty-four-year-old aunt's love life was more interesting than her own. She wasn't sure if this was amusing, pathetic, or both.

She deposited three slices of Olivia's homemade brack on a platter. "Speaking of the men of Ballybeg, how's Aidan? For a woman whose husband was recently savaged by Chihuahuas, you're remarkably chipper."

"He's in a foul mood," said Olivia with a scowl. "His face is a fright. He's already looking up plastic surgeons."

Fiona cocked an eyebrow. "Would his foul mood be the reason you're hiding out here?"

Her friend laughed. "Perhaps. Frankly, all the men in my life are giving me grief at the moment. I'm on the verge of packing my bags and heading off to a female-only commune."

Fiona poured tea into three cups and handed one to her aunt and another to Olivia. "You sound stressed. Have your brothers been up to mischief again?"

Olivia rolled her eyes. "They've been suspended for a week for spraying graffiti on the walls of their school gym. Seriously, what sort of eejits do that to their own school?"

"Any time you want to escape, you're always welcome at ours."

"Thanks, Fee. I might just take you up on that offer."

Fiona took a sip of her hot tea, liberally laced with sugar. "I'm more of a coffee than a tea drinker, but I must admit this hits the spot."

"I don't know how you can drink that awful black stuff," Bridie said with a shudder. "It's like putting tar through your bowels."

Fiona laughed. "You must admit there's been an upturn in business since I embraced the twenty-first century on your behalf and got a functioning coffee machine."

"Harrumph! The stuff coming out of the machine is no better than instant—just a lot more expensive. I don't know what people are at today. They come in here looking for frothy milk and tiny cups of coffee that don't hold a thimbleful of liquid." She shifted her substantial weight to her good hip. "Well, you know what they say about a fool and his money. At least I'm benefitting from their frumduddery."

Olivia looked at Fiona questioningly. Fiona simply smiled. Bridie was renowned for her original vocabulary. Her theory was that if the Oxford dictionary was allowed to add new words to the official English language on a regular basis, then she was entitled to invent a few herself. Most people dared not contradict her, and thus Bridie's speech was peppered with words of her own creation.

The Major, who had studied English at Cambridge before embarking upon his army career, was one of the few souls brave enough to call her on it. Not that Bridie paid him the slightest heed.

"This definitely hits the spot." Olivia took a generous

mouthful of brack. "I don't want to think about the amount of calories it contains."

"As if you need to worry about your weight." Fiona gave a scornful laugh. "It never ceases to annoy me that you can eat the most incredible amounts of junk and stay slim. If I so much as look at a piece of chocolate, my arse expands."

"Personally, I think being thin is overrated," Bridie said. "What real man wants to roll around with a bag of bones?"

"To be frank, Ballybeg is short of real men," Fiona said with a grin. "I don't think we need to worry about being too skinny to attract them."

"Fiona's right," Olivia said. "There's no decent talent in this town. We'll have to go to Cork City one of these nights and hit the clubs. I wouldn't say the men there are much better than they are here, but at least there's less of a chance you went to primary school with them, shagged them, or have assessed them and dismissed them as wanting."

Fiona laughed. Bridie made an unconvincing attempt to look scandalized but quickly gave it up as a lost cause.

"Hello, ladies." Fiona jerked around at the sound of the familiar deep voice. "Hope I'm not interrupting anything."

28

Gavin's heart performed a slow thump and roll. Fiona had crumbs on her chin. She looked adorable. Flushed, awkward, and utterly kissable.

He'd barely seen her over the past few days. After spending Monday in bed with a cold, he'd been working double shifts at the pub, leaving Wiggly Poo to be dog-sat by the O'Mahonys. With Fiona equally busy at the Book Mark, they hadn't had a chance to spend more than a few minutes in each other's company.

He'd missed her. Missed her warm smile and dirty laugh, missed her kisses and the little sound she made in the recesses of her throat when he nibbled her earlobe.

After much soul-searching, he'd reached a decision. He was going to tell her how he felt. Yeah, it was utterly mad, what with the divorce proceedings underway and his ex-fiancée living in the same town. But if he didn't take the chance before she left Ballybeg, he'd never know what might have been.

He nodded to Olivia and Bridie and took a seat at James Joyce, his preferred table at the Book Mark Café.

"Well now, and if it isn't Mr. Maguire." Bridie greeted him cheerfully, her trademark tight gray curls enlivened by a pink rinse. Bridie changed her hair color about three times per year, alternating between peach, pink, and purple. "Still on for painting the shop?"

"I'll be as good as my word." His grin was wide. Painting the shop would be an excellent excuse to spend one-on-one time with Fiona. "How about after Christmas? Say, from the twenty-sixth? We'll need at least a day to pack up the books, then another day or two to paint. Will that give you enough time to get sorted?"

Bridie nodded. "I think we can manage." She turned toward Fiona. "What's wrong with you, missy? Have you lost your manners? I'm sure Gavin would like a cup of tea."

"Yeah, sure. Milk or sugar?" Fiona's was worrying her lip ring. He'd noticed she fiddled with it whenever she was flustered.

"Actually…" He cast a rueful glance at Bridie. "I'd prefer a coffee." He winked at Fiona.

She dropped her gaze to the coffee machine. "Regular? Espresso? Cappuccino?"

"An espresso will do fine."

She was looking pale and tense. *Damn.* Had he given her his cold? He hoped not.

"I'll never understand why young people today are mad for coffee."

Bridie regarded the new coffee machine with suspicion. He wondered if she expected it to jump up from the counter and launch an attack. "I'm surprised to see you in here, Bridie. Aren't you supposed to be resting at home?"

"Yes," Fiona said with emphasis, placing his espresso in front of him. "She is."

He smiled at her, their fingers brushing. She flushed and pulled her hand away. "Why don't I give Bridie a lift home after I've finished my coffee? I need to shower and change before my shift at the pub."

"I don't need mollycoddling," snapped Bridie.

"Yes, she does," Fiona and Olivia said in unison.

"What can we do for you, Gavin?" Bridie asked. "Are you here for the coffee or have you come to buy a few Christmas presents?"

"I was hoping Fiona could recommend more books to me. My library's a little sparse at the moment, and I flew through the last batch she gave me."

"Anything in particular you're in the mood for?" Fiona asked.

He drained his espresso. "Crime fiction. I've finished Jonas's latest mystery, and I'd like something in a similar vein."

She moved into the book room behind the café and pulled a box out from underneath one of the book display tables. "If you're not set on buying a brand-new book, we've had a few people bring in used mysteries and thrillers. I haven't had a chance to sort through and price tag this box yet. Do you want to have a root through it?"

"Yeah, fantastic."

"Speaking of books, will you bag me up a few Mills

and Boon?" Bridie heaved her heavy frame into the book room, wincing as she did so.

"Do you need another painkiller, Bridie?" Fiona asked in concern.

"Ah, no. I don't want to get addicted to those things like Nessy O'Flaherty. Ended up in a loony bin, she did."

"I think Mrs. O'Flaherty's problems were a little more serious than taking a few painkillers after a major operation," he said wryly.

Fiona smiled at him, displaying her adorable dimples. He'd always been indifferent to dimples, but somehow, she made them the most attractive sight he'd ever seen.

He rooted through the box of books, selecting a few Agatha Christie mysteries he hadn't read as well as a popular thriller by a Swedish author.

Bridie had selected an armful of romance novels. "There's no point in running a bookshop if I don't get to sample the wares every now and again."

"Why don't I carry those out to my car? Seeing as I'm driving you home."

"You're as stubborn as Fiona. I think I can manage to heft a few M&B, lad."

He carried his books to the counter.

"On the house," Fiona said. "Especially as you're painting the place."

He shook his head and placed a twenty-euro note on the counter. "Don't turn down trade, Fiona."

"Can I have a word with you before you take off?" she said, lowering her voice.

"Sure. Let's get Bridie settled in the car first."

Once Bridie was ensconced in the passenger seat of

the SUV, he closed the car door and turned to Fiona. "What's up?"

She was fiddling with her fingers now, twisting them to and fro. "I've had time to think over the past few days—"

He broke into a smile. Excellent. She'd reached the same conclusion he had. Happiness swelled his chest.

"—and I've decided this needs to stop."

His smile faded. "Eh?"

"Us. You and me and whatever it is we have between us." There was a tremor in her voice. "Bridie's on the mend, and I'll be leaving Ballybeg soon. When Bridie's doctor gives her the all clear, I'm booking my ticket to Australia. The trip won't be as long as I'd planned, obviously, but I intend to spend the last weeks of my sabbatical traveling."

"And after?"

"And after I'll return to Dublin and my real life."

Her real life. The sentence hit him like a kick to the kidneys. He reeled backward and opened his mouth to object. The words never made it from his brain to his vocal chords.

"If you two are finished flirting," Bridie yelled through the car window in a voice loud enough to carry down the street, "I'd like to go home and read a romance."

~

After Bridie left with Gavin, Fiona wandered into the shop in a daze. She felt wretched, but it had to be done. What choice had she had? It wasn't like they had a future together. Unlike the couples in Bridie's romance novels, she and Gavin would not live happily ever after.

Olivia was packing her stuff. "Fee," she said in a low voice, "now Bridie's gone, I have the info you asked for."

A woman entered the shop and waved to them before heading into the back room to browse through the books.

"Well," she whispered in response. "Don't leave me in suspense."

"The file contained copies of both your grandmother's last will and the one she made soon after your dad died. The earlier one divided her estate evenly among you, Bridie, and Bernard. It was witnessed by Aidan's former secretary and a friend of your grandmother's named Marie Taylor. The later will was made roughly two months before she died. It left everything to Bernard and was witnessed by Deirdre and Ann Dunne."

"Pretty much as we'd expected."

"Yeah, but there's one thing that bothers me—" Olivia stiffened as the customer browsing the books walked through the café to the front entrance.

When the door clanged shut, Fiona asked, "What bothers you?"

"According to the first will, the land you would have inherited is the plot on which Bernard is building the new shopping center."

29

On the morning of Christmas Eve, Fiona awoke to the smell of freshly baked mince pies. She lay in her bed for a few minutes before emerging from under her duvet, staring at the ceiling and turning over the thoughts that had been troubling her for days.

Was she imagining something odd about her grandmother's last will? Were her niggling suspicions down to jealousy because Bernard and his family had so much in comparison to her and Bridie?

It wasn't like either one of them was starving. Bridie owned the cottage and the building on Patrick Street. If the Book Mark went belly-up, she had those assets to cushion the blow. Fiona's teaching job paid enough for her to afford the mortgage on a small apartment in Dublin, and she was renting it out for the months she was supposed to be in Australia.

But the suspicions remained. Her grandmother

wouldn't have cut her and Bridie out of the will. It didn't ring true. The most obvious explanation was the least palatable—Bernard had engineered a forgery. Her blood boiled at the notion, rage rising like molten lava. If she could prove he'd done it, she'd make him pay—for Bridie's sake as well as her own.

Thanks to the Internet and a few phone calls, she'd narrowed the search for the mysterious Ann Dunne down to a likely candidate in County Clare. If she wanted to prove the will was a forgery, she'd need to pay her a visit. But that, alas, would have to wait until after the holidays.

Blinking with the sleepiness borne of a restless night, she got up and wandered toward the kitchen.

Bridie was sitting at the kitchen table, flicking through the TV listings in the newspaper. A batch of mince pies was cooling on a wire rack on the kitchen counter.

"Mmm…" Fiona moaned in appreciation and reached out a hand. "Those smell divine. Can I have one for breakfast?"

"Get away with you, missy," replied Bridie, swatting her with the business section. "Of course they're not for breakfast. I've invited a couple of people over for Christmas dinner. I'll serve them with mulled wine as a snack."

"Hey, I'm not complaining. I love both mince pies and mulled wine." Fiona fixed a cup of strong black tea and poured cereal into a bowl. "So who's coming?"

"Harrumph." Her aunt looked decidedly shifty.

Her eyes narrowed in suspicion. "Who did you invite?"

Bridie shoved a poorly wrapped package across the

kitchen table. "Your Philip fella called round about a half hour ago. He left a Christmas present for you."

Fiona regarded it as one would a venomous snake. She opened it gingerly. It contained a playbill and a couple of free tickets to Philip's pantomime. "I'll pass these on to Liam O'Mahony as a thank-you for his help the night of the vandalism. He can take his grandson to the panto."

Across the table, her aunt was still looking nervous. A sneaking suspicion slithered down Fiona's spine. "What does Philip's visit have to do with your Christmas Eve drinks party?"

Her aunt shifted in her chair.

"Bridie, what did you do?"

"It was him, not me." Bridie crossed her arms across her chest in a defensive gesture. "The fecker invited himself for Christmas Dinner. He laid the guilt trip on me. Said his father had turfed him out, that he had to stay in Cork for the panto and would have to spend Christmas all alone."

"You could have said no."

"I did say no, but I was so stunned it took me a minute to react, and he was already halfway down the street."

"Ah, Bridie. The only person whose company I'd enjoy less is Bernard's."

"Come on. Where's your sense of Christmas spirit? Why don't we do the lad a good turn?"

"Oh, no. Don't shove this off on me. This is your fault, and I'm leaving it to you to sort out."

"Sure, it'll be grand," Bridie said with determined cheer. "We'll get him drunk and let him pass out in the living room. We'll feel we've done our bit for mankind, and he'll—"

"Have a hangover?" Fiona cleared the table and packed her bag for work. "You pretend to be an absolute dragon, but at the end of the day, you're a total mush."

"Why don't I invite a few extra people round to act as buffers? I know the Major's not keen on spending Christmas with his daughter's family."

"You do that," she said dryly. "Make sure you get as many as we can feed. I don't care if they're fossilized. Get them to come. With a bit of luck, the golden oldies will scare Philip away."

The peal of the doorbell broke through Bridie's laughter. "I'll get it," Fiona said.

When she opened the front door, a red-faced Olivia and a sheepish-looking Kyle and Ronan stood on the doorstep.

It took her a fraction of a second to size up the situation. "Do you boys have something to say to Bridie about her shop window?"

They exchanged guilty glances. Their sister prodded them in the back. "Yes, they do. Right, lads?"

The boys nodded in unison.

Fiona stood aside. "In that case, you'd better come in."

They trooped into the kitchen with obvious reluctance. Olivia bristled with embarrassment. "I don't fucking believe this, Fee. Of all the stupid things for them to go and do!"

At the sight of her visitors, Bridie raised both bushy eyebrows. "Will I make more tea?"

"No, thanks," Olivia said. "We're not staying long. Kyle and Ronan have something to tell you."

Ronan danced on the balls of his feet. Kyle cleared his throat. "We...well...we sort of..."

"Broke the Book Mark window," Ronan finished.

"And the door," Kyle added and bit his lip.

"Is that so?" Bridie's face was devoid of expression. "Would you boys care to tell me why you trashed my shop?"

"It was an accident," they said in chorus.

"The daft eejits got hold of a bottle of vodka and were out drinking on the night of the storm," their sister said.

"We were drunk." Ronan's cheeks burned as red as his hair. "Not that it's an excuse. Anyway, it was too far to walk home in the floods, so we decided to take shelter. The Book Mark seemed as good a place as any."

"After downing a bottle of vodka between you, I'd imagine breaking into my shop seemed like a logical decision."

"We're really sorry, Miss Byrne. We totally screwed up. When the shop door wouldn't open properly, we busted the window."

"And then the alarm went off and scared the bejaysus out of us," Kyle said. "We scarpered before the cops arrived."

"My parents will pay for the damages." Olivia drew a pen and notebook from her handbag. "Here's my father's phone number. Tally up the costs incurred and let him know what he owes you."

Bridie took the piece of paper and gave a stiff nod.

"What should I say to Garda Glenn? He's in charge of the case."

Olivia paled and stole a glance at Fiona.

"Since he realized he can't pin it on Sharon," Fiona said hurriedly, "Garda Glenn has no suspects. Frankly, I doubt he's devoting a lot of time to finding out who broke into the Book Mark. Why burden him with more paperwork?"

Bridie considered for a moment, then inclined her head. "All right. We'll keep this to ourselves."

"Aw, thanks, Miss Byrne," Kyle said.

"We're really sorry," added his brother.

Bridie held up a palm. "Not so fast, boys. I'm not letting you off the hook that easily. The walls of the café were damaged during the storm. Fiona and Gavin are due to paint them after Christmas. I expect you two to help."

"Yeah, defo," they said. "We can paint."

"And I want you to help me tend my garden for a couple of months come spring. After my operation, I'll have trouble bending for a while. I'll need someone to help me weed and dig my flower beds."

"That sounds more than reasonable," Olivia said. "Right, boys?"

Her brothers nodded in reluctant agreement.

As they trudged out of the cottage, Olivia turned to Fiona. She was flushed with embarrassment and lacked her usual poise. "I can't believe they did this. If they keep up their antics, I swear they'll give me gray hairs."

"It's not your fault. Let's get together after Christmas, okay?"

Her friend nodded. "Sure. Dinner's on me."

"In the meantime, call me if you need to vent."

Olivia enveloped her in a floral-scented hug. "Thanks, Fee. It's so good having you back in Ballybeg."

"I'LL HAVE a pint of the black stuff."

"Coming right up." Gavin grabbed a pint glass from under the bar counter and prepared the Guinness. He did it slowly, letting it sit, then topping it up, then letting it sit a while longer. Most barmen rushed the job these days, but not in Ruairí MacCarthy's pub.

"Here you go." Gavin set the pint in front of the heavyset man and input his order.

He'd been working there for a few weeks now and had developed an easy routine. It wasn't the job he'd dreamed of, true, but the staff were a laugh and the punters mostly decent folk. Plus the opportunity to work on the plans for the pub renovation provided an excellent distraction from his worries. He and Ruairí had finalized the plans, sticking as closely to the original look of the pub back when it first opened in 1927. The first stage of the renovation was due to start in January, right after the Christmas and New Year rush.

"Managing all right, Gav?" Ruairí was polishing glasses and surveying his domain.

"I'm grand."

"You're a shite liar."

"Ah, you know how it is. I should be relieved someone wants to buy the cottage."

"But?"

"But I wish they wanted to buy Clonmore Lodge

instead." The offer had come through the previous evening, ensuring he'd not had a wink of sleep. It was lower than the asking price, but unless a miracle occurred within the next couple of weeks, he'd have no choice but to accept.

Last week, he'd used the money he'd saved from the sale of the BMW and his severance pay to reimburse the Byrnes their share of the wedding costs. He was down to the wire. The money he earned at the pub kept food on the table. His earnings from the renovation job would cover a few mortgage repayments on Clonmore Lodge and keep the bank at bay for a couple more months. After that, he was fucked.

"We'll be run off our feet in the next hour or so. Take a break while you can." For a man of few words and even fewer demonstrative gestures, Ruairí was a shrewd judge of people.

"Right-o," he said.

"And help yourself to some food from the kitchen."

Gavin grabbed a plate from the kitchen and sat down at one of the tables out in the pub. Although the customers were quick to approach him for a chat while he was working, they respected his space when he was on his break. He appreciated the peace. It gave him time to think, and thinking was an activity he'd been doing a lot of these past few days.

He bit into the thick bread of the sandwich and gave an appreciative moan. The cheese, chutney, and ham combo hit the spot. His gaze strayed to the local newspaper lying abandoned on the table next to his. Splashed across the front page was a photograph of Bernard Byrne,

Aidan Gant, and a couple of other men. Gavin reached for it and skimmed the article.

> *Local property developer, Bernard Byrne, introduces the new design director for their soon-to-be constructed shopping center. Declan O'Keeffe said he was "Honored to be approached by Mr. Byrne back in June and delighted to start work on this ambitious project."*

Gavin choked on his cheese. What the actual fuck? Bernard approached O'Keeffe in June? The lying, scheming bastard.

He'd promised Gavin the position as far back as April, yet never got round to formalizing the arrangement. Had he ever intended to sign those papers?

Gavin forced his food down his throat. He knew the answer to that question. Bernard's plan was to dangle a carrot in front of his eager son-in-law-to-be, only to yank it away the moment he returned from his honeymoon. Why should Bernard pay him a higher salary when he was aware Gavin's loyalty to Muireann made him unlikely to quit in favor of a more lucrative position?

"Penny for your thoughts."

Gavin jerked at the sound of Bridie's voice. "You wouldn't want to hear them. Trust me."

She lowered herself onto the stool opposite his, grimacing as she did so.

"Are you okay?" he asked. "Should you be in pain this long after the operation?"

"Ah, I'm grand. The damp weather always makes my

arthritis worse. But I'm not here about my hip. I have a favor to ask of you."

"Fire away."

"I'm after letting that young pup Fiona used to go out with persuade me to invite him round for Christmas dinner. Fiona wants backup, and I've promised to find a few more guests. Unfortunately, most people already have plans. Can I count on you to come to our rescue?"

He laughed. "Consider it done."

"I'm not dragging you away from prior commitments?"

"Ah, no. The O'Mahonys invited me round to theirs, but I said I'd go over for lunch on Stephen's Day instead, right before Fiona and I start clearing the Book Mark."

"Excellent." Bridie heaved herself to her feet. "You can bring your little dog if you like."

"Are you sure? He's not exactly tame."

Bridie leaned heavily on her cane. "Any dog that loathes Deirdre and her rats as much as I do is more than welcome in my home."

30

Christmas Day dawned bitterly cold with a piercing wind.

Fiona helped Bridie prepare the last trimmings for the meal and mount the last of the numerous Christmas decorations.

"Doesn't the place look grand?" Bridie beamed at her handiwork.

"It's—" she struggled to find a tactful phrase, "—festive."

Her aunt preferred tack to taste when it came to Christmas decorations and quantity over quality. The Christmas tree sagged under the weight of china figurines and tinsel. Colorful streamers adorned the ceiling. The crowning glory was the light-up Virgin Mary strategically placed in the hall to scare the crap out of unsuspecting visitors.

"Who did you find to invite for Christmas dinner?" she

asked, sliding a ginormous turkey into the oven. "I need know how many places to set."

"A few people. The Major. Philip. Oh, and Gavin Maguire."

"You invited Gavin?" She jerked with such ferocity that she burned her hand against the side of the oven. "Ouch!"

"Best get your hand under cold water."

Fiona shook her sore hand and held it under the ice-cold stream from the tap. "Why did you invite Gavin?"

"He's a neighbor, isn't he? Besides, despite your ageist comment about not caring if the guests were fossilized, I thought you might appreciate people your own age."

She narrowed her eyes in suspicion. "Is this another one of your matchmaking attempts?"

"Now, haven't I already said you should steer clear of the lad?" Bridie's innocent expression was faker than her latest hair color. "In the romantic sense, that is. Besides, aren't you well able to find a decent man yourself? You've told me so often enough. Not that you've actually found one, mind."

Fiona bit back a laugh. "Thanks for the vote of confidence."

"It's kind of Gavin to offer to give up his Stephen's Day to help you box books, not to mention him helping you paint the shop."

She slathered ointment on her injury. "Guilt is a great motivator. He feels responsible for trusting that drunken eejit in Vegas to remember not to register our marriage."

"Harrumph," Bridie said. "Who's making him feel

guilty? You are, missy. Why didn't you make sure the man wouldn't register the papers?"

Fiona looked up in exasperation. "Because I assumed Gavin had taken care of it."

"In other words, you both messed up, and you're equally to blame for the consequences."

"Bridie—"

"No." Her aunt grabbed wine glasses from the cupboard and set them on the table. "You're an adult, Fiona. You, and you alone, are responsible for sorting out your life. If you don't want that nincompoop Philip here for Christmas dinner, why didn't you turf him out of the Book Mark weeks ago? You clearly *do* want Gavin in your life, so why on earth are you sabotaging your one shot to put things right?"

"It's...complicated."

Her aunt rolled her eyes and threw her arms heavenward. "Life's complicated. Get used to it."

Fiona flicked on the kettle and made another cup of tea. Bridie was exasperating. And the most exasperating part was how right her aunt was. Why hadn't she told Philip to feck off the moment he walked into the Book Mark? She should have made sure Drew Draper shredded the marriage papers that morning in Vegas. As for Gavin, she never should have kissed him in the cave, let alone slept with him. She knew how she felt about him, and she should have known better than to think she could keep their relationship a casual fling.

She sipped her hot tea and stared out at the weak winter sun. Christmas was a difficult time of year for her. The forced cheer and festivities acted as a sharp reminder of the family she'd lost. Clearly, she'd let the stress of the season cloud her judgment.

In a few days, the New Year would begin, bringing with it the chance of a fresh start for all of them. By the end of January, she'd make her belated escape from Ballybeg and head to Australia for the adventure of a lifetime. It was what she'd always dreamed of. So why did the prospect leave her feeling hollow inside?

AT ONE O'CLOCK on Christmas Day, Gavin pressed the doorbell of Bridie's cottage. Wiggly Poo danced at his feet, tail wagging, tongue lolling.

Fiona opened the door. For a moment, he forgot to breathe. She was wearing a knee-length black corduroy skirt and a formfitting green roll-neck pullover and was absolutely gorgeous.

"Come in." She stood to the side to let them pass. He brushed against her on his way in and saw her intake of breath. They stared at one another in awkward silence, neither sure how they should proceed.

Wiggly Poo had no such reservations. He launched himself at Fiona.

"Hey," Gavin said. "Down, boy."

Fiona laughed and bent to pet the little dog, giving him an excellent view of how nicely her skirt accentuated her curves. If only it were just her curves that had such an affect on him. In the days since their talk outside the Book Mark, he'd missed her like crazy.

"As you can see, we failed obedience school," he said. "Or rather, he did. We've to retake the class next month."

"You don't say?" She grinned at him, and his heart skipped a beat. "Come through to the kitchen. The Major's already here."

"Merry Christmas, Gavin," Bridie said. "Will you have a glass of mulled wine?" She was already sloshing a generous amount of the potent red liquid into four mugs.

"Hello, Major," he said, taking a mug from Bridie.

"Fancy one of these scrumptious mince pies?" the Major asked, handing him a tray. "I believe Fiona made them."

Fiona laughed. "Under your granddaughter's strict instructions. I wasn't born with Olivia's knack for pastry, alas."

"Nonsense," the Major said. "You've done splendidly. If the smell wafting from the oven is any indication, your roast turkey will also turn out a treat."

The doorbell rang, and Fiona excused herself to answer it. A minute later, she returned to the kitchen, her posture tense.

"Hello, folks." Philip sloped into the room behind her, standing closer to Fiona than Gavin liked. He'd made zero effort with his outfit—ripped jeans and an ancient pullover. His hair looked as though it had seen neither shampoo nor a brush in the last few days. His gaze roamed over Fiona's body in lewd appreciation. "Nice outfit, FeeFee."

Gavin's free hand balled into a fist.

"Wish I could return the compliment," she said, taking a step away from Philip.

Wiggly Poo growled at the new visitor and bared his teeth.

Philip backed into a chair. "I'm not exactly a dog person."

"Apparently, neither is he." Fiona crossed her arms across her chest. "How come you didn't go home to Dublin for Christmas?"

The guy shrugged. "I'm performing in the matinees over the next couple of days. There's no time to make it to Dublin and back."

"Your family won't come to Cork?"

He flushed. "Actually, we're not on speaking terms at the moment."

"Fiona!" called Bridie. "Can you help me with the turkey? I think it's done."

The guests trooped into the tiny dining room and took their seats. The Major's prediction about the turkey proved accurate. It was delicious, as were the various side dishes.

Gavin was having seconds when Bernard Byrne barged into the house. His face was red, his eyes were bloodshot, and the whiskey fumes were evident to everyone.

"Bernard?" Bridie asked, getting to her feet. "What are you doing here? Why didn't you ring the doorbell?"

Bernard stubbed a sausage finger on the festive tablecloth. "You!" he snarled and lunged at Gavin.

He held Bernard at arm's length, the smaller man going wild from his efforts to get in a punch. Seeing his owner under attack, Wiggly Poo raced to the rescue. He launched himself at Bernard and sank his teeth into his ankle.

"Argh!" Bernard roared "Get that animal off me."

Fiona grabbed a piece of turkey from the table and waved it at Wiggly Poo. "Come on, boy. Look what I've got for you."

Not releasing his grip on Bernard's ankle, Wiggly Poo considered his options. Continue to gnaw the nasty's man's leg, or eat some yummy turkey? He let Bernard go and bounded toward the meat.

"Traitor," Gavin said.

"My foot." Bernard was scarlet with rage. "I'll get gangrene."

"What the feck is wrong with you?" Bridie demanded. "Why did you come barging into my house on Christmas Day?"

Bernard opened his thick lips to speak, panting through the pain. "Muireann's pregnant."

31

"Muireann is pregnant?" The floor shifted under Gavin's feet like a rocking vessel. He swayed before righting himself. "That's not possible."

His words were as much a prayer as a statement. A wave of panic crested in his chest. She couldn't be pregnant. He couldn't be the father. Why the hell did this have to happen now?

Bernard's beady eyes narrowed to slits. "I'll expect you to pay up, you blaggard. I'll bleed you dry, so help me God."

"You're already bleeding me dry," he said wearily. "You and Gant have seen to that. Where's Muireann now?"

"I don't know," the man muttered. "She told us she was pregnant, then took off in her car."

"Probably couldn't take your roaring," snapped Bridie.

Bernard glared at her. "How's a father supposed to

react when his daughter tells him she's pregnant by a someone who can't marry her for another four years?"

"You could have listened to her." Gavin tasted bile but swallowed past it. "Did she actually say I'm the father, or did you make an assumption? Because if I am the father, she must be around five months pregnant. I'm no expert, but she doesn't look over halfway through a pregnancy to me."

"She didn't need to say you were the father. Sure, who else would it be?"

Fiona exchanged a significant glance with Gavin. "Muireann was abroad for weeks. Why couldn't she have gotten pregnant while she was away? Like Gavin said, she certainly doesn't look anywhere near five months pregnant."

Bernard's face went from scarlet to purple. "Are you calling my daughter a slut? That's rich coming from you."

"That's enough." Bridie moved toward her brother. "I won't have anyone slut shamed in my house. Not Fiona and not your daughter. If Muireann slept with someone on holiday, she was free and single and entitled to do so."

Bernard opened his mouth to let out another roar, but Bridie checked him. "I said that's enough. Come on, I'll drive you home. There's no use in fighting with Gavin until we find Muireann and know more about the situation."

Without waiting for him to protest, Bridie dragged her brother out of the cottage.

Silence descended upon the assembled company. Fiona was green with worry. Philip looked smug. The Major's aged eyes were more sunken than usual.

Gavin took a ragged breath. What if he was the one making assumptions? What if Muireann truly was expecting his child? It wasn't as if he knew anything about pregnant women.

Fiona put a hand on his arm. "I'll go next door with you."

"Ah, there's no need," he said, still shocked but rallying. "I'm grand. Stay here with your guests."

"Bollocks. You're far from grand. You're in need of a stiff drink. And frankly, so am I." She grabbed a bottle of vodka from her aunt's drinks cabinet and turned to the remaining dinner guests. "I won't be long. In the meantime, help yourselves to sherry trifle."

"No problem, dear," the Major said. "Take all the time you need. We can let ourselves out if necessary."

Philip wore an insouciant smirk. "If I'd known your family get-togethers were this entertaining, FeeFee, I'd have come down with you to Ballybeg years ago."

Her expression went from rigid to enraged in the space of a millisecond. "By the time I get back, I want you gone, Philip. And don't bloody call me FeeFee."

"Ah, now, I was only having a laugh. You're overreacting."

"If Fiona wants you gone by the time she comes back," said the Major smoothly, "you will be gone. I'll make certain of it."

"And if you need any help getting rid of him, I'm more than willing to assist." Gavin whistled for Wiggly Poo to come. For once, the puppy obeyed. He'd give him a doggy treat when they got home. Fiona looped her arm through his, and they stepped out into the bitter December cold.

Back in his cottage, Wiggly Poo made a dash for his basket and was snoring within seconds.

Gavin slid into a kitchen chair and stared at his hands.

"You okay?" Fiona sloshed vodka into shot glasses and placed one before him. "You've gone so white you're rivaling me for the crown of palest person in Ballybeg."

He could barely get the words out, had to clear his throat a couple of times. "It can't be my baby."

"You sure about that?" Her hands shook around her glass, but her voice was steady.

"I won't know until I speak to Muireann, but we haven't had sex since a couple of weeks before our non-wedding." He downed his shot in one, relishing the burn of the harsh liquor as it snaked its way to his stomach.

Fiona clasped her trembling hands. A smorgasbord of emotions flitted across her face: shock, disbelief, hurt. "Did you know this was a possibility before we slept together? Luca made that comment about Muireann and pregnancy when you guys came by the Book Mark. I didn't place much emphasis on it at the time."

"No, of course I didn't know she was pregnant. I'd never have let things get this far with you if I'd had any suspicion she might be carrying my baby. We weren't planning on trying for a family for a while after the wedding—or at least I wasn't."

"But?" Her green eyes were filled with tears. "Luca's comment wasn't a coincidence, was it?"

"Not exactly. The morning of the wedding, Muireann mentioned her period was late. I was less than thrilled, to be honest, but we'd planned to have kids eventually, and I know I would have gotten used to the idea."

Fury flashed across Fiona's face. "So you did know she might be expecting."

"No. Please hear me out. The day I collected my stuff from Clonmore Lodge—the day she trashed my stuff—she told me I didn't need to worry because she wasn't pregnant after all."

"And you believed her?"

"Well, yeah. I had no reason to doubt her word."

Fiona finished her shot and then refilled their glasses. "What a mess."

"Yeah. The understatement of the decade." He stood and began to pace his small kitchen. "My relationship with Muireann is over, and there's no going back. But if I did get her pregnant, I can't abandon my child. I won't be like my father."

"Your father?" She looked up. "You've never talked about him to me before."

He stared out the kitchen window at the starry sky. "I don't mention him because I try to forget he ever existed. Long story short, he took off when my mother was eight months pregnant. By all accounts, he was a loser. Given my mother's subsequent taste in boyfriends, I'm not surprised. We were probably better off without him in our lives, but it didn't feel like that when I was growing up."

"You're a good man, Gavin. If that baby is yours, I'm sure you'll make a great dad." She stood, scraping her chair over the terracotta-tiled floor. "I'd better get back to Bridie's. Will you be okay on your own?"

No, he thought, *please stay*. "Sure. Get back to your guests. Any problem with Philip, let me know."

Fiona bent to scratch Wiggly Poo's sleeping head. "You're a good doggie for biting Bernard. I'll be sure to get you a nice, juicy bone next time I'm at the butcher's."

"Two o'clock suit you for tomorrow?"

Her head jerked up in surprise. "Surely you don't still want to help out with painting the Book Mark? Kyle and Ronan can help me pack up the books. They're due to help paint anyway. You should concentrate on tracking down Muireann."

"I can do both. I made a promise to Bridie, and I intend to keep it." He fumbled in his trouser pockets for his phone. "I'm going to try calling Muireann now."

"All right," Fiona said. "But if you need to meet her tomorrow afternoon, no worries."

"Thanks, Fiona." He took her hands in his and planted a kiss on her springy curls. "I'm sorry. For everything."

~

"Hmm…" Bridie said, standing in the doorway of Fiona's small room, "you're very dolled up for an afternoon hauling boxes."

Fiona jumped at her aunt's voice. She'd been staring critically at her reflection in the mirror, searching for flaws. "I'm only trying on a few outfits. Nothing wrong with that, is there?"

She pulled off the shirt she'd been trying on and threw it on the bed. This was stupid. She was stupid. She and Gavin might be destined to remain man and wife for the next four years, but he'd never truly been hers, nor would he ever be. Even if Muireann's unborn baby wasn't his, he'd never told her he loved her. The only one of them foolish enough to lose their heart was she.

"Ah, love." Her aunt stepped into the room and closed the door. "Don't cry."

She rubbed her eyes and blinked. "I'm not crying. My contacts are acting up."

"And I suppose your sinuses are also acting up? Come on," Bridie said coaxingly. "Sit down on the bed beside me."

Her face crumpled, and the tears began to flow. She sank down onto the saggy mattress beside her aunt, wracked with sobs.

Bridie put her arm around her shoulders. "There, pet. A good cry will do you the power of good."

She leaned into her aunt's sturdy form and surrendered to her emotions. Bridie let her get it out of her system, then handed her a fresh tissue to blow her nose.

"I shouldn't be this upset," she said between honks. "It's my own stupid fault for letting myself fall for him again. I should have learned my lesson the last time."

Bridie squeezed her hand. "Take it from one who knows—chances at true love are few and far between in this life. Don't give up on Gavin yet."

She gave a bitter laugh. "Did you not hear what Bernard said? Muireann's pregnant. If she's a few months pregnant, the baby might very well be Gavin's."

"Let's break this down into what we do know, rather than what we don't. According to Bernard, Muireann announced she was pregnant over Christmas dinner. They had an argument, and she stormed out. Bernard, being the eejit that he is, automatically assumed Gavin had to be the father and hared off to confront him."

"Muireann's been back in Ballybeg for weeks," Fiona mused. "We know she saw Gavin at the Christmas Bazaar, and I'm sure she's had plenty of opportunities since then to hunt him down and tell him she was pregnant. Why didn't she?"

"Exactly." Bridie drew the word out for maximum emphasis. "Muireann's not the type to suffer in silence. If she thought there was any possibility of Gavin being the father of that child, she'd have gone straight to Aidan Gant and started financial negotiations for the baby's upkeep."

Her aunt had a point. She recalled her cousin's gaunt appearance and concave stomach that morning outside the Book Mark, not to mention her peaky appearance at the Christmas Bazaar. Didn't some women end up losing weight during pregnancy due to extreme morning sickness? "There's no point speculating," she said aloud. "Until Muireann reappears, we won't know when her baby is due. I agree, though, that it's totally out of character for her not to tell Gavin if she thought he was the father."

"Fiona, apart from this business with Gavin, how are you coping being back in Ballybeg? I realize it's hard for you being here. I'd hoped you might find it cathartic, but perhaps I was way off the mark."

She hesitated for a moment before replying, gathering her thoughts. "To be honest, it's been better than I expected—drama notwithstanding. It's certainly not how I'd planned to spend my sabbatical, but I'm enjoying spending time with you and rekindling my friendship with Olivia. We've kept in touch over the years, but we don't see one another that often. When I get back to Dublin, I intend to change that."

"Having you in Ballybeg is good for Olivia." Bridie's brow furrowed. "I worry about the girl. Before you came back, I never saw her out and about socializing with people her own age."

"She's cagey about her relationship with Gant. I don't get the impression she's happy in her marriage but she doesn't go into details. All I can do is be there for her and hope she'll confide in me if she needs to."

"That's what friends are for."

"Listen, Bridie, would it be okay if I went away for a couple of days after we finish painting? We'll need to wait a couple of days before opening the shop to give the paint fumes time to dissipate. I could ask The Major and Mrs. Cotter if they'd look in on you."

"Of course, love." Her aunt squeezed her hand. "I'm in far better shape than I was when I first got out of the nursing home. I might see if Nora Fitzgerald would be willing to stay over. She's always looking for an excuse to escape that useless lout she married."

"You're sure? If so, that would be fantastic."

"Are you off anywhere nice?"

Telling Bridie the whole story about tracking down Ann Dunne was tempting, but she'd rather not say anything until she knew she'd found the right person. "Just a couple of days in Clare. I know some people there."

"Clare's a lovely part of the country," her aunt said. "You'll have fun."

Fiona stood and rooted through her wardrobe until

she located an old black sweatshirt bearing the faded logo of a rock band she'd once liked. She slipped it on and began gathering her stuff for the day.

"Are you sure you want to do this today?" Bridie asked. "Gavin would understand if you canceled."

No, she definitely did not want to see him today. She wanted to curl up under her duvet and hide from the world. She took a deep breath. "I'll be fine."

Bridie gave her a hug. "You're a good girl. It'll all work out for the best. You'll see. If he looked at me the way he does you, I'd be sorely tempted to turn into one of those jaguars."

For a moment, Fiona was flummoxed. Then enlightenment dawned. "I think you mean a cougar, Bridie," she said with a smile.

"Yeah, that's the term. One of them big cats. Sort of like that Samantha in *Sex and the City*. Always running after hot young men, she was. Nabbed them, too."

Fiona was temporarily bereft of speech. "You've seen Sex and the City?"

Her aunt raised an eyebrow. "Hasn't everyone? Nora Fitzgerald has the DVDs. We used to watch them after bingo on Friday nights." She looked wistful. "Pity they don't make them anymore."

Fiona placed a light kiss on her aunt's plump cheek. Bridie smelled of face powder and Estee Lauder's Youth-Dew. "Do you have everything you need before I leave?"

"Sure, go on, girl. If I need anything, I can give Nora Fitzgerald a bell. The number of times I've looked after her blasted cat, I'd say she owes me one."

"In that case, I'll be off. See you later." Fiona stepped outside into the roaring wind.

32

Gavin was waiting for her on the doorstep of the bookshop. God, he was gorgeous, even with dark bags under his eyes and stubble on his jaw. He leaped to his feet when he saw her. "Hey, Fiona."

His smile was tinged with regret. She itched to kiss it away.

"Gavin." They stared at one another for a beat before she opened the door to the Book Mark. "Do you fancy a cuppa before we get started?" She slung her bag on the counter. "It'll be our last opportunity to use the kitchen until the painting is finished." Not to mention their last opportunity to be alone together. Tomorrow, Kyle and Ronan would be underfoot.

Gavin hesitated for a fraction of a second, then relented. "Okay. Why not?"

She put on the coffee machine and prepared Gavin's usual extra strong espresso. For herself, she opted for a cappuccino. "I'm afraid we have no fresh-baked goods today. I do, however, have some leftovers from Christmas." She extracted an airtight container from her carrier bag. "Do you fancy a mince pie?"

"Uh, sure." He'd chosen his favorite seat and was drumming his fingers on the table. She'd noticed he did that when he was nervous. She fiddled with her lip ring and added milk and sugar to the tray.

After placing the tray on the table, she slid into the seat across from him. "How are the O'Mahony's? You went there for your Stephen's Day lunch, right?"

"Yeah. Turkey casserole." He reached for his coffee cup. "Liam and Nuala are fine, but Jonas isn't doing too well. Luca's mother left them just before Christmas and didn't leave a forwarding address."

"Crap. Poor little Luca. How's Jonas coping?"

Gavin grimaced. "Single fatherhood doesn't suit him. Luca's autism diagnosis suits him even less. There's talk of him moving back to Ballybeg with Luca."

"Where would they live?"

"With Liam and Nuala initially."

"Wow." Fiona shook her curls. "Their predicament certainly puts our crazy Christmas into perspective."

"I'll say."

He stared at her. She stared at him. He cleared his throat. She cleared hers.

"This is ridiculous, Gavin. To use the words people dread to hear, we need to talk about us."

His gaze latched on to hers. "I know."

Clasping her hands, she turned the silver rings on her

fingers round and round. "We shouldn't have let…whatever it was between us…develop. It was a mistake."

A muscle tensed in his cheek. "I don't agree."

"You don't?" Her hands froze mid-twirl, and she blinked in confusion. "Why not?"

He flexed his jaw and leaned back in his chair. "The time we spent together opened my eyes, Fiona. You made me realize that my outlook on life was skewed. I was so intent on not repeating the mistakes my mother made that I mistook a passionless relationship for one that was stable and secure."

She heard her own intake of breath. "You never loved Muireann?"

He shook his head. "No, I did love her. Part of me still does. I even thought I was *in* love with her, and maybe I was for a time. All I know is that the emotion I felt for her was tepid in comparison to what I feel for you."

Her heart pounded against her ribs. How did she react to that statement? Ask him if he was *in* love with *her*? She took a deep breath and focused on the vital question. "Will you go back to her if she is pregnant with your child?"

"If she'll take me, yes." His gaze dropped to his coffee cup. "I can't be like my father, Fiona. I won't abandon my child, and I don't want to be a part-time dad. That's the dilemma Jonas is facing at the moment, and I'm pretty sure that's why he and Susanne haven't made a clean break."

"Will you tell her about us?" she asked, her voice a whisper.

"Living in a town this small, I'm sure she's heard

rumors already. But yeah, I'll be honest with her. I'm not going to lie and say nothing happened between us."

The silence stretched, taut with tension and unspoken words.

She reached for her coffee spoon, turned it over in her hands, and then replaced it on her saucer. "I take it you haven't spoken to Muireann yet?"

He pushed an uneaten mince pie around his plate. "I've tried. Her phone is switched off."

"Does anyone know where she is?"

"I called everyone I could think of. I finally got Brona to say Muireann was in Clare."

"Clare?" she asked in surprise. "What's she doing there?"

"Thinking, apparently." Like the sweet treat, his espresso lay untouched before him. "Brona said she'd gone to a little bed and breakfast in Doolin for a couple of days."

"Muireann needs to pick better friends," Fiona said. "I can't imagine any of my friends betraying a confidence."

"Yeah, well. You know Brona. She's as discreet as a flashing neon sign." Gavin shoved his plate away. "I'm planning to drive to Clare the day after tomorrow, once we've got this place painted. I want to talk to her in person."

"Wait a sec," Fiona said slowly, "I'm planning to go to Clare in a couple of days, too. If I recall correctly, Lisdoonvarna isn't far from Doolin."

"You are?" He frowned. "Business or pleasure?"

"Neither." She pulled a face. "I'm looking for a woman

who might have helped my uncle forge my grandmother's last will."

"Hmm," Gavin said, his expression neutral.

She laughed. "You don't sound surprised. Do you know anything about it?"

"No and no. But I wouldn't put anything past Bernard." He stood. "Let's get started, eh? The sooner we get cracking, the sooner we can go home."

And away from one another was the thought left unspoken. Perhaps she was being paranoid.

They moved into the book room and assessed their strategy.

"Wow," Gavin said, looking around. "I knew there were a few books in here, but the prospect of boxing them all puts it in perspective."

"Yep," she agreed. "We'll be kept busy for a few hours."

"Where should I start?" Gavin asked.

Damn the man. Why did he have to look so appealing when she was no longer allowed to touch him? "Why don't you start with the crime fiction section?" she said. "And I'll start over here with the children's books."

"Sounds good. You want me to keep the books in alphabetical order?"

"As far as possible, yes. It will make putting them back on the shelves a thousand times easier."

She cranked up the music and they got to work. The music was loud and heavy—perfect for avoiding conversation.

They worked fast. Each box they filled brought them closer to one another. His presence was a constant reminder of what they'd shared over the last couple of months. He hummed to music, off-tune. The temptation to pull off his sweater and feel the muscles beneath was overwhelming, and the subtle scent of his aftershave teased her nose and reminded her of waking up next to him after a night of hot sex.

Within a couple of hours, they'd amassed a neat pile of boxes in the middle of the room, and Fiona was a quivering mess. When she reached for a book, her hand accidentally brushed against his and their eyes met. Her skin burned from the sexual tension, and her pulse went into overdrive.

Time stood still.

He reached for her and cupped her chin. His sky-blue eyes were warm with lust and soft with tenderness. Her gaze dropped to his mouth. She felt as much as saw his lips move toward hers.

No...this is madness.

She stumbled backward. "Gavin, I—"

He blinked, shell-shocked. "I'm sorry. I shouldn't have done that."

"No, I'm sorry. I shouldn't have responded."

They were silent for a moment, then started to laugh.

"Constantly apologizing," he said. "How very Irish of us."

"True." She shifted her weight from one foot to the other.

Gavin swayed on the balls of his feet. "Listen, Fiona. If you want a lift to Clare, I'm leaving at eight o'clock on Monday morning."

~

GAVIN SHIFTED gears as they left the outskirts of Ballybeg behind them. The morning was cool and crisp, and there hadn't been a drop of rain so far.

Out of the corner of his eye, he watched Fiona in the passenger seat of the SUV. She oozed tension, coiled tighter than a spring.

In stark contrast, Wiggly Poo—snoozing on the backseat in his travel basket—was the picture of tranquility. The picture was deceptive. Last night, he'd savaged Gavin's best running shoes.

"Any requests for music?" he asked, noticing the faint stress lines on Fiona's pale forehead.

"What?" She turned to him, her emerald green eyes startled. "Oh, music. Play whatever you feel like listening to."

He switched to a punk rock playlist.

The drive to County Clare wouldn't take long. Three hours, tops. And if the traffic stayed as quiet as it had been thus far, they'd make it in less.

The signs for various towns flashed past. Bandon, Cork City, Blarney.

"You don't want to stop off and kiss the Blarney Stone, do you?" he teased.

"Hell, no," Fiona said, horrified. "That thing's probably riddled with germs. Besides, it's not even a real legend. I suspect the owners made it up to attract tourists."

Gavin laughed. "And which of our many Celtic legends and superstitions do you believe?"

She blushed and then bristled defensively. "I believe in fairy trees."

"Seriously? Have you ever left offerings?"

She glared at him. "I studied History and Celtic Folklore in university. Did you know that?"

"I knew you were a history teacher. I didn't know you'd also studied folklore." He smiled at her. "That's cool. I know next to nothing about stuff like that."

"Yeah. My dad was an amateur expert in Celtic mythology and folklore, and I inherited his interest. I even toyed with the idea of staying on at university and becoming an academic, but jobs are scarce in academia and rarer still in such a specialized area."

"Speaking of Celtic myths," he said, "did you know Bernard and Aidan Gant want to raze a fairy tree to build their shopping center?"

"I heard about that." Her stress lines deepened. "No good will come of it. And from what I can tell, there's no reason they can't shift the location of the supermarket a half a kilometer farther down the road."

"No, there's not, but Bernard's a stubborn bastard. A local activist group sealed the tree's fate the moment they sent him a letter. Once he received that, he was determined not to budge. Look, I don't know that I buy into the myths, but enough people do that I think their beliefs ought to be respected. Besides, many of them are the very locals Bernard's expecting to shop at the center. From a structural point of view, moving the building a bit farther down the road would make absolutely no difference."

"Like you said, Bernard's stubborn." Fiona shook her head. "He'd take an axe to the tree himself if no one else were willing to."

They lapsed into silence, content to listen to music and retreat into their thoughts. The unsettled feeling in

Gavin's stomach grew worse with every kilometer that brought them nearer to Doolin. The idea of not being with Fiona anymore was tearing him apart. If he wasn't the father of Muireann's baby, he'd tell Fiona how he felt about her. Life was too transient to screw up the best thing that had ever happened to him. She made him laugh, she made him smile, she made him *feel*.

"We're making good time," she said, indicating the sat nav. "Not much traffic today."

More town signs flashed by: Mallow, Charleville, Bunratty. An uncomfortable thought settled in Gavin's brain. In all the years he'd spent studying and working his arse off for Bernard Byrne, he'd enjoyed a few foreign holidays that were the status symbol of the New Ireland. But how much had he seen of his own country? He'd joked with Fiona about the Blarney Stone. Had he ever seen it? And what about Bunratty Castle, another famous Irish tourist attraction?

"Have you ever been to the Burren?" he asked, referring to Ireland's world-famous karst landscape and home to many native flowers and ancient tombs.

"I went once on a school trip," she said. "Doolin's in the heart of the Burren, right?"

"I think so. Sorry for rambling. I was thinking about all the famous foreign places I've traveled to over the years, yet I've seen very little of my own country."

She smiled. "Isn't that always the way? Here I am planning a world trip, but I haven't seen a fraction of the sites tourists flock to Ireland to visit."

They bypassed the city of Limerick and wound their

way up the rugged west coast until they reached Doolin, a small fishing village near the Cliffs of Moher.

"Are those the Aran Islands?" Fiona asked, pointing to a faint craggy mass far out to sea.

"I believe so," he said. "Doolin operates a ferry service out to the islands during the summer months."

"Another famous Irish place I've never visited."

He smiled at her. "Maybe we'll come back in the summer and go out to visit the islands."

*Or maybe he'd be greeting his first child...*the sharp reminder made his stomach churn.

Past a cheerily painted pub, Gavin pulled into the car park of the small bed and breakfast they'd booked for the night. "Where did you say this Ann Dunne lives?"

"Lisdoonvarna."

He checked the map on his sat nav display. "Not far from here, then."

"No."

They sat in the car, the engine still running.

"And Muireann is also staying in Doolin?" she asked.

"Yeah. Her bed and breakfast is down near the harbor."

"How are we going to do this? Divide and conquer?"

"Sounds good to me," he said. "You take the SUV to Lisdoonvarna, and I'll visit Muireann by foot."

She got out of the car while he was unloading their overnight bags from the boot. She reached up and kissed his cheek. "Whatever happens in the future, I can't regret the time we spent together over the past couple of months. If I feel guilty about anything, it's that I don't feel guilty enough."

He reached for her and pulled her to his chest. "I feel

the same," he said, smelling the soft scent of her shampoo. "No regrets."

33

Ann Dunne lived several kilometers outside the spa town of Lisdoonvarna in a large detached property set on a respectable plot of land.

Fiona parked across the road. Her fingers were tingly and ice cold—a sure sign she was anxious. Was she making a massive mistake? After all, she hadn't a clue what she was going to say to the woman. Should she blurt it all out and hope for the best? Or take a more subtle approach? Even if she persuaded Ann to confess to wrongdoing, what would she do with the information? Go to the police?

Dragging oxygen into her lungs, she climbed out of the car. At the front gate, she pressed the buzzer. There was no response.

She let a couple of minutes elapse, pacing back on forth in a nervous jig. Then she pressed the buzzer for a second time.

A static voice came through the intercom. "Yes?"

"Ms. Dunne? My name's Fiona Byrne. I'd like to speak to you."

"Who?"

"Fiona Byrne. Bernard Byrne's niece."

There was a pause, then more static crackle from the intercom. "I'm not feeling too well today. Can't this wait?"

"No," Fiona said. "It can't wait. If you recognize my name, you must have a fair idea why I'm here. What's it to be, Ann? A quiet chat between the two of us, or would you prefer I come back with the police?"

After a fraction of a second, the buzzer sounded, and she pushed open the wrought iron gate.

She exhaled in a gust. She was bluffing, of course. Without concrete evidence, the police would laugh her out of the station. But with a bit of luck and a lot of bravado, perhaps she could persuade the woman to incriminate herself.

Ann Dunne was waiting on the doorstep of her spacious bungalow. After weeks of picturing a fairytale witch, it was a shock to find herself faced with a tiny, bird-like woman with silver-gray hair and faded blue eyes. Despite her expensive perfume, the unmistakable odor of illness hung about her like a shroud.

"My heart," Ann said, reading Fiona's expression. "You'd better come in out of the cold."

She wavered on the doorstep before following the woman into the house.

The bungalow was a relatively new build with large rooms and floor-to-ceiling windows. The decor was tasteful—soft pastel colors and carefully chosen antique furniture. It was what Bernard and Deirdre's house might have looked like if either of them had taste.

Ann led her into the living room and motioned for her to take a seat in the bay window. Fiona paused by the fireplace to admire a ceramic bowl fashioned after a seashell.

"My son is an artist," Ann said. "He does some ceramics, but oil paintings are his passion. These are all his." She pointed to the striking oil paintings of Irish landscapes that adorned the walls. Bold brushwork and subtly blended colors brought the familiar settings to life in a new and vibrant way.

"He's talented," Fiona said honestly.

"But I'm guessing you didn't come here to talk about Damian's artwork." Ann had a shrewd glint in her eye.

"No," she said. "I did not."

Ann indicated a glass coffee table on which a tea tray lay. "I'd just made a pot of tea when you rang the buzzer. Would you care to join me?"

"Um..." Fiona blinked. This was *not* going the way she'd expected. "If it's not too much trouble."

"Not at all." The older woman fetched a second cup and saucer. When she'd poured the tea into the delicate porcelain, she handed one to Fiona. "I suppose you're here about your grandmother's will."

Fiona raised an eyebrow. "You don't beat about the bush."

"Nor did you," Ann said with a small smile. "You threatened to sic the police on me."

Fiona placed her teacup on the glass table. "If we're being direct, I'll get straight to the point. Did you witness my grandmother's last will?"

"You're asking the wrong question, Fiona. You should ask if I saw your grandmother write and sign her own will."

"Well, did you?"

Ann took a sip of Earl Grey and considered Fiona over the rim of her cup. "No, I did not. But I did sign a blank piece of paper for your uncle."

"You're admitting it?" Her voice rose a notch. "Just like that?"

Ann shrugged. "Unless a miracle occurs, I'm dying. Bernard Byrne can't hurt me or my son anymore. What does it matter if I tell you the truth?"

"Okay, let's back up here for a sec." Fiona leaned forward in her seat. "I was expecting you to deny everything and chuck me out on my arse. Why did you sign that piece of paper in the first place?"

"For reasons I won't bore you with, I needed the money. Bernard offered me a once-in-a-lifetime payout I couldn't afford to refuse."

Fiona glared at her. "Did it mean nothing to you that you were cheating my aunt and me out of our rightful inheritance?"

"I only learned of that part later. I knew Bernard was up to something with his mother's will, but I didn't know what."

Oh, no, thought Fiona. She wasn't wiggling out of it *that* easily. "What about the other elderly patients you're alleged to have cheated?"

"Rubbish." Ann's face darkened. "I was a good nurse, and I get on well with old folk. Some of the other staff at the places I worked resented my easy rapport with the patients. Yes, a few of them gave me small gifts, but none were worth much. The most I ever received was a small bequest in a patient's will that covered the cost of a summer holiday for me and my son."

"And yet you weren't averse to committing a crime in return for a large payment?"

Ann's mouth hardened. "As I said, I needed the money."

"For what? To buy this fancy house? I wouldn't define a house like this as a need."

"No. My son bought the house for me a couple of years ago. The money Bernard gave me is long gone. I used it to deal with a family crisis. I'm not proud of my part in robbing you and your aunt of what was rightfully yours, but I'd do it again if it meant achieving the same outcome."

"And you're not willing to divulge what you used the money for?"

Ann shook her head. "It's private and not relevant to your situation."

Fiona glowered at her. She couldn't work out if the woman was deliberately trying to provoke her, or if she was on the level. Either way, she wasn't leaving until she had a signed confession. "Where is this going, Ann? I'm assuming your family crisis is no longer an issue."

The older woman blanched. "No, thank goodness."

"In that case, would you be willing to go on the record?"

"Sign a police statement?" She shook her head. "I don't mind telling you the truth in person, but I'm not prepared to do anything that could sully my son's reputation."

"A verbal confession is no good to me. I need leverage I can use against my uncle."

"I understand that. Bernard's threats don't concern me anymore, but I have no intention of getting a police record."

Fiona bit her lip in frustration. She hadn't come this close to nailing her uncle only to retreat at the first hurdle. "Look, can't we come to some arrangement? If you sign a sworn statement witnessed by your solicitor, I'll promise not to press charges against you for your part in defrauding us of our inheritance."

The older woman's mouth quirked. "I'm to accept your word on the matter? No, if you want me to put anything in writing, I expect you to do the same."

"Fair enough. When are we going to do this? I'm only in the area for a couple of days."

Ann's smile was wan. "To use the hackneyed phrase, there's no time like the present. If you give me a lift, my solicitor's practice is in Lisdoonvarna. Let me give her a call to see if she can squeeze us in today."

GAVIN HAD no problems finding the right bed and breakfast in Doolin, and even less trouble persuading the chatty landlady to give him Muireann's room number and to look after Wiggly Poo for a few minutes. It was just as well he wasn't one of the many serial killers or sexual deviants who populated Jonas's murder mysteries.

Her room was upstairs along a narrow corridor. He

paused in front of door number four and knocked. "Muireann?"

Rustled movement came from within, and then the door opened a crack. Her face was puffy from crying, and her hair hung lank around her thin shoulders. "Did Brona tell you where I was?"

The sight of her looking so wretched cut him to the quick. "Yeah. And your dad paid me a visit. I wanted to see how you were."

Her laugh was hollow. "You mean you wanted to see how pregnant I am."

"That, too." He glanced around the hallway. "Can I come in for a few minutes?"

She shrugged but opened the door fully. As she stood aside, her dressing gown gaped at the neck revealing her bony clavicle.

"Jaysus, Muireann. You look awful. Do you need to see a doctor?"

His ex pulled her dressing gown closed. "King of the compliments, aren't you? For your information, I've already seen a doctor. I have nothing more sinister than a combination of stress and morning sickness."

"I can't help you with the morning sickness, but if I can do anything to alleviate the stress, tell me."

"Bar inventing a time machine and erasing your marriage to Fiona, there's nothing you can do to help," she said with a bitter laugh. "If you can find space to sit down, do. Let's get this little chat over with."

Her room was clean and cozy and absolutely crammed with furniture. Muireann's clothes were strewn in a haphazard fashion across the floor. She hadn't bothered to unpack her suitcase.

Gavin cleared toiletries off a chair. "What's going on?" He watched her tired face and tried to read her emotions.

She sat on the edge of the bed and twirled a lank strand of hair around her index finger. "Let me sum it up for you, Gavin, and you can be on your way. You're not the father."

His shoulders sagged, and he exhaled the breath he hadn't realized he was holding.

"You needn't look *quite* so relieved," she said dryly. "Besides, you must have known you couldn't have gotten me pregnant. What did my father tell you to have you haring up to Clare?"

"Not much. He was too busy swinging his fists."

This time, her laugh was genuine. "That sounds about right. For what it's worth, I'm sorry. He turfed me out before I had the chance to tell him you weren't the father."

"He said you stormed out."

She shook her head. "Typical. And my mother's reaction was equally characteristic. She sat stock-still with Mitzi and Bitzi on her lap and said absolutely nothing."

His jaw tightened. "If I could retrospectively give them a mental slap, I would. They're clueless."

"I don't know why I expected better from them. All they're concerned about is the potential scandal."

"In this day and age? It'll be a two-day wonder, and then no one will give a damn." He leaned forward in his seat. "If I'm not the father, may I ask who is?"

She fingered a cigarette, then tossed the pack into the

wastepaper basket. "A man I met in Brisbane. It was just a fling."

"What are you going to do?"

"That's what I came up here to decide. All I know is that I'm keeping the baby. How I'll support us and where we'll live is an open question."

"Is it helping?" he asked. "The time to think?"

She shrugged. "Ask me in a few days. It's definitely easier being away from Ballybeg. There's no one to hassle me here and no one to judge me."

"Whatever happens, whatever you decide," he said, "I'll always be your friend. I want you to know that."

"I'm not ready to be your friend yet, Gavin. I'll get there, eventually, but not today."

"Fair enough. You have my number if you want to talk."

She gave a tight nod. "Despite being a total eejit, you're a good man at heart. I wish things could have turned out differently. For what it's worth, I'm sorry I wrecked your stuff."

"Forget about it," he said and meant it. "Water under the bridge."

"My time away from Ireland and Ballybeg showed me my life in a new light. I realized that while I was mad as hell with you for humiliating me, I didn't actually *miss* you in the way I'd expect to."

Gavin bit the inside of his cheek. "I deeply regret the way I humiliated you on our wedding day. You deserved better from me."

"I blame my father for that," she said. "If he hadn't

started bellowing in the vestry, we might have kept the specifics quiet."

"Would that have made any difference to the outcome?"

"Probably not." She drummed her fingertips on the bedside table, then stood and extended her hand. "Thanks for checking up on me, but I'd like you to leave now."

He swallowed and nodded. "Okay, Muireann." He stepped forward and gave her a hug. At first, she was rigid in his embrace, but then relented. He kissed her forehead and drew back. "Take care of yourself."

She nodded and hugged her arms around her body. "Good-bye, Gavin."

34

When Fiona got back from visiting Ann Dunne, Gavin and Wiggly Poo were waiting outside their B&B, the former desperately trying to control the antics of the latter. That dog was so damn cute. She wasn't much of a dog person, but the curly-haired pup had grown on her—as had his master.

Tugging the puppy away from the cat he'd found to terrorize, Gavin strolled over to the car window. His gait was confident and he exuded positivity. Obviously, his talk with Muireann had gone well.

She rolled down her window, and he leaned in. "Want to go for a walk?" he asked.

He was close enough to kiss. She stared at his soft pink lips. "Where do you want to go?"

Flipping his phone open, he checked the map app. "We could head out to O'Brien's Tower on the Cliffs of Moher. According to the map, it's only a few minutes' drive."

"Yeah, okay. Hop in."

They used the short drive to the cliffs to catch up on their respective afternoons.

"Apart from your relief at not being the father of her baby, how do you feel about the way you left things with Muireann?"

His brow creased in thought. "I don't know. Hollow? I mean, a few months ago, we were planning on getting married. Now we don't even miss each other, and we're not sure there's so much as a friendship to salvage. Were we going through the motions for all those years?"

"Sometimes you need to see things in a different light to truly see them, you know?"

"Yeah, I guess you're right," he said. "I worry about how she'll manage as a single parent. Up until this point, she's led a pampered life."

"She's always been a baby person, though. Way more than me—if I have a biological clock, it's far from ticking. I'm thinking it'll do her good to have independence from her parents."

The road wound around the cliffs, each bend bringing a view more spectacular than the last. Millennia of erosion had given the Cliffs of Moher their stark drops and jagged shape. The Atlantic crashed and foamed at their base, its deep blue-green water stretching all the way from the cliffs to the American continent. "The view is breathtaking," she said. "When I get back from Australia, I'm taking a vow to visit at least one Irish place of note per year."

"I know what you mean. Seems a shame to miss what's on our own doorstep, so to speak." He leaned back and gave Wiggly Poo a scratch through the bars of his carrier. "How do you feel about getting a signed confession out of Ann Dunne?"

"Stunned, to be honest. I hadn't expected her to capitulate so easily. Makes me wary of her, if that makes sense."

"What's her connection to Bernard? Merely a random nurse he happened to meet at his mother's nursing home?"

"Or one of his many mistresses?" she finished for him with a smile. "Yeah, I've heard the rumors of his extramarital adventures. As for whether or not Ann was one of them, I haven't a clue. She indicated she was a single parent. No idea who the father of her child might be. She might have had an affair with my uncle, but she's too shrewd not to have gotten a regular monthly payment out of him if there was any chance her son was his."

O'Brien's Tower grew from a dot in the distance to an imposing sight. Fiona found a parking space at the side of the road, and they got out.

As it was low season, the Cliffs of Moher had the barest straggle of visitors, and there was no queue for the tower. From the top turrets, they could see far out over the Atlantic. Wiggly Poo was indifferent to the view and settled down at Gavin's feet for a scratch.

She shivered in the bitter wind, and he slipped his arm around her shoulders. Their eyes met, and she forgot to breathe. "Just making sure you're warm," he said with feigned innocence.

"Yeah, right, Maguire." Her mind told her to step away, to leave this at the friendly-banter stage, but her heart—

not to mention other parts of her anatomy—was rooted to the spot.

They watched the sun set over the cliffs in a brilliant blaze of reds and oranges and yellows. "It's beautiful here," she said, staring out over the sea. "It's a moment of perfection you wish you could bottle and keep forever."

"Yeah," he said softly. "And maybe you can. Keep it forever, I mean."

Her head jerked up and collided with his nose. "Oh, sorry."

They stepped apart—him smiling, her flustered.

"I'm..." She sought for a word that would stem the rising tide of panic. "Hungry."

He blinked.

Feck. What a way to react to his romantic gesture. *Okay, deep breaths.*

"Why don't we go out for fish and chips in Doolin?" he asked. "Our landlady gave me a recommendation for a place by the harbor."

Her stomach rumbled, making them both laugh. "Guess I'm hungry. Okay, come on. Let's go for the cholesterol special and wash it down with Guinness."

On the walk back from dinner, Gavin reached a decision. If Fiona got flustered every time he tried to tell her how he felt, he'd have to *show* her. It was time to put his seduce-and-declare-undying-love plan into action.

"Those fish and chips hit the spot," he said, sliding the key into the lock and opening the door to their room at the bed and breakfast. "I'm giving Mrs. O'Leary a nice tip for that recommendation."

"Yeah, the food was delicious, but I'm now freezing." Fiona huddled into her winter coat, red-nosed and with her scarf pulled tight around her neck.

"Hey, it was your idea to eat them outside, not mine," he said with a laugh, tossing the key onto the nightstand. Wiggly Poo bounded straight to his basket and snuggled up with Ducky, his favorite dog toy, held in his jaws.

"I know eating outside in this weather was a crazy thing to do, but the view over the harbor was so gorgeous I wanted to savor it." She shrugged off her coat and scarf and hung them by the entrance.

"If you're cold, I'm more than willing to warm you up."

"Oh, you are, are you?" she laughed. "Completely without an ulterior motive, I'm sure."

"Of course," he said, closing the distance between them. "Come here."

He bent to claim her sexy lips. The kiss was soft, hot. She gave a little moan and slipped her arms around his back. He pulled her closer.

Her tongue slid into his mouth. She tasted of gin, peppermint, and something uniquely her own.

He increased the pressure, intensifying the kiss. Her breathing shifted from labored to short, sharp bursts. This felt good. Too damn good.

They crashed against the mahogany dressing table. Gavin slid his hands through her dark curls and felt the beat of her heart against his chest. In an instant, Fiona tugged his shirt free from his pants and danced her fingers up his torso, slowly at first, then gathering pace.

She moved her hands up toward his nipples and playfully tugged on one. "I like," she said and claimed it with her mouth.

"Ah." He groaned and moved his hands beneath her T-shirt, emitting a low laugh when he reached her bra and traced its familiar lacy pattern. "Dare I hope this is the sexy red lace bra with the matching knickers?"

She released his nipple and smiled up at him. "You'll have to wait to find out."

Her fingers fumbled with his shirt buttons, sending one bouncing off the glass mirror of the dressing table.

"Steady on," he said with a laugh.

"They're fiddly." Another button ricocheted off the dresser.

They stumbled against the wall, him tugging up her T-shirt, her fiddling with the clasp of his belt. They might be tipsy, but their fingers knew the steps to this dance.

His belt opened, and she shifted her efforts to the button and zip. He groaned as she slid her fingers into his trousers and touched his erection. She stroked the tender flesh of his penis, and he let out a low hiss. She slid to her knees, and his erection hardened in anticipation.

"No," he said, catching her arm. "I want to kiss you first."

Her eyes widened, then a smile curved her full lips. "Then I'd better get naked, hadn't I?" She took a step back and, in one fluid movement, pulled her top over her head and flung it to the side.

Sure enough, underneath her T-shirt, Fiona wore a red lace bra.

Her eyes met his and held his gaze. Slowly, deliberately, she unbuttoned her jeans. She tugged them over her hips and down her legs.

Gavin's blood pounded. Her knickers did match the bra. *Jaysus.* He was a lost man.

Biting her bottom lip, she reached for the clasp of her bra. Gavin's heart rate kicked up a notch. The V of her top had given a glimpse of the barest hint of creamy cleavage, but nothing beat the real deal. Fiona's full breasts were lush and begged to be touched.

She let the bra dangling from her fingers drop to the floor. Her mouth smiled an invitation.

Gavin closed the distance between them, and his fingertips met silky skin. Damnation.

"Lose the knickers," he said.

Her eyes widened, and her mouth opened and shut. She laughed and hooked her thumbs into the sides of her underwear. She slid the knickers over her hips to display those gorgeous buttocks that had been his not-so-secret obsession since she'd inadvertently revealed them at Clonmore House.

Fiona let her knickers drop down her legs, then kicked them off her feet in an elegant dance.

"On the bed," he said in a growl.

This time, she didn't hesitate. She lay on the floral cover, one arm flung out to the side, the other teasing a pebbled nipple. Her breathing was low and shallow. "And now?" she asked, her eyes cloudy with desire.

"And now," he replied, settling between her legs, "Relax."

He kissed her breasts, nipping her nipples. She gasped

and pulled on his hair, letting the fingers of one hand trace the vertebrae in his neck.

He kissed a path to her stomach and drew his tongue in an erotic circle around her navel. Her belly was perfect. Rounded with a little flesh. She was gloriously feminine, and very, very sexy.

Gavin let his tongue slide south, exploring her soft, neat curls while his fingers kneaded her buttocks.

She arched when he bent to tease her clit. "Oh. Oh, my." She exhaled a breathy moan.

Her taste was a delicious mix of sweet and salty. He nibbled her, making her gasp.

"Don't. Stop."

Her breathing grew rapid, shallow. He kept up the pressure, relishing the feel of her mounting orgasm.

"You. Inside me. Now."

"Your wish, madam, is my command."

He rolled on a condom and pushed inside her, savoring her slick tightness.

Fiona arched her hips, welcoming him.

He stilled for a moment inside her, letting her grow used to his presence. Their eyes met, and she smiled at him, teasing him. She moved her hips invitingly, and he began to thrust.

It felt good. Amazingly good.

She parted her lips, then licked them, and he bent to claim them in a passionate kiss

He ceased to think, gave in to the erotic rhythm and increasing pressure.

Then she gasped and cried out as she orgasmed. He

kept the pressure up until the last wave receded, then succumbed to a volcano of bliss.

"Fiona," he said when they'd more or less returned to Planet Earth. "I'm sorry about Vegas. For running out on you, I mean."

"S'okay." She yawned sleepily. "You're forgiven."

"No, seriously. I owe you a major apology, and not just for the Drew Draper screw up. It all happened at lightning speed, and it was intense. I'd always had a soft spot for you, but the Vegas trip tipped it into new territory. I wasn't ready to admit I'd fallen in love with you. Rather than giving us a chance, I took the coward's way out."

She opened one eye. "Is this one of those shag-her-senseless-then-quickly-admit-emotional-attachment moments?"

He roared laughing. "Guilty as charged."

"Ah, men. Such eejits." Fiona propped herself up on her elbows. "Let's be honest, Gavin. Even if you hadn't run for hills eight years ago, it probably wouldn't have worked. The timing was wrong. I needed the chance to develop self-confidence, and you needed to see that love and passion aren't synonymous with turmoil and chaos."

"I'd never felt so drawn to anyone before. Frankly, it scared the crap out of me."

Her eyes twinkled with amusement. "In other words, *I* scared the crap out of you."

"You were so—" he struggled to find the right words, "—vulnerable. Intense."

"Add insecure and needy to the list, and you've got my younger incarnation summed up." She grinned at him, and he had the urge to trace the curve of her smile with his index finger.

"Where do we go from here? I don't want these days in Clare to be it for us."

She leaned forward and kissed his cheek. "Let's worry about our future later. First, I need to confront Bernard."

35

Bernard Byrne was not having a good day. His niece was making damn sure of that—and relishing every millisecond of his discomfort.

With Garda Brian Glenn sitting to her right, Fiona smiled across the conference table at her uncle and Aidan Gant. Bernard's toupee was off-center, as sometimes happened to him in moments of great stress. This meeting definitely qualified.

"So you see, Bernard," she said, handing him a copy of Ann Dunne's sworn statement, "you have no choice."

Bernard stared at the paper as if it were laced with anthrax.

"Aidan assures us he had *nothing whatsoever* to do with the forged will." Fiona gave Aidan a significant look. She knew damn well he was in this business up to his balls, but unlike Bernard, he'd been smart enough to cover his arse. "Garda Glenn assures me there's enough evidence to charge you, but as I'm sure Aidan will agree, settling out of court is in both our best interests. The Irish judicial system being what it is, it could take years to sort out, and the only winners would be the lawyers."

Bernard licked beads of moisture from his upper lip. "What are you suggesting?"

"That you pay me and Bridie the value of the land you stole from us at the price we would have gotten had we sold it right after Nana died."

His eyes bulged. "But that was during the property boom! It's not worth anything like that amount now, nor was it before."

"Tough shit, Bernard. Those are my terms—along with three other stipulations." She smiled at him, enjoying prolonging his agony.

"What stipulations?" He dabbed sweat from his forehead with a monogrammed handkerchief.

"Firstly, the fairy tree stays. There's no reason you can't build your shopping center a few hundred meters down the road."

Bernard and Aidan exchanged glances. "Fair enough," Aidan said—he would agree to pretty much anything as long as it didn't jeopardize his stake in the shopping center, and Fiona was perfectly happy to play that card for all it was worth.

"Secondly, you buy out Gavin's share of Clonmore Lodge."

"This is outrageous!" A vein in her uncle's temple bulged.

"All right," Aidan said, shooting his client a warning look. "What's the final stipulation?"

"It's in both our best interests if those details don't

reach Garda Glenn's ears." Fiona winked at Brian. During the drive from the police station to Aidan Gant's offices, she'd filled him in on the particulars. While she doubted he'd be solving organized crime anytime soon, he'd proved surprisingly quick on the uptake regarding her uncle.

Flashing her a grin, Brian pushed back his chair and stood. "I'll just nip to the loo. Don't break any laws while I'm gone."

After Brian closed the door, Fiona turned to Bernard. "My final stipulation is this: I want whatever evidence you've conjured to frame Gavin for stealing money from your company. *All* copies of said evidence. You promise—in writing—not to jeopardize Gavin's career in any way. Understood?"

Bernard's nostrils flared, and he turned an interesting shade of puce. He opened his mouth as if to say something, but Aidan put a firm hand on his arm. "What if Bernard doesn't agree to your terms?"

"Then this will not only go to the courts, but to every tabloid in the country. How do you think Deirdre and Muireann will feel about being dragged into a scandal? And as for you, Aidan, how do you think your political pals will react to the news of your most prominent client and future business partner forging his own mother's will and cheating his sister and orphaned niece out of their inheritance?"

Bernard slid a look of appeal to Aidan. Aidan ignored him.

"Bernard will be delighted to take the deal," he said

smoothly. "Put the specifics in writing, and I'll get on it right away."

After confronting Bernard at Gant's, Fiona's adrenalin spike plummeted. She'd spent the two days since their return from Clare orchestrating today's confrontation. It had left her drained of energy and all out of sass. Needing to be somewhere she could be alone and clear her head, she went to the place that had been her refuge in times past—the Book Mark. Sitting in the familiar surroundings, now freshly painted and decorated, she tried to make sense of her racing thoughts.

One thing was clear: she had to make a decision. At Bridie's hospital appointment that morning, the doctors had given her the green light to go back to work on a part-time basis when the shop reopened for business tomorrow. By the end of January, she'd be back full-time.

After months of willing this day to come, Fiona was free to rebook her ticket to Australia. So why wasn't she whisking out her phone and making the call? Was she truly contemplating taking the biggest gamble of her life and staying in Ballybeg with Gavin?

When she heard the jangle of the Book Mark's door, her heart jumped. Philip stood on the threshold, shifting his weight nervously from foot to foot. In his left fist, he clutched a bunch of drooping yellow roses. She knew what he was about to say before he opened his mouth.

"FeeFee, we were so good together. Please give us another chance." He held out the bunch of flowers.

She squinted at the ribbon binding the stems. "If you selected a bouquet to symbolize our relationship, you chose well. But if your intention was to woo me, you need a refresher course on chivalry."

"Eh?" He glanced uncertainly at the flowers.

"The black ribbon, Philip. It's a dead giveaway—literally."

He stared at her blankly, then his gaze dropped to the tired bouquet. He flushed as realization dawned.

Fiona crossed her arms over her chest. "Whose grave did you rob? I know memorial flowers when I see them, and I'm sure as feck not accepting them as a peace offering."

His eyes darted from side to side before settling on the faded wood floor. "I didn't think."

"You never do." She sighed. "Honestly, I'm not sure if I should laugh or cry. I think I'll roll with laughter—it's better for the heart."

"Isn't it the thought that counts?"

"Not when the thought involves nicking flowers off a grave." She pressed her tongue against the roof of her mouth. "Why are you in Ballybeg, Philip? It's not because you're in love with me. Hell, I'm not convinced you find me attractive."

His head shot up. "Of course I'm in love with you. Sure, you're a great shag."

She made no attempt to hide her eye roll. "For an actor, your courtship technique needs improvement."

"Come on, FeeFee. What do you want me to do? Serenade you?"

She held up a palm. "Don't call me that. My name is Fiona."

"But it's my pet name for you."

"Which I've always hated. And you lost the right to call me anything once you shagged Rachel Monroe. How long was it going on for, Philip? How many others were there?"

He flushed and shoved his free hand in his jeans pocket. "You knew about Rachel? I'd wondered if you'd found out. Why didn't you say something about it when you broke up with me?"

"Because I didn't want to give you the satisfaction of humiliating me any farther than you already had."

His Adam's apple bobbed. "She meant nothing to me, I swear, FeeF—Fiona. It was just sex, nothing more."

"Why did you cheat on me?"

"I dunno. I acted on impulse. I was stoned and angry with you."

"Not *that* stoned, apparently," she said acidly. "Why were you angry with me?"

"You kept nagging me about getting a part-time job and saving up for the trip."

"You said you *wanted* to come to Australia with me."

He gave one of his half shrugs. "I did. But I wanted to earn the money through acting."

She puffed her cheeks out and exhaled. The man was exasperating! "You hadn't acted in months. Not since your soap character was killed off in a fiery car crash."

"I had auditions, though." He tossed the flowers onto a table. "I knew my luck would turn."

"Obviously, it didn't. If it had, you wouldn't be down

in Cork playing the role of Dopey in a Christmas pantomime."

"Come on, Fiona. Give us another shot. I miss you."

She shook her head. "What you miss is someone organizing you, cleaning up after you, washing your clothes, and bailing you out every time you get yourself into a financial mess. You're almost thirty years old. A grown man. You ought to be ashamed of yourself."

"Oh, come on. It was only the once with Rachel. Are you really going to let one indiscretion wreck what we had together?"

"Yes, I am. Rachel was only the catalyst. We should have broken up a couple of years ago. Be honest, for once. We were bored. I know I was. Weren't you? Surely we both deserve better than a partner who bores us. We stayed together because we didn't want change. I stayed because finding someone new seemed like too much of an effort. I was approaching my late twenties, and all my friends were settling down, getting married, and starting families. I guess I didn't want to be the odd one out. You stayed with me because it was convenient. I was the perfect mother substitute, right down to washing your laundry."

"I doubt my mother would know how to operate a washing machine," he muttered. "Our housekeeper takes care of that."

A reluctant laugh escaped her. "Well, you know what I mean. We were never meant to be anything more than a stopgap relationship. If you think you love me, you're deluding yourself. If you truly felt that way about me, you'd have treated me a damn sight better than you did."

He remained silent, squirming awkwardly on the spot. She felt no need to fill the void. Eventually, he shifted. "I guess I'd better be going."

"Yes, I think that would be best."

"Can we keep in touch?"

"No," she said without hesitation. "I'm not angry with you anymore, but I don't want to be your friend."

His mouth opened and closed, fish-like. "Fair enough. But if you change your mind—"

"I won't," she said firmly. "Good-bye, Philip."

He gave a feeble salute and exited the shop.

She picked up the limp bunch of flowers from where he'd dropped it and fingered the frayed black ribbon. Philip would never know it, but he'd just done her an enormous favor. While he'd presented her with a stolen bouquet and mouthed meaningless platitudes, she'd come to a decision.

Grabbing her handbag from the counter, she tossed the flowers into the bin. It was time to make peace with her past and embrace her future.

36

Gavin stepped out of O'Dwyer's Jewelers and fingered the box burning a hole in his pocket. It contained a gold Claddagh ring. He'd considered buying one for Muireann when he first planned to propose to her. However, his subtle probing as to whether or not she liked the idea of wearing a traditional Irish wedding band had quickly disabused him of the notion. His former fiancée would settle for nothing less than a diamond-studded extravaganza.

Clutching Wiggly Poo's lead, he crossed Patrick Street and stopped in front of the Book Mark. The little dog whined with excitement and tugged on his lead in an effort to race to the shop door.

"Steady on, mate." At the same moment Gavin pushed on the door, it opened from within. He found himself nose-to-nose with Fiona. A very startled, sweetly-scented Fiona.

"Hey," she said, blinking. Her face creased into a smile.

Cupping her chin in his hand, he took in her lovely face with its smattering of freckles, admired her soft hair and feminine curves. He'd never seen anyone more perfect in all his life.

His heart was performing an Irish jig. This was his chance—perhaps the last chance he'd have—to tell her how he felt. "Will you come for a walk with me? Wiggly Poo needs an airing. We could head down the beach. The tide's out, and..." Why was he babbling? If he didn't get a grip, he'd screw this up. *Again.* A post-coital declaration wasn't good enough. Fiona deserved a touch of romance.

"Yes," she said decisively. "A walk would do me good. We can catch up on what we've been up to over the past couple of days."

He enclosed her hand in his free one and kept a grip on the dog's lead with the other. They walked toward Beach Road and took the stone steps down to the strand.

Wiggly Poo scrambled down the slippery steps with more speed than grace. Gavin hurled a small ball through the air, and the puppy shot after it.

"Aidan Gant phoned earlier," he said, catching Fiona's eye. "Apparently, Bernard has agreed to buy back my share of Clonmore Lodge. I don't suppose you know anything about his sudden change of heart?"

Her green irises twinkled with merriment. "Perhaps."

"Ah, Fiona. Isn't the knight in shining armor supposed to slay the dragon and rescue the princess?"

She gave him a playful shove. "You're reading the wrong fairytales, Maguire. In Celtic mythology, the heroines kick arse."

They took the route toward Craggy Point. Wiggly Poo

darted across the sand to bark at seaweed and other known enemies.

"You're looking very pleased with yourself," she said as they scrambled over some lichen-encrusted rocks. "Care to share?"

"If Bernard buys my share of Clonmore Lodge, I won't need to sell the cottage. And as the cottage doesn't have a mortgage, I can live on far less than I needed to earn before."

She raised an eyebrow. "Is that a positive change?"

"As far as I'm concerned, yes. I'm enjoying working on Ruairí's pub renovations. Before Christmas, Liam O'Mahony mentioned he's looking for an architect to collaborate with him on house renovations and the like. I gave him a call this morning and said I was interested. Between working with Liam and the few lecturing hours at the university, I'll earn more than enough to support myself and Wiggly Poo."

Her warm smile set the butterflies in his stomach free. "Would you be content working on smaller domestic projects like house renovations and extensions?" she asked.

"For the moment, yes. The experience certainly won't hurt my C.V."

When they reached Craggy Point, Wiggly Poo was thrilled to discover an enormous clump of seaweed to attack. Meanwhile, Gavin had no difficulty in locating the cave Fiona had shown him a few months ago.

She blinked in confusion when he led her into the cave. "Why are we here?"

"Do you remember our first kiss?" he asked. "The first one this decade, I mean."

She smiled, displaying her dimples. "Of course. I got sentimental and showed you my parents' carving."

"Feel like getting sentimental all over again?" He tugged her down the passage. "See," he said, withdrawing a piece of flint from his coat pocket, "I came prepared."

Her eyes widened. "What are you doing?"

"Carving our names into the cave wall, my sweet. Why do you think I dragged you all the way out here?" He scratched their names high up on the wall, well past tide level. Then he added the final flourish to his creation—a small Cupid's bow and arrow.

"You're daft," she said, blushing.

He grinned. "Not daft. In love."

He heard her intake of breath.

Slipping his hand into his coat pocket, he extracted the ring box and slid to one knee. "Fiona, I screwed up in Vegas, but I'm not going to make the same mistake in Ballybeg. Will you give our relationship a second chance?"

"Are you asking me to stay in Ballybeg?"

He wanted to kiss away the tremor in her voice. "I'm asking you to stay with *me*. I just told you Liam's offered me some freelance work. If I do a good job on the pub renovation and whatever Liam gives me over the next few months, I'll have a solid foundation to set up on my own in Dublin, Cork, or wherever else we decide to live. I don't mind doing the distance thing for a while, especially if you need more time to make up your mind about where you want us to settle."

She worried her lip ring. "What about my trip to Australia?"

"I've already thought about that. As it happens, Liam's taking a couple of weeks' holiday in March. That coincides with the university mid-semester break. Now that Jonas is moving back to Ballybeg with Luca, I've offered him the use of the cottage to write while we're in Australia. In return, he'll look after Wiggly Poo."

Her lips parted but she made no sound.

"Of course," he said hurriedly, "all these plans are worth naught if you won't have me."

She laughed. "Of course I'll have you, you daft eejit. Now get up off that damp floor and kiss me."

"Wait a sec." He flipped open the jewelry box. "I almost forgot to give you this."

"Oh!" She gasped. "It's gorgeous."

He slipped the Claddagh ring onto her finger. It was the perfect fit.

"How did you know my size?" she asked, admiring her new ring in the soft sunlight.

"I asked Bridie to nick one of your rings and measure it. She was thrilled to assist."

"Oh, I bet she was." Fiona's grin was wide. "Thank you, Gavin. It's perfect."

"I love you, Fiona Byrne. You can regard this ring as whatever you want—friendship ring, engagement ring, or wedding band. I'm willing to do whatever it takes to stay in your life this time."

She grabbed him and smacked a kiss on his lips. "And I love you, Gavin Maguire. I've loved you for years. And as for where we live, well…I've kind-of sort-of enjoyed reconnecting with people here. In fact, the principal of Glencoe College asked me if I was interested in a teaching position starting next academic year."

"And what did you say?"

She gave him a wink. "I said I'd think about it."

At the sight of his faltering smile, she laughed. "I'm teasing you. Of course I said yes. You're stuck with me whether you like it or not."

Gavin drew her into his arms and kissed her thoroughly. "I'm thrilled to be stuck with you. So," he whispered into her ear, "Shall we go tell Aidan Gant the divorce is off?"

EPILOGUE

Two Months Later
Wilsons Promontory, Victoria, Australia

From: fiona_byrne@telcom.ie
To: livlongandprosper@imail.ie

Hi Liv,

I'm sending you this e-mail from Wilsons Promontory, an Australian national park south of Melbourne. The picture I've attached is of a wombat. One of those little suckers snuck into our tent last night and scared the bejaysus out of me. It was just like being back in Ballybeg and dealing with Wiggly Poo's stealthy schemes to get into our bed.

So far, Australia's exceeded my expectations times a million. The weather, the people, the wildlife—and my travel companion! Gavin and I haven't had one single fight since we got here. LOL! Okay, he begs to differ. When he produced a flask of Long Island iced tea on what was supposed to be a romantic picnic on the beach, I reacted by gagging. Even after all these years, I can't smell that stuff without feeling sick. So he downed the lot himself and was deservedly hungover the next day.

Thanks for your gossipy e-mail. Ruairí MacCarthy has a secret American wife? Holy crap! I did not see that one coming. He was kind of cagey about why he left Manhattan, but that's wild. I need more details!

Hope you're surviving Aidan's mayoral campaign and haven't strangled any political wives. We'll go out for drinks when I get back, okay?

Love and Kisses from Down Under,

Fee xoxoxo

—THE END—

•Thanks for reading ***Love and Shenanigans***. I hope you enjoyed Gavin and Fiona's story!

•Want more Ballybeg? ***Love and Blarney*** (Ballybeg, Book 2—a novella) features Ruairí the grumpy barman and his estranged American wife. **You can read *Love and Blarney* for FREE if you sign up for my mailing list**. **http://zarakeane.com/newsletter**

•I also have **an active reader group**, **The Ballybeg Belles**, where I chat, share snippets of upcoming stories, and host members only giveaways. I hope to join you for a virtual pint very soon!

•You can connect with me on Facebook, Twitter, or via email zara@zarakeane.com. I love hearing from readers!

Now Available.

Read for FREE if you sign up for Zara's newsletter!

http://zarakeane.com/newsletter

Falling for her husband...

When stockbroker Ruairí MacCarthy left Manhattan to deal with a family crisis in Ireland, he never intended to stay away. Twelve months and a bitter break-up later, he's replaced his three-piece suits with jeans and exchanged his Wall Street career for a job managing his family's pub. When Jayme, his estranged American wife, blasts back into his life weeks before their divorce becomes final, Ruairí must decide if home is really where the heart is.

LOVE AND BLARNEY
CHAPTER ONE

Ballybeg, County Cork, Ireland

If Jayme King wanted a metaphor to sum up the mess she'd made of her marriage, finding herself on a flooded Irish road blocked by sheep seemed pretty damned appropriate.

The wipers of her rental car swished back and forth at a frenetic pace. Heavy traffic and even heavier rain had turned what should have been a two-and-a-half-hour drive from Shannon Airport to Ballybeg into a four-hour ordeal. According to the GPS, she'd almost reached her destination…*almost* being the operative word.

Jayme sighed and regarded the ovine roadblock. An elderly man in an olive-green raincoat and tweed cap was herding the sheep. He waved a walking stick at her in a friendly gesture. The sheep inched their way from a pasture on one side of the road to a metal building on the other. If they didn't hurry their furry asses across, she'd lose what little control she had over the standard transmission. Why hadn't she remembered to specify an automatic when she'd made the reservation? But how was she to know the Irish regarded stick shifts as the norm? Remembering to stay on the left side of the road was bad enough. Throwing a third pedal into the equation had turned her impromptu road trip into a nightmare.

She drummed the steering wheel and glanced at the dashboard computer. Nearly nine thirty. If she made it to Ballybeg within the next few minutes, she'd check into her accommodation before hunting down the man she'd traveled over three thousand miles to find.

At the thought of the task ahead, her stomach went

into a free fall. What would he say when he saw her? How would he react? And how much would it hurt if he rejected her a second time? Her fingers tensed over the wheel.

Finally the last sheep reached its destination. The farmer doffed his cap at her and disappeared into the metal shelter. Grinding the gears, she shuddered into motion. She didn't want to spend the rest of her life wondering *what if?* She'd already wasted months on tears and regrets. It was time to learn to live again.

RUAIRÍ MACCARTHY, manager and proprietor of MacCarthy's in Ballybeg, surveyed his domain. The pub had the flair of an Ireland long gone but far from forgotten. The bar was the old-fashioned kind—stained mahogany edged with a tile inlay. He danced his fingertips over the faded wood counter, each scratch a reminder of a previous generation of customers.

Not bad. Not bad at all, especially considering the state of the place when he'd taken control thirteen months ago. Once the renovation was complete, the pub would look similar to when his great-grandfather had hung his shingle over the door in 1927.

He whistled cheerfully, an old tune he couldn't place but couldn't get out of his head. Yeah, life wasn't perfect—not by a long shot—but in comparison to this time last year, things were good.

A fist pounded on the front door.

He paused in the act of polishing a pint glass and

frowned. Probably kids messing around. They'd know someone would be in the pub by now, readying it for opening time. He refocused on the task at hand, polishing the glass until it lost its dishwasher dullness and sparkled under the pub's dim light.

This evening, he was knocking off early. And he couldn't bloody wait. The moment the clock struck five, he'd chuck the keys of the kingdom to his sister Marcella and head to Cork City. He smiled to himself and pictured his date. Laura Corrigan was a leggy brunette with generous breasts and a ready smile. But most important, Laura was a laugh. She didn't take herself—or him—too seriously. In short, she was exactly what he needed after the implosion of his marriage. For his first date in years, he was glad it was with someone who was more potential friend than future soul mate. And if their relationship developed into more than friendship, he'd take it one step at a time.

Bang. Bang.

He swore beneath his breath. Could it be one of his sisters? If so, he was in no mood to rush to the door.

"We're not open." His voice was gruff enough to deter whoever was pounding on the pub door before opening time.

Another bang.

For feck's sake. Surely no one in Ballybeg was *that* desperate for a pint. Grumbling, he placed the glass on the counter and tossed his polishing cloth beside it. He shoved up the counter flap and maneuvered his large frame through the gap.

Bang, bang.

"Keep your hair on," he growled. "I'm coming." Through the stained-glass slats in the oak door, he spied a small figure.

Ah, hell.

He loved his sisters, he truly did. But being their go-to person for every disastrous situation they got themselves into was exhausting. What would it be this time? Was Sinéad's renegade boyfriend in jail and in need of bail money? Had Sharon's boss finally come to her senses and fired her? He slid the bolts and braced himself, not to mention his bank account, for the latest episode in the MacCarthy family soap opera.

His chest collided with his visitor's petite form. She took a step back in alarm. He blinked through the heavy rain. She was a small woman and fine-boned, judging by the way her oversized raincoat enveloped her tiny figure.

"Our opening time is the same as every other pub in Ireland," he said, not unkindly. "Ten thirty."

"I'm not here for a drink." One slim hand, wearing a large diamond ring, pushed back the hood to reveal a mane of honey-streaked brown hair and a very familiar heart-shaped face.

His heart rate kicked up a notch when his brain registered who was standing on the doorstep. "Jayme?" His voice was a croak.

"Ruairí." She pronounced his name in the light singsong way of a foreigner who'd tried hard to master which of the many syllables went up in intonation and which went down but hadn't quite gotten it right.

Air exited his lungs in a whoosh. "What are you doing here?"

She tilted her sweet little chin, revealing the cleft he'd once loved to trace with his tongue. "Ask me in and maybe you'll find out."

His feet reacted before his head could process her words. He stood aside and let his estranged wife step over the threshold.

Now Available.

Read for FREE if you sign up for Zara's newsletter!

http://zarakeane.com/newsletter

ALSO BY ZARA KEANE

BALLYBEG SERIES

Love and Shenanigans

Love and Blarney

Love and Leprechauns

Love and Mistletoe

Love and Shamrocks

BALLYBEG BAD BOYS

Her Treasure Hunter Ex

The Rock Star's Secret Baby

The Navy SEAL's Holiday Fling

Bodyguard by Day, Ex-Husband by Night

The Navy SEAL's Accidental Wife

TRISKELION TEAM (DUBLIN MAFIA)

Final Target

Kiss Shot

Bullet Point

MOVIE CLUB MYSTERIES

Dial P For Poison

The Postman Always Dies Twice

How to Murder a Millionaire

ABOUT ZARA KEANE

USA Today bestselling author Zara Keane grew up in Dublin, Ireland, but spent her summers in a small town very similar to the fictitious Ballybeg.

She currently lives in Switzerland with her family. When she's not writing or wrestling small people, she drinks far too much coffee, and tries—with occasional success—to resist the siren call of Swiss chocolate.

zarakeane.com
zara@zarakeane.com

ACKNOWLEDGMENTS

I'm enormously fortunate to be surrounded by family and friends who have always encouraged my writing career. To name them all would take up more pages than anyone would care to read, so I'll confine myself to those without whom *Love and Shenanigans* never would have been finished, let alone published.

Many thanks to Kate Garrabrant for suggesting I give NaNoWriMo a shot back in November 2009; to my wonderful critique partner, Magdalen Braden, for always telling me the unvarnished truth; to Janet Webb for encouraging me to write a romance set in Ireland; to Nadia Lee for patiently answering numerous newbie questions over the years; to Rhonda Helms, editor extraordinaire, for her excellent suggestions on story development and character arcs and for reining in my comma abuse; to Gwen Hayes for her wonderful Fresh Eyes Critique; to Trish Slattery, April Weigele, and Michele Harvey for beta reading and proofreading the book; and to Anne and Linda at Victory Editing for the thorough proofread.

Last but definitely not least, thank you to my family for always believing in me and for encouraging me to live my dream.

LOVE AND SHENANIGANS

Published 2014 by Beaverstone Press GmbH (LLC)

This book is a work of fiction. The names, characters, places, and incidents are products of the writer's imagination or have been used fictitiously. Any resemblance to persons, living or dead, actual events, locales, or organizations is entirely coincidental.

EBOOK ISBN: 978-3-906245-00-3

PRINT ISBN: 978-3-906245-38-6

Printed in Great Britain
by Amazon